Shockadelica

Jon O'Bergh

Book Baby

Pennsauken, NJ

Author website
obergh.net

Front cover designed by Jon O'Bergh

Printed and bound in the United States

About the Author

Jon O'Bergh is an author and musician who loves a good scare. He received a Bachelor of Arts in Music from the University of California at Irvine. A fan of ghost stories and horror movies, Jon has published several books, including the psychological thriller *The Shatter Point*. He has released over a dozen albums in a variety of styles. After many years living in San Francisco and Washington, D.C., he now spends most of his time with his husband in Toronto.

About the Bone Man

The Bone Man has released his debut album *Box of Bones*. The music is available on all streaming platforms or for purchase from online music sites.

Box of Bones – Album Song List

1. The Beast Within
2. Frankenstein Monster
3. Bone White
4. Sorceress
5. Slipping Away
6. Zombie
7. Devil in the Night
8. Midnight Succubus
9. The Vampire's Kiss
10. Box of Bones
11. Invisible Spirit
12. Night on Bald Mountain

Prologue: Scream

Kendall

The scream woke Kendall Akande, piercing the haze of a strange dream in which he struggled to control a careening car. The ensuing silence made him wonder whether it had indeed been part of the dream. Then he heard the second scream, its muffled sound close by. More of a shout really, not quite the shrill pitch familiar to him from watching so many horror films. It could have come from the apartment above him where his best friend Jenna Chen lived, but for the fact that it had the distinct quality of an older woman. He removed his Blanche Devereaux—the nickname he gave his sleep mask, after the freewheeling retiree from his favorite eighties sitcom, *The Golden Girls*—and groped for the light switch on his bedside lamp. The light hurt his eyes, and he winced as he looked at the time: 12:34 a.m.

He heard shuffling above him. The screams must have also awakened Jenna. He picked up his cell phone and called her. She barely had time to say "hello" before he blurted out, "Girl, did you hear that scream?"

"Yeah. Sounds like it came from your floor."

A door opened down the hall, followed by a commotion. Kendall rushed to the peephole with the phone pressed to his ear. "Something's happening in the hallway."

He heard hammering on a neighbor's door, and recognized the voice that shouted, but the peephole provided only a view straight across the hall to Elliott Bernbaum's apartment. "It sounds like Mrs. Gupta. She must be pounding on Rooney's door."

"Stay there. I'm coming down."

"Do you think it's safe?"

"Please. You know I grew up in Regent Park. Before gentrification."

Kendall heard Rooney open her door, followed by Mrs. Gupta's agitated story about something inside the walls. Rooney tried to calm her and asked if she wanted to call the police. Mrs. Gupta hesitated, probably realizing how ridiculous the notion would sound to the officers. Across the hall, Elliott opened his door and leaned against the frame with his arms crossed. The peephole's fish-eye perspective exaggerated his belly. Strands of his hair stood askew at sleep-sculpted angles. Kendall unconsciously patted his own hair, grateful that his short sponge twists were not in such disarray.

Morvena Delacroix, a former model of an advanced but indeterminate age, emerged from her apartment upstairs like a spider sensing something tapping a thread in its web, and called out, "Hello? Hello? What's going on?" The slightest noise always drew her out, whatever the hour, especially during the night. Ever since she had moved in two months earlier, Kendall and Jenna had tried to alter their habits to avoid disturbing her, closing the building's heavy front door with extra care and tiptoeing through the hall. Still, noises inevitably drew Morvena from her lair.

Kendall retrieved his silk robe and tied it around his body. By the time he opened his door, Jenna had reached the bottom of the stairs, and he joined her in the hallway. Mrs. Gupta reiterated her story about something in the walls.

"Mice, maybe?" suggested Jenna.

"No, no. Like something with huge claws, or nails on a chalkboard. And the sound of breathing."

Elliott pushed himself away from the doorframe and stepped all the way into the hall. "You know the rumors about this building, eh? That it's haunted?" Jenna shot him a stern look, which did little to deter him. "No, really. It has a sketchy past. I've heard things myself."

Mrs. Gupta frowned.

Kendall clutched the lapel of his robe, uncertain whether to be afraid or exhilarated. He raised his eyebrows and glanced toward Jenna. In unison they muttered "Podcast." Kendall clarified that he and Jenna recorded a bi-weekly program called Shockadelica in

2

which they discussed horror films, books, and related topics. Their very own haunted residence would make a great episode.

Elliott nodded toward Morvena, who had just reached the bottom of the stairs. "With your super-sensitive hearing, I'm surprised you've never heard any ghosts."

"I hear plenty of things. This building is so noisy. People going up and down the stairs, talking on the phone, toilets flushing. And now shouting in the middle of the night."

Rooney smirked. "Maybe what Mrs. Gupta heard was your pounding on the floor above me. You've got me scared to use my own bathroom during the night."

Kendall gently touched Mrs. Gupta's elbow. "Tell you what. Why don't you come to my apartment and I'll brew you some tea— some relaxing chamomile. We can't let you go back to your place in your condition."

Mrs. Gupta thanked him. He extended the offer to the others, but all declined except Jenna. She put her arm around Mrs. Gupta and guided her into Kendall's apartment.

As he rummaged through the kitchen for mugs and tea, Mrs. Gupta fidgeted with her hands. "Do you think this place really is haunted?"

"How long have you lived here?" asked Jenna.

"Five years."

"Have you ever heard anything before?"

"No, but..."

"Exactly. No ghost would wait five years to reveal itself."

"Then what was it?"

Jenna shrugged. "I won't insult you by suggesting it was a dream, or your imagination. I certainly don't know the answer, but there could be any number of explanations."

"Such as?"

"Such as..." Jenna looked up at Kendall for help.

Kendall spun his hand through the air in an effort to help birth an idea. "Such as...water pipes. We've all heard them shudder in this old building whenever someone turns on the tap."

Jenna nodded. "Or—or Morvena banging on the floor, like Rooney said. You know the walls are so thin you can hear your neighbors breathe." She looked up mischievously at Kendall. "Maybe you heard Kendall snoring."

Kendall stuck out his tongue at her as he placed three mugs on the table.

"But it's a quiet building, despite what Morvena says," continued Mrs. Gupta. "No late-night parties or loud music. Those other sounds never bother me, the sounds of people going about their lives. This was different. Not like anything I've ever heard before."

A quick glance from Jenna convinced Kendall they were thinking the same thing. What if Mrs. Gupta was losing it? Her husband had passed away a couple of years ago, shortly before Jenna had moved in. Kendall knew Mrs. Gupta to be a sensible woman, always smartly dressed, with a dignified bearing that projected calm control. Perhaps the loneliness and stress had started to take their toll. Perhaps something beneath the surface had boiled up and melted the cool facade.

Kendall sat at the table and pulled his robe tighter around his legs. "So tell us again, what exactly happened?"

Mrs. Gupta recounted how she had been awakened by noises, a soft scratching that came from the wall directly behind her bed. At first, she just lay in bed, listening. Then she heard a long, drawn out scratch, like sharp claws being dragged across a metal pipe. Once that stopped, she heard breathing. As if the walls themselves were breathing.

Kendall furrowed his brow and placed his elbow on the table so he could rest his chin in the cup of his hand. Mrs. Gupta was not the kind of person to have a suggestible imagination. Yet his bed was on the other side of the wall from her bedroom, and no sound had woken him. Maybe she *had* heard him in the throes of sleep—even if such sounds had never woken her before.

Mrs. Gupta continued her account, explaining how she got up and slid her feet into the slippers resting beside the bed. At that moment, she heard a disembodied voice whisper, *I'm watching you.* That was when she screamed and looked anxiously around the room.

4

Then the voice added, *I'm going to enjoy watching you die*. At that point she screamed again and fled the apartment.

Kendall wondered if he had been talking in his sleep. He suffered from a recurring nightmare, and such a statement would not have been out of place in that particular dream. The only problem was that he had not experienced the nightmare in months, and certainly not when Mrs. Gupta screamed. He asked if the voice came from the same place as the other noises.

"I believe so. But my back was to the bed at that point, and it just seemed to be everywhere in the room."

"And you're certain that's what it said?"

Mrs. Gupta assured them she had heard those very words. She rested her hands on the table, one hand protectively covering the other. "I know it's hard to believe. It sounds...preposterous. I understand."

The kettle began to whistle, rescuing Kendall from having to think of something to say. He patted Mrs. Gupta's hands and rose to attend to the tea. No one spoke as he brought the kettle back to the table and filled the mugs. He told Mrs. Gupta this would help her relax, and she offered a weak smile.

Jenna swept some loose strands of hair behind her ear. "The important thing is, you're okay, and we're here if you need us."

Mrs. Gupta noticed Jenna's fuzzy green slippers with cartoon eyes and smiled. "I like your slippers. They remind me of something my granddaughter would wear."

Jenna stretched out her leg and playfully rotated her ankle. Kendall frowned and addressed Mrs. Gupta as if Jenna was not present. "Cute, yes, but the poor child here has absolutely no fashion sense when it comes to her own wardrobe. And she calls herself an artist. I can't tell you how many years I've labored in vain to help her see the light." He modeled his leopard print slippers with their sleek cut and open heel. "These, on the other hand, are the epitome of good taste."

The repartee seemed to relax Mrs. Gupta. They talked about her children. The son lived just outside Toronto in Brampton with his wife and two kids. The daughter owned a condo in one of the many high-rises dotting the waterfront corridor. Mrs. Gupta expressed pride in her daughter's accomplishments in the financial sector, but worried that her independent streak and devotion to her job would interfere with being able to settle down and raise a family. Between the effects of the tea and the conversation, Mrs. Gupta grew more relaxed. At last, she said she was ready to return to her apartment, and Jenna offered to help her settle in.

A short while later, as Kendall was washing out the mugs, he heard a soft knock on the door. Jenna stood at the threshold when he opened the door, but shook her head when he swung the door wider to invite her in. "I just want to let you know Mrs. Gupta's bedroom checked out fine. No more sounds."

"So what do you make of it all?" asked Kendall in a hushed voice.

"I don't know. I hate to blame it on stress, or a combination of imagination and something she actually heard. That's the logical explanation. Then again, if the building really is haunted... We should find out more from Elliott."

"And if there's an interesting history we can turn it into a podcast."

"Exactly."

"Wait. What's the matter? I know that look."

Jenna shifted from one foot to the other. "I just find it really hard to believe ghosts actually exist. I mean, I love reading ghost stories and watching horror movies, but it's like fantasy, you know what I mean?"

"My aunt believes in ghosts. She has plenty of stories from Nigeria, before she came to Canada. My mother, on the other hand, doesn't like to talk about anything superstitious."

"And what do you believe?"

"I believe it's late, and if I don't get my beauty rest, I will be a ragged mess in the morning."

Jenna mock-pinched his stomach. Kendall feigned outrage with a loud "Ouch," then hunched his shoulders in fear that he might have reawakened Morvena. The two friends tittered at the prospect.

Kendall whispered, "Five dollars you can't make it upstairs without rousing the beast."

"You're on," she whispered.

Kendall listened as she crept up the stairs. He heard her door shut above him, followed by the soft pad of her feet over the ceiling, and shook his head. "Damn, she's good."

1

Excerpt from Shockadelica Podcast
Episode 24: Review of *American Horror Story*

Jenna: Let's talk about the new season of *American Horror Story*. It's titled *Cairo*—which locals pronounce "kay-ro"—and takes place in a real ghost town in Illinois. Well, it's not completely a ghost town, but it's mostly abandoned. The buildings are boarded up and falling into decay.

Kendall: I think the premise is great. The small number of residents who still live in the town try to revitalize it by capitalizing on its reputation as a ghost town. So they build a horror museum and offer ghost tours to try to draw tourists, only people start disappearing.

Jenna: I like the mummy that comes to life, which cleverly ties into the town's name. That was freaky-deaky.

Kendall: I thought it was a little too obvious. Like they were stretching to include it. How do you think *Cairo* compares to past seasons of AHS?

Jenna: I quite like it so far. Especially the socio-political spin. It's a commentary on economic distress in the Midwest and fear.

Kendall: And don't forget the town's real history of racial strife and prejudice, which many people blame for Cairo's demise.

Jenna: All that context gives the story more heft. More power.

Kendall: It's not just about horror.

Jenna: Exactly.

The Nightmare
Kendall

Cabbagetown. Such an unfortunate name for a neighborhood that, in all honesty, possessed a good deal of personality. Kendall knew about its origins, that the name started as a British epithet for the area where Irish immigrants used narrow front-yard gardens to grow cabbages and other vegetables. The British considered such behavior most unfashionable. Though the cabbages were long gone, the branding issue over the name lingered. Originally established as a Toronto suburb in 1840, its mix of prosperous streets, middle-class homes, and blue-collar enclaves was eventually absorbed into the city, pushing the suburbs farther out. Cabbagetown began to decline in the nineteen-twenties and -thirties, spending half a century as an undesirable part of town before its rediscovery and rehabilitation. A classic story of urban renewal. Now some of its residents proudly displayed the neighborhood's very own flag, which mimicked the red maple leaf of the Canadian flag with a dark green cabbage head set in a white background between two green rectangles.

The narrow lanes and alleys that crisscrossed Old Cabbagetown charmed Kendall, reminding him of a world from another time, secluded from the glass and steel skyscrapers downtown. Streets bustling with shops and streetcars mingled with darkly shaded lanes as quiet as the old Necropolis at the eastern edge of the neighborhood. To the east of busy Parliament Street, with its shops and restaurants, lovingly maintained brick Victorians crowded shoulder to shoulder along the streets, as dense as roosting bats. The homes stood sturdy and proud of their heritage. By contrast, the houses to the west tended to stoop in slight disrepair. Front steps splintered. Posts leaned and lintels sagged. In reality, the demarcation was not so absolute, and the two realms bled into each other; nothing in the world is ever as absolute and pure as people wish things to be. When Kendall watched a chic woman with an expensive bouquet pause at the door of a flower shop while a bent, elderly woman with a tattered hem passed, dragging her shopping cart, he realized that was the perfect representation of Cabbagetown.

The building where he and Jenna lived sat on a quiet lane, just west of Parliament Street. An old, two-story apartment structure, it still retained a hint of Victorian charm despite the faded, peeling paint on the bay windows and the gray grime streaking the brick facade. Five cement steps, chipped and cracking, led up to the recessed entry. On the transom, gold letters shadowed in black spelled out *Covington Terrace* in lacy script. Ionic columns on either side of the porch supported a lintel with a small, plant-crowded balcony. The broad edifice squatted atop a basement, whose windows peeked aboveground like skittish schoolchildren spying on the neighborhood.

Kendall had moved into the building only eight months earlier, thanks to a tip from Jenna when she learned the tenant below her would be moving out. Kendall communicated his interest to the landlord, Arthur Turnbull, before the unit even went on the market. He knew that Turnbull did not keep the building in great repair, but the rent was affordable and the location convenient—within walking distance of The Village, where Kendall sometimes appeared in drag as La Chandelle.

His first-floor apartment looked out on an overgrown backyard garden that grew wilder each year because, naturally, Turnbull could not be bothered to hire a gardener. Kendall called it the Jungle and found inspiration in its unrestrained abandon. He had strung up a netting of Chinese lanterns over the small, paved area immediately below his bedroom window, and installed a table and chairs where he held court with friends on summer evenings.

Kendall was in a cheerful mood because it was the start of autumn, his favorite time of year. Although autumn officially would not start until the Equinox, Kendall embraced the season immediately following Labour Day. He thrilled at the start of the academic year at the University of Toronto, which signaled autumn's arrival with the Week of Welcome and culminated in a street festival for students on St. George Street. As nature prepared for her annual decrescence, here culture and the pursuit of knowledge were

11

blooming afresh. By the arrival of spring in May, the two would have traded places: nature would be exploding as students felt exhausted and spent.

On this particular day, Kendall had enticed Jenna to visit the Bata Shoe Museum to check out an exhibit on Hollywood style. "We'll get to see the shoes worn by Marilyn Monroe and Elizabeth Taylor," he enthused, anticipating that their walk would take them through campus. Despite Jenna's short legs, she walked with determination, and Kendall struggled to keep up. In a handful of trees, he could detect the hint of fall, the green just starting to drain from their leaves even though peak color was still at least six weeks away. How the trees had perfected their timing even though the weather remained pleasant enough for shorts always amazed him.

They passed a store window filled with boughs of yellow and orange leaves, autumn-themed ceramic ware, and doll-like scarecrows with straw poking out from their sleeves. Orange was his favorite color, which is why he had dyed his twists the color of flames. He paused to pose in front of the window, and Jenna said, "You'd fit right in."

Kendall crooked his arm through hers. "I've been thinking about our podcast on Covington Terrace. We could start by interviewing Elliott, get some basic background. We need to do some research into the building's history. We could interview Turnbull—visit him on Ward's Island. Then check with the other neighbors to see if anything odd has ever happened to them." He counted off the tenants for each of the apartments: himself, Elliott, Rooney, and Mrs. Gupta on the first floor; and Jenna, Morvena, a vacant apartment, and an older lady with a little dog on the second floor.

"Don't forget the apartments in the basement. I don't know who lives there, though."

"I thought it was just the laundry room and storage lockers down there."

"There are two apartments, plus the boiler room, lockers, and some supply rooms." They stood on a corner waiting for the light to change. "It's strange when you think about it. Passing neighbors in

12

the hallway, you say hello, maybe comment on the weather, but you don't really know them. I've lived there for just over a year now, and they might as well be strangers."

They reached the museum and bought their tickets.

"Robbie broke up with me," Kendall blurted out as they entered an exhibit room with subdued lighting. "He said I wasn't masculine enough."

"And that was a surprise to him? Well, I always thought he was a jerk, and that just clinched it."

Kendall studied a velvet-covered platform chopine from sixteenth-century Italy and read the description aloud. *"The chopine was so tall that the wearer could not walk unaided.* Now, that's my kind of shoe."

"Are you avoiding your feelings?"

"No."

"It's just that you glossed over what Robbie said about you. I know that was hurtful."

Kendall bent close to study the beading on another shoe. "If I worried what everyone thought about me, I'd never be able to get out of bed in the morning."

In fact, Robbie's comment had wounded him, more so than if it had come from a stranger. They had only been seeing each other for several months, but Kendall had become rather attached to Robbie. Yet he knew Jenna was right. Robbie was a jerk. Pretentious, with a self-conferred crown of superiority, constantly putting down people and their opinions. Kendall had tolerated Robbie's jibes with uncharacteristic passivity, as if he bought into the lie that Robbie was better than him. Normally, Kendall would not have tolerated such disrespect. The fact that he had allowed Robbie to get away with it suggested old feelings of inferiority from his childhood still lurked below the surface. How difficult it was to completely banish such fears of inadequacy. How intractable were society's judgmental prejudices.

Jenna paused in front of a preposterously elevated Vivienne Westwood platform shoe in embossed red leather.

Kendall looked over her shoulder. "That's the kind of shoe Naomi Campbell made famous when she fell over on the runway."

"Ankle-breakers."

"No one ever said being stylish was safe."

They came across an illustration of a Manolo Blahnick shoe with small dog bones stacked in a column up the front.

"I can see you wearing that for Halloween," said Jenna.

"I'm still looking for ideas for what I should wear this year. Whatever it is, it has to be spectacular."

Kendall melted when they came to the end of the exhibit and he spotted the Beth Levine stilettoes worn by Marilyn Monroe. Simple and elegant, with a point that was not too harsh, and a uniform cherry red except for the small buckle the muted shade of aged brass. The shoe's interior matched the color of the buckle. He thought about the contrast between the ostentatious Manolo Blahnick—unquestionably over the top—and the classic, refined Beth Levine. They both reflected a different part of his personality, and he had difficulty choosing a favorite between the two. Then again, who said one had to choose?

That night, Kendall's recurring nightmare returned for the first time in several months. Perhaps Mrs. Gupta's experience had gotten under his skin and reawakened old fears. Watching horror movies rarely bothered him, but what she had experienced was real life. It had happened right next door, on the other side of the wall from where he slept. The nightmare always began with a diffuse anxiety. Sometimes he would be driving a vehicle but the steering wheel and brake would not respond to his maneuvers. Sometimes he would be running through empty city streets, pursued by an unseen enemy. However it began, eventually he ended up standing in the dark, his hands and feet tied so he could not run away. Firelight illuminated the faces of the men gathered around him, anonymous faces etched in anger. One man—or sometimes more—wore a wooden mask atop his head that made him tower above the others. A white cloth fell like a shroud beneath the headdress, hiding the man's face. The mask was a brown orb with black triangles for its eyes and slashes on the cheeks, giving the impression of a giant African jack-'o-lantern. Coils of hair protruded up and out from the forehead of the mask like frozen snakes. The masked figure danced and twirled as embers lifted out of the flames and vanished into the night. Then a blade flashed in the hands of one of the men. At that point Kendall would awaken in terror.

As usual, the dream followed its trajectory to the point where the knife glinted in the firelight. Kendall woke up with a gasp. After removing his Blanche Devereaux and turning on the light, he went to the bathroom to splash warm water on his face, and looked in the mirror. The face staring back still had an ashen look. He said aloud, "It was only a dream," but its reappearance still disturbed him. A bath would soothe his nerves. The pipes shuddered as he turned on the tap, and the water came out in a torrent. He poured scented bath salts into the bubbling water, then set several candles around the tub, waiting for it to fill.

Years ago he had done research to try to understand the persistence of the dream. He knew that anxiety and depression could trigger nightmares. He read once that recurring dreams signify the existence of something stressful in one's life that one has not acknowledged. That theory sounded reasonable. But he had never been able to link the dream to anything specific. Once, he consulted a psychic who claimed to be able to interpret dreams. After gathering facts about his past, she said the dream represented his grief over his father's death when he was a toddler. He found the psychic's interpretation unsatisfying. And the explanation did nothing to prevent the dream from coming back.

He lowered himself into the bath, closed his eyes, and leaned back against the porcelain, placing a hot washrag over his eyes. Tranquil music at a low volume played on his smartphone. The water felt good, made him forget about the disturbing images from the dream. He tried to remember his father, but nothing came beyond the photo of the white man standing next to his mother, taken on their wedding day. Helen Akande had worked hard to raise her only child after Kendall's father died in an accident. She had always been there

15

for him. Helen had not pushed him out of the house at sixteen, unlike what happened to fellow drag queen Tipsy Hedrin. Helen came to his performances and clapped proudly, telling the patrons around her, "That's my son." She had insisted he attend college, just as she had in Lagos. "I don't care what you study or where you go. But you *will* go to college. A good education is essential, not only to earn a good living, but as a safeguard against falling victim to prejudice and superstition."

He heard footsteps above him. Jenna was up. A minute later, his phone chimed and he read the text: *Are u up?* He dialed her number.

"I heard the water running," she said upon answering the call.

"I had my nightmare and needed a distraction. Sorry if I woke you."

"No, that's okay. I'm sorry about your dream."

"I just can't figure out why I still have it after all these years. I'm sure it's playing on an endless loop in hell."

"Maybe all the talk of a haunted building triggered it. And I wouldn't doubt that Robbie's rejection stirred up feelings of vulnerability."

"That's possible."

"You still up to going with me tomorrow to see my grandmother?"

"Yeah, sure."

"You won't be too tired?"

"Only if you're planning on visiting her at dawn."

"Okay. I just want to give you an out if you need it."

They chatted for a few more minutes before ending the call. Kendall slid lower into the water so it covered his shoulders, his knees bent into a chevron. Was it possible the building was haunted? He imagined himself halfway on the spectrum between his credulous aunt and skeptical Jenna. He was open to the possibility, but had so many questions. Why would some ghosts linger in this world while others moved on? Why did they manifest only sporadically? If they were incorporeal, how did they make sounds like footsteps and scratching in the wall? If they did not have bodies and vocal cords, how could they laugh (or was that just a movie cliché?), let alone say something like *I'm going to enjoy watching you die*?

Stop thinking about ghosts, he told himself, and turned his attention to his Halloween outfit. He envisioned something sexy, feminine, uncommon, but realistic. He wanted to create the height of illusion, so onlookers would think he was a real woman. No wild fantasia or clever joke this year. The dress was key—he would build the look around the dress. But he needed a fabulous idea capable of turning heads. An idea started to take shape in his mind. It would be a complicated dress to make. But it would be gorgeous, and unforgettable.

A Ghost Story

Jenna

Twice a month, Jenna journeyed across town to visit her grandmother in Happy Gardens. She mocked the name each time she told Kendall about the visits, describing how the facility mimicked a small town to soothe dementia patients. Grandmother Lily—or as Jenna called her, LaoLao—had been there for the past year, ever since her condition had worsened.

"Happy Gardens—such a stereotypical name," Jenna complained.

"And what would be better—Sunset Last Stop?" Kendall countered. "A little reminder that their days are numbered?"

"You know what I mean. It's just so phony. Everything about the place is phony. There's about as much happiness there as on the dark side of the moon."

Kendall ignored the bait. "Apart from the place, how do you feel about these visits?"

Jenna looked out the window of the streetcar as it pulled away from the stop, its bell chiming. "They're so hard. Sometimes she thinks I'm my sister, or my mom, so I don't even get the satisfaction of credit for spending time with her."

"But that's not the important thing."

"No, you're right. I'm always the dutiful granddaughter. On the worst days, though, it bothers me that she thinks I'm a total stranger."

"Yet you still go. Because you're able to show her that someone cares and is willing to spend time with her. It's not about the past, or the future. It's about the present."

"Oh, that sounds *so* Zen."

Kendall gently elbowed her. "Stop being so cynical. You get this way every time you visit Grandma Lily."

They lapsed into silence for a few minutes. Happy Gardens gave Jenna the creeps. Each of the residences, constructed with the facade of a clapboard house and porch with a rocking chair, surrounded a central square in imitation of a traditional town. A fountain gurgled in the center of the square, but since the entire space was enclosed like a huge warehouse, the water echoed in the ominous way that splashes echo in an indoor pool. Green artificial turf lined the street. Windows gaily decorated with fake shutters and window boxes with plastic flowers faced the square. Light coming in through clerestory windows illuminated the ceiling, which was painted blue with puffy white clouds. As night fell and the daylight dimmed, old-fashioned streetlamps came on and LED lights that dotted the ceiling began to twinkle their artificial starlight.

She had read the literature, about how this imitation of the past soothed patients, how even those beset with terrors would relax without the need for medication like Haloperidol. The fiction was so much kinder than drugs or restraints, but it rankled her all the same. She had argued with her mother, who scolded, "Would you rather she be content like this, or drugged into docility?" Jenna had no comeback to that question. What bothered her was how everyone participated in the fiction, telling Lily that her husband was away at the office rather than buried in the cemetery, or leading her to the make-believe bus stop when she said she wanted to go home, even though no bus would ever arrive. Then, after half an hour, when she no longer remembered why she was sitting on the bench, a relative or a nurse would escort her back to her residence.

"I just hate lying," Jenna said. "I have a pathological aversion to lying."

"Don't think of it as lying," Kendall said, examining his nails. "Think of it as creative storytelling to spare someone needless pain. What do you think of this color? I tried a new brand."

Jenna looked at his outstretched hand but barely registered the image. "It's fine."

"Fine? Is that all you have to say? You don't even care." He snatched back his hand.

"I'm just distracted. No, really, I like it. It's—very autumnal."

"Good observation. It's called *Autumn Glaze*, as a matter of fact. You're redeemed. I think I'll wear it with my dress for Halloween."

"Do you have a design in mind?"

"In my head. I haven't sketched it out yet. But it will be slinky, silvery, and sparkly."

"You're going for a cool femme fatale vibe, then?"

"Picture a cross between Barbara Stanwyck and Pam Grier."

"That is some combination."

Lily was sitting on her porch when they arrived, still as a statue, with a vacant look on her face. She appeared startled when Jenna called out to her.

"It's Jenna, LaoLao." The bewildered look remained, so Jenna added, "Nancy's daughter." She sat down in the other chair while Kendall leaned against the railing. "This is my friend, Kendall. Do you remember Kendall?"

Lily looked at Kendall for a moment before nodding.

Under her breath, Jenna muttered, "Great, she remembers you but not me."

"I know who you are. Jenna. Nancy's daughter."

Kendall laughed. "All right, Miss Lily. You tell her."

Lily directed her next comment to Kendall. "I watch her like a hawk when she was little. Always get into mischief."

"Do you want to go inside, LaoLao, so Kendall can sit down, too?"

19

"No, I'm fine, diva," Kendall interrupted. "Let's not disturb the moment."

Jenna took Lily's hand and held it lightly with her other hand resting on top. She relaxed, realizing that this would be one of the better visits. It was hit or miss, these visits with Lily. The times when Lily's memory clouded over left Jenna feeling drained, and more and more such visits had become the norm. But today, Jenna could see a bit of the woman she had once known peeking through: the telltale sarcasm (which Jenna had inherited), and the firm independence that had provided such a strong role model when Jenna was little. She had always aspired to be like Lily. Perhaps that was why the deterioration of Lily's mind and the obliteration of her personality hurt Jenna so deeply. She took it personally.

"Did the mail come yet?" Lily asked.

"No, LaoLao. It's Sunday. There's no mail on Sunday."

Jenna told her about an important project at work, which entailed a suite of ads covering the entire exterior of streetcars and colorful tunnels where passengers walked in subway stations. Lily had always taken such pride in Jenna's career and artistic talent. She listened attentively to Jenna's description of the bright colors and shapes, then asked, "Did the mail come yet?"

Jenna looked up at Kendall, imploring for help. He kneeled down to be at Lily's same level. "Yes, Grandma Lily. Jenna sent you a letter telling you that she would be visiting today. And she wrote about a personal art piece she's been working on that you would love. It's a huge tree of life showing the whole family: your mom and dad, your children, and their children, your brothers and sisters, all the branches full of leaves reaching up to the sky, and roots anchoring the tree deep into the earth. Beautiful shades of brown and green, and a perfect blue sky with a blazing sun as bright as the light bulbs on a vanity mirror."

Lily smiled. "Oh, how wonderful. Where is it?"

"The letter? We'll show it to you later when we go inside."

Jenna regained her footing. "Do you remember the time you took me and Beth to Centre Island? We had so much fun." Jenna recounted how they had walked around the petting farm, and how she became enamored by one particular sheep with the dramatic contrast between its fluffy white fleece and its black face and legs. The fleece had felt so soft, like clouds, and she imagined she lived in a castle in the sky with the sheep as her companion. Ornate bridges connected the clouds, just like the little pedestrian bridges between the isles comprising the Toronto Islands. She imagined her grandparents living on one cloud, her parents on another, and she would visit them with just a quick walk over any bridge.

"Yes, and you had a fit when we did not let you go on the log ride twice." Lily made a face of mock disgust, then leaned toward Kendall. "So willful. I think she get that part from me. Not from her mother, always obedient."

Jenna pretended to be hurt. "You're saying I wasn't obedient?"

"When it suited you."

Kendall laughed. "And she hasn't changed one bit."

"No fair. You're ganging up on me."

A dark cloud seemed to descend on Lily, and she suddenly announced, "Ma came last night."

"What do you mean, she came?

"She appear at my bedside. I ask her, Why do you come, Ma? But she say nothing. Ghost Month is almost over. Maybe I neglect her spirit, and that is why she came."

"Now, LaoLao, you were a good daughter. Ma would have no reason to chastise you."

"No, I am neglectful. I have nothing to give her."

"Then we need to bring her something," said Kendall.

Jenna pulled out some money and handed it to Kendall. "See if you can find some food in the vending machine."

"What kind?"

"Anything. It doesn't matter. Just get a variety. Okay, LaoLao, Kendall is going to buy some food for Ma and we'll leave it out on a plate for her, so everything will be all right."

"Oh, thank you, Nancy. You are a good daughter. Always so obedient."

Jenna looked at Kendall and grimaced. He scampered away in search of food.

Lily gripped Jenna's hand. "You must be careful of the hungry ghosts. You know spirits live for a while after death until they fade away, and you must always pay attention to them until they leave."

"I know." Ma had been dead for almost twenty years. Lily's lapse into the past, as if Ma had passed away just recently, disturbed Jenna, who found the time travel disorienting. She tried to distract Lily by talking again about the fictitious tree of life project, although her improvisatory powers could not match Kendall's. Then she made the mistake of mentioning the roots, which reminded Lily about Ma. Another round of worry ensued.

Kendall returned with a handful of snacks: small bags of potato chips, a candy bar, and a bag of peanuts.

"Look, LaoLao, Kendall has brought some food for Ma. He's going to put it on a plate inside, along with this twenty." She handed Kendall the cash and tried to convey with a look what she hoped he would do. Kendall winked in return. "After he comes back out, we'll wait a while here on the porch, then check to see if she came. I'm sure she'll be happy with what we brought her."

Lily relaxed and sank back into her chair.

A frail woman with a bent frame shuffled by in slippers and black pants that ended above her ankles. She lit up when she saw Lily on the porch. Jenna offered her the chair, but she shook her head.

Lily rested her hand on Jenna's arm. "Mrs. Shin, this is my daughter, Nancy."

Jenna was about to protest, but Kendall returned at that moment and nudged her elbow. Instead, she bowed her head. Mrs. Shin clapped her hands together in delight and said, "Oh!" Jenna could not determine if Mrs. Shin recognized her from a previous visit or was just being polite, because that was the extent of Mrs. Shin's vocabulary. She had lost the ability to speak due to a stroke, but she could infuse that one word with enough shades of meaning to communicate reasonably well.

Jenna introduced Kendall and explained that they were offering food to the hungry ghosts. Mrs. Shin said "oh" with a different intonation to indicate she approved greatly and a nod of her head to suggest how lucky Lily was to have such a wonderful daughter who honored the traditions.

Kendall asked Mrs. Shin if she had any photos of her children to share. She let out a dejected, drawn out "oh" and shook her head. Noticing Kendall's nails, she took one of his hands to inspect it up close. A mischievous smile spread across her face.

"It's called *Autumn Glaze*," said Kendall. "Do you like it?" Mrs. Shin nodded, then looked at her own hands and sighed. "I take it you don't get the opportunity to dress up much. But I tell you what. Next time I come, I will bring you a bottle of *Autumn Glaze*."

Mrs. Shin brought her hands to her cheeks but was too overcome to even say *oh*, and contented herself with just opening her mouth like a carp.

Jenna nudged Lily to her feet. "LaoLao, let's see if Ma came yet." The group entered the housing unit. On the table sat a large dish with a dusting of potato chip crumbs, surrounded by open wrappers. Jenna gave Kendall a smile of gratitude. "Look! She came and took the food. And the twenty, too."

Lily swayed with joy. "Oh, thank you, thank you."

Mrs. Shin shouted "Oh!"

Jenna watched Kendall scroll through his phone. She knew what would come next, now that he had an audience assembled in an upbeat mood. A rendition of Diana Krall singing "Peel Me a Grape" started. Kendall turned up the volume and grabbed a shawl off the sofa as a prop for his best imitation of a blasé chanteuse. As he mimed the words and twirled the end of the shawl, Jenna thought about Lily's mental decline, how it had started with insignificant things. At first, Lily had trouble finding the right word in the middle of a conversation. She would switch to Mandarin, and then Jenna's mother would supply the right word in English for Jenna's benefit. It was easy to write off these early incidents as memory lapses in her non-native language. Then she lost interest in playing mahjong with her friends and sat home all day. More words began vanishing from her vocabulary, even in Mandarin. Jenna cried the first time Lily failed to recognize her. She suspected the worst, which the doctor confirmed. Jenna watched the woman she loved slipping away, becoming someone else. That was the cruelest of all, to watch someone become unrecognizable. Eventually, the Lily that Jenna knew would be erased. No more flashes of lucidity or familiarity. What remained would be a stranger. The thought frightened Jenna more than any horror story she knew.

At the conclusion of the performance, the three women applauded. Jenna noticed a serene smile on Lily's face.

Kendall and Jenna gave their goodbyes. As they left, Jenna leaned into him and said, "Thanks for everything. Especially the bit with the food."

"That wasn't me. I left the unopened packages on the plate."

Jenna pushed him affectionately. "You—!" She held out her hand. Kendall laughed and slapped the twenty-dollar bill in her palm.

Murder House

Kendall

"So, Elliott, tell us what you know about the building's haunted history."

Jenna posed the question as she and Kendall sat in Elliott's apartment, the first time either of them had been in there. Even though he lived directly across the hall, Kendall had only glimpsed the interior for the first time the night Mrs. Gupta had screamed, catching sight of a few items behind Elliott's hulk. Kendall had seen a gray sofa facing a flat screen TV. The glimpse had felt like trespassing, or like unexpectedly coming across someone's underwear in the basement dryer. Now here he was, sitting on that very sofa. Although it was mid-afternoon, the smell of breakfast still hung in the air—Kendall identified sausage and greasy eggs— mingling with something a bit stale.

Kendall remembered that embarrassing evening several months earlier when Elliott had seen him coming home in drag. Elliott had done a double take, then returned Kendall's nod without a word. Impossible to guess what Elliott had been thinking. Surprise, of course. But that was understandable. Kendall had not been able to read anything else into Elliott's expression, whether disgust, disapproval, curiosity, or amusement. The few times they encountered one another in the hallway, Elliott would always nod, but they had never stopped to talk or introduce themselves. Kendall only knew Elliott's name from the slip of paper displayed in the mailbox.

Elliott wore a faded gray Toronto Blue Jays shirt, the lettering and logo veined with tiny spider web cracks from innumerable washings. He entwined his fingers and rested them behind his head, pondering Jenna's question. "Well, let's see. The building is late Victorian, probably eighteen-eighties or -nineties. As far as I know, nothing unusual happened during its earliest decades—at least nothing that survives in historical archives. Only when Cabbagetown fell on hard times did bad things start to happen. The first incident took place in 1932. A man named William Monmouth lured vagrants to his apartment and murdered them. Five in total."

Jenna recorded the details on a notepad. "What did he do with the bodies?"

"Chopped them up and buried them in potato sacks in the backyard in the middle of the night. A neighbor got suspicious and reported his nocturnal activities to the police. He killed himself when they came to question him. Slashed his own throat. They discovered a journal filled with drawings of a creature with the body of a man and the head of a horned goat. In the journal, Monmouth claimed that the goat-man had taken over his body and ordered him to kill undesirables."

"I don't even want to ask which apartment," said Kendall.

"Don't worry. It wasn't either of yours. He lived above me, in apartment six. No one ever stays in that unit for long. As soon as the lease is up, they're gone. It's hard for Turnbull to keep it rented. And there must be something negative about the space that turns off many prospective tenants. I've seen it sit vacant for long periods, which is uncommon for Toronto."

The apartment had indeed been on the market for over a month. A *For Rent* sign in red block letters had appeared at the beginning of August near the building's entrance. Fortunately, the apartment had been occupied at the time Kendall moved in, or he might have ended up there instead of his current apartment. He shuddered thinking of the prospect.

"You don't look like someone who would believe in such tales," said Jenna.

Elliott scratched an itch below the head of the blue jay on his chest. "It doesn't bother me, if that's what you mean. But the story gets worse. Cabbagetown was already sliding into decline when Monmouth lived here, and people considered the area pretty sketchy, populated by people on the fringe of society." He glanced at Kendall when he said this, but then must have felt guilty because he corrected himself. "I mean, there was nothing inherently wrong with these people, they were just mistreated and marginalized. Those were not especially enlightened times. Anyway, a mentally unstable woman moved into the apartment where Monmouth had lived. One night she jumped out the window and landed smack on the flagstones."

Kendall grimaced, thinking of his garden court with the Chinese lanterns, just steps away from where she hit the ground. "She died there?"

"No, she survived. For a while. Died several days later in the hospital. But she kept saying *he* had pushed her."

In unison, Jenna and Kendall said, "Who?"

"She described a man with the head of a horned goat. Monmouth's ghost."

Kendall shot Jenna a look of remonstrance. "Ooh, child, if you had gotten me into that apartment instead of the one I'm in now, I'd have killed you."

She laughed. "Unless Monmouth's ghost got you first."

"Of course, the Monmouth murders were notorious at the time," continued Elliott. "She could have heard about the goat-man from news reports, and in her fragile mental state imagined something."

Jenna lifted her pen and twirled it in her fingers. "And after that, anything else?"

"Nothing that made it into the papers."

Kendall asked Elliott if he had heard or seen anything strange in the building.

"I've heard footsteps when the apartment was vacant, and other strange noises and knocking sounds. The woman who used to live upstairs a couple of years ago, Alyssa—before the last tenant—she told me she started hearing a weird thump every night at the same time, very soft but close by, repeated at regular intervals. No one could figure out what would be causing the sound."

"What happened to her?" asked Jenna.

"I don't know. One day she was just gone. Police came to interview folks, but I don't know if they ever found out what happened to her."

"And what about the last tenant?" asked Kendall.

"She only lasted one year, the length of her lease. I did hear her shout out once in the middle of the night. Whether it was a bad dream or something else, I don't know."

The news of the murders, the death, and the disappearance made Kendall wince. Whether or not the ghost was real, these things had happened. A man had murdered five people in apartment six. Residents had been haunted by visions and sounds. Mrs. Gupta had heard a voice in the walls. He looked at Jenna for signs that she mirrored his concern, but she seemed unperturbed. "What about all of the other people who've lived in that apartment?" he asked.

Elliott shifted in his chair. "Nothing that I know about. But people don't talk to each other all that much here, as you probably know. Every building has its own personality, shaped by the people who live there and by other qualities in the design. Some places are really cold. Some places are neutral but indifferent. Some places everybody knows each other, like a village, or an extended family."

Kendall spotted an issue of *Architectural Record* on the coffee table. "I just figured it out. You're an architect."

"Not what you expected, eh? I mean, for me to be living in an old building like this? It's a beautiful structure, though, if you can get past the disrepair." He sat up with enthusiasm and pointed to the walls and ceiling. "Look at the wainscoting and the crown molding in this room. The high ceiling and bay windows. Classic Victorian. Real craftsmanship. You don't see that kind of detail much in contemporary interior design." He relaxed back into the chair. "Plus, I enjoy being in a historic architectural district like Cabbagetown. I did as much research as I could on the building after I moved in. I like to get to know the buildings where I live, their unique history and design."

"Is there anything unique thing about the design of this building?" asked Jenna.

Elliott thought for a moment. "I'd love to know more about its original design and subsequent renovations. Unfortunately, the city no longer has the original records for residential properties built prior to the twenties. And they won't release other records without the owner's permission. If you get the chance, though, check out the boiler room. Turnbull keeps it locked, but there's something you'll find interesting if you can ever get in. I saw it once when he brought in some outside help to repair the boiler. I won't spoil the surprise."

As they concluded the conversation and rose to leave, Elliott tossed out one last comment. "You might also be interested to know that Monmouth's grave is in the Necropolis. Someone cared enough to ensure that he had a nice plot—his parents, I'd guess. Although, Lord knows, it must have devastated them to learn what he had done."

"Can you give us a clue what's in the boiler room?" asked Jenna.

Elliott laughed. "Let's just say it enhances the story I've told you."

In the hallway, Kendall did not try to hide his annoyance, but lowered his voice to a whisper. "Why so coy about what's in the boiler room?"

Jenna shrugged. "I guess, like he said, he didn't want to spoil the surprise." Kendall crossed his arms and grumbled. Jenna nodded down the hallway. "Do you want to come with me to talk to Rooney?"

"No, I think I'll pass. I've got to get ready to go over to my mom's."

She started down the hall. "I'll let you off the hook on one condition—if you promise you'll interview Morvena."

Kendall frowned. "Diva, you drive a hard bargain."

The Girl Next Door

Rooney

Rooney Xavier positioned her smartphone on the tripod, then took a seat facing the camera. She smoothed her lap as if brushing away non-existent lines on the citrus-yellow pants that hugged her legs. She adjusted the magenta-rimmed glasses that matched her lipstick, a superstitious routine she repeated at the start of every filming. She liked to wear glasses because it made her appear more trustworthy. Her legs were pressed tightly together, and her hands rested flat on her lap, a momentary calm before they started tracing their butterfly paths through the air. She glanced one last time at the bulleted talking points on the scrap of paper to her right before pushing the paper out of sight. When she turned back to the camera, she inhaled and lifted her head while parting her lips like an anchorwoman. The words tumbled out effortlessly.

"Hi, folks. Tina Swayne here, with a review of Mom's Eatery. I stumbled on this place recently and thought I'd give it a try. And you know what? Amazing. I've been back, like, three times already. They have the best burgers in town, and the fries are to die for. The prices are reasonable, and the service is excellent. They have two locations—one on Bloor Street in the Annex, and the other on Queen Street East in Riverdale. I've tried both locations, and they're equally impressive. If you're looking for the juiciest, most scrumptious burgers, you've got to try Mom's Eatery."

She got up to review the video, then went into the bedroom to change into black slacks and a white top with a lacy collar. After wiping off the magenta lipstick, she applied a sober, matte finish lipstick close to the color of actual lips while leaning in toward the mirror. She fixed her black hair into a bun, then stepped back for final approval. Thinking she still looked a bit too young, she donned a pair of black-rimmed glasses. Once seated before the camera, she made a last gesture, undoing the top button of her blouse. This time, the hands emerged not as butterflies but as honeybees, zipping methodically from flower to flower as she made her points. She moderated her voice to sound older, more business-like.

"Hi. My name is Alison Merryweather, and I'd like to tell you about Alliance Property Management. I first utilized Alliance a year and a half ago when I was seeking someone to manage two residential properties I own. I was unhappy with the company I had originally employed, and after reading the positive reviews on Alliance's website, decided to give them a try. My only regret is that I didn't use Alliance from the very start. Their level of professionalism and competence truly places them at the top of their class. I have been one hundred percent satisfied with their service. Don't make my first mistake and be seduced by a cheaper service. Because you get what you pay for. I'm absolutely certain you will be as pleased with Alliance as I am."

Rooney edited each video to remove the dead space at the beginning, but restrained the impulse to polish up the quality. She wanted them to look competent but not too slick. After verifying that money had been transferred to her account, she posted each testimonial online.

The knock on the door startled her. She jumped up to stash the tripod, placed the phone on the coffee table, and shouted, "Coming!" She peered through the peephole and recognized one of her upstairs neighbors. Although they had introduced themselves at one point, she was not sure she remembered the name—was it Jessica, or perhaps Jeanie? Something like that. They had traded greetings several times while passing in the hallway. Once, the young woman had asked her when she would be finished using the washing machine in the basement. That had been about the extent of their interactions, because Rooney was always rushing somewhere, hurrying down the front steps, rustling up clients.

"It's Jenna," the neighbor said through the door. Thankfully, Rooney would be spared the embarrassment of having to ask the neighbor again for her name. She remembered just in time to remove her prop glasses before opening the door halfway.

"Wow, you're all dressed up," said Jenna.

"Yeah, um, I wanted to try on this dress for a date this evening." She brushed back a loose strand of hair that has fallen into her face, but made no effort to open the door further.

"Looks great on you."

Rooney thanked her, then asked what Jenna wanted, but the words came out too quickly, a breathless *whadyuwan*.

"I won't keep you, but I just wanted to know if you'd seen or heard anything strange. Kind of like what Mrs. Gupta experienced the other night. Elliott says the building has a haunted history, as you know."

"No, I've never noticed anything odd, and I've been here for three years." The itch to return to her work made her hesitate at first to prolong the conversation, but curiosity won out. She opened the door a bit more, and her shoulders relaxed. "Why, have you?"

Jenna shook her head and laughed. "Hardly. And even if I did, I grew up in a tough neighborhood where we had worse things to worry about than ghosts, so it wouldn't bother me."

A sudden impulse to be hospitable dropped out of nowhere. Although unsure where the impulse came from—maybe it was because she and Jenna were close in age—she opened the door wider. "Would you like to come in?"

"I don't want to hold you up if you're busy."

"No, really. It's fine. I have a little time."

Jenna stepped into the apartment. Rooney worried about being judged as she noticed Jenna looking around the room. Thank God she had stashed away the tripod. She sat on the couch to signal that Jenna was welcome to stay a while.

Jenna took a seat. "Did you grow up in Toronto?"

"No. Barrie. I moved here to go to college. You?"

"Yup. Third generation. My great-grandparents fled the Communist Revolution in China and brought their children here. My mom was born in St. Michael's Hospital. Where did you go to school?"

"George Brown. I got a degree in marketing." Rooney knew this was a lie—she left college without graduating—but she had used the line so often on her website and in conversation that she felt it should be true. She straightened a pile of magazines sitting on the coffee table. "What about you?"

"OCAD."

"Ontario College of Art and Design?"

Jenna nodded. "That's where I met Kendall."

"Isn't that the crazy building with the big black-and-white pixelated box propped up on stilts in the shape of giant colored pencils?"

"That's the one."

"It looks like it could topple over at any minute. Makes me nervous every time I walk by." She leaned back and crossed her arms. "So what is this podcast I heard you mention the other night?"

"It's something Kendall and I started two years ago. We're both really into the horror scene. I can send you the link. We just talk about stuff, review books and films, sometimes interview people."

Rooney nodded, thinking to herself that she did not like horror one bit. She hoped Jenna did not ask about her own endeavors. None but her closest friends knew about her for-pay testimonials. At least she suspected that no one else knew. Anyone who recognized her face and saw one of the videos (for which she charged a premium; the written testimonials were quicker and easier to fake) would of course figure it out. She decided to steer the conversation in a different direction. "Can I ask you something? Do you have as much trouble as I do getting Turnbull to fix problems in the building? I told him, like, two weeks ago about my leaky kitchen faucet, but no one has shown up yet to fix it. You'd think he would be concerned about the cost of his water bill. I've never known such a negligent landlord."

"Yeah. I had a problem with one of the cabinet doors. After waiting a month, I finally decided to fix it myself."

"The oven has not functioned right for a year. I think it's the thermostat. A slight turn of the knob means the difference between undercooking and burning something to a crisp. I've complained over and over. Luckily, I rarely use it."

"But the rent is really reasonable."

"I know. And the longer I stay, the higher the rent goes up on vacant apartments elsewhere, so it becomes harder and harder to move." A brief lull ensued, and Rooney noticed Jenna looking around the room. To fill the silence, she blurted out, "I'm so fed up. I should do something to get back at Turnbull. Maybe that will wake him up."

"What do you mean?"

"Oh, I don't know. Hit him where it hurts. Like his rental income."

"Well, just don't tell me. That way I can plead ignorance if asked."

The two laughed. Then Rooney sensed a shift in Jenna's demeanor, the way she inhaled and crossed one arm to grip her elbow that signaled the imminent launch of a delicate question. Rooney cringed, expecting something intrusive about her line of work. Instead, Jenna asked if Rooney knew about the building's history. Relieved, Rooney shook her head. Jenna shared what she had heard from Elliott, about the murders and the mysterious fall, the doomed second floor unit in the back. Rooney watched Jenna as the story unfolded, wondering if she was being tested. The tale sounded implausible, but then she was naturally skeptical about everything, and knew you could not assume anything was real. When the story finished, she waited for a clue from Jenna to provide whatever it was she thought Jenna wanted to hear: derision, incredulity, hope, excitement.

Jenna offered her own opinion first. "Personally, I don't believe in ghosts. It's fun to imagine the possibility, but I just don't see how they can exist."

Rooney tagged on to Jenna's comment. "Me, too. They always turn out to be fake."

"But I'm open to being convinced otherwise. What would you do, if it turned out our building really is haunted?"

Rooney shrugged. "It would take something extraordinary to convince me."

Rooney's cell phone buzzed. Jenna excused herself, saying she should get back to her apartment, and stood. Rooney nodded, picking up the phone, and said to Jenna, "Talk to you later." Rooney enjoyed giving the impression she was so busy she needed to cut short the visit, and exaggerated her interaction with the caller. As Jenna reached the door, Rooney glanced at her and smiled her camera smile, lifting her eyebrows to signal goodbye.

After Jenna left, Rooney paced the apartment, talking to her friend. She went to the sink to look at the pile of dishes—she was not even sure why—then turned away and walked back to the coffee table to pick up a magazine. The cover showed a row of people of various ages meant to convey a range of Toronto types: the young hipster, a retired couple, a mother with a baby, a young man with a guitar. The headline read, "Toronto's Rental Market Is Downright Scary." She was only partly listening to her friend, because an idea had just occurred to her, thanks to Jenna's inquiry and Mrs. Gupta's scare.

She dropped the magazine and moved toward the bay window, where she noticed a man standing on the front walkway, studying his phone. He faced the street, a baseball cap pulled tightly down on his head, so she could not see his face. From the way his clothes draped his strong build, she guessed he was in his early thirties. The back of his neck between the collar of his T-shirt and his auburn hair was deeply tanned, with a crease slicing across. Bronzed biceps peeked out from his short-sleeved shirt. He probably worked outdoors. A young woman approached him from the sidewalk, extending her hand. After he turned around to escort her to the front door, Rooney realized he was Wade Turnbull, the landlord's son. She had seen him sporadically over the years, when he had come to repair a leaky pipe in the washroom or replace a faulty smoke detector. Such visits had

34

been rare, as far as she could tell, but then she did not keep tabs on everyone in the building, unlike the nosy, annoying woman who recently moved in above her with the improbable name Morvena.

The woman outside was smiling in that over-eager way when one wants to make a good first impression. The buzz of their voices floated into Rooney's living room, and for a moment she lost track of her own conversation. She had to ask her friend to repeat the last comment. As Wade and the woman approached the front door, he looked up and saw Rooney. *Fat chance I can get him to fix my faucet or oven today*, she thought, but attempted a smile just in case.

She heard their voices echo in the hallway outside her door. The woman must have come to look at the vacant apartment. Their voices faded with the sound of their footsteps on the stairs, one heavy, the other a gentle tap-tap.

Rooney calculated that she had ten minutes or less to wrap up her call, and began to plot how she could waylay the visitor out of Wade's earshot. She cracked open her door, trying to split her concentration between her conversation and listening for their return. Rooney missed something her friend said. She resisted requesting the comment to be repeated and instead laughed along, though she had no idea what she was laughing about.

She heard a door shut down the hall and peered out, even though she knew it could not be Wade returning so soon. True enough, Elliott Bernbaum strode down the hall, stuffing his keys into his pocket. He offered a half-smile when he spotted Rooney, but at that moment she was distracted by her conversation and failed to respond to Elliott's smile. How difficult it was to juggle one's attention. Although their eyes met, Elliott had already passed by the time his gesture registered, and she was left with the image of his smile withering. Then he was out the front door, which swung slowly shut behind him on its pneumatic arm before closing with a solid bang. Above her, she heard Morvena scamper to the window to investigate the cause of the noise.

Footsteps on the stairs announced the imminent return of Wade and the young woman. Rooney cut short her call with "Hey, can I call you back? I've got to go." She waited until Wade was almost in front of her door, then opened it. "Oh, hi. I was on my way out, but if you have a minute, could you take a look at my leaky faucet?"

Wade's face remained impassive, a blank slate she could not read. He blinked a couple of times. Up close, Rooney remembered he was sort of good-looking. Not the kind of handsome you would pick out in a crowd, but with an insouciance she found sexy.

"Can it wait?" he asked. "I'm kind of in the middle of some business right now."

"Well, actually, I complained to your dad, like, two months ago, and it still hasn't been fixed." Rooney eyed the young woman, hoping this negative tidbit would discourage her tenancy. She could tell that the woman did not want to appear impatient with her prospective landlord, which gave Rooney the confidence to press her request. "Please. At least take a look at it, then you'll know what you'll need when you return."

Wade looked her up and down, then without a word ambled into the apartment. "It's in the bathroom," Rooney called out after him. She turned back to the woman and smiled her sincerest smile, which was not really sincere at all. "So, are you looking at the apartment?"

"Yes. The rent is a bargain. Plus it's a top floor unit."

Rooney stepped into the hall and pulled the door almost shut behind her. She lowered her voice. "He did tell you why the rent is so cheap, didn't he?" The woman shook her head. "Something really bad happened there years ago. A man murdered a bunch of people, chopped them up in the tub." The woman grimaced. "Everyone in the building knows the apartment is haunted. I've even heard strange noises myself. That's why the landlord has so much trouble keeping it occupied."

The young woman's eyes widened, then she furrowed her brow. "Why do you stay?"

"The bad energy stays in that apartment. I've never noticed anything in mine. But everyone who's lived there has horrible stories to tell. I just thought you'd want to know before renting it."

Wade pulled the door open, startling Rooney, who still had her hand on the doorknob. "The faucet in the bathroom is fine."

"Oh, did I say the bathroom? I meant the kitchen. Sorry."

"I'll come back and fix it." He held up a clipboard with a completed form and turned toward the young woman. "I'll check your credit and let you know later today."

She looked at Rooney as she said, "No rush."

2

Excerpt from Shockadelica Podcast
Episode 2: Origins

Jenna: People want to know how we came up with the name
            Shockadelica.
Kendall: You mean how you stuck a fork in the toaster while
            dressed up like Jane Fonda in *Barbarella*?
Jenna: No, silly, the real story.
Kendall: Oh, okay. Well, my mother was a huge Prince fan.
            "Shockadelica" is a song about a woman who is so
            seductive the singer thinks she might be a witch. And he
            can't tell if things are real or a mirage. He sings in this
            artificially tweaked, cartoonish voice that for some reason
            really appealed to me as a kid whenever my mom played
            it.
Jenna: Prince didn't actually come up with the name, did he?
Kendall: No. A fellow musician, Jesse Johnson, titled his album
            Shockadelica. Prince was disappointed to find out there
            was no song on the album with that name—how could
            you come up with such an awesome title and not make it
            a song, too?—so he decided to write his own song.
Jenna: And when you proposed it as the title for our podcast
            about all things horror, I was, like, that's perfect.
            Something shocking. A little retro.
Kendall: With a hint of drag. It would make a great drag name.
Jenna: And the lyrics are so appropriate.
Kendall: See, everything ties together.

39

The City of the Dead

Kendall

By mid-September, summer already seemed a distant memory. The weather had cooled appreciably—still pleasant, but the blue sky and verdant trees tricked you into imaging it was warmer outside than it actually was: not warm enough for a short-sleeved shirt but not yet cool enough for a coat. And while some people might treat autumn as a straight slide downward toward winter, Kendall understood it was more like a seesaw. This day just happened to be on the up part of the cycle. At least the cloudless sky kept the day from being moody. A good day to visit the Necropolis, the city's mid-nineteenth-century cemetery.

As they left Jenna's apartment, Morvena opened her door. "Would you like to come in for cocktails and a cigarette?"

"Sorry," said Kendall, "but we're on our way to—on our way out." Better not to let her know their business. She was nosy enough without handing her a clue.

"Oh, that's a shame. Well, another time, then."

She hovered at the top of the stairs, watching them descend. Kendall could feel her eyes peering down on them, the spider watching its prey wiggle out of the web. Only after they had left the building did he feel comfortable talking. "She is so odd."

"At least you don't have to live on the same floor as her."

"Did you hear her the other night, when there was a party on the next street?"

"You mean when she went to the fire escape and shouted, *This has got to stop*?"

"Yes. I feel sorry for her, always hounded by the slightest sound."

"I think she's just lonely. She later told me that if they were going to make so much noise, at least they could have invited her over."

Jenna reported that she had spoken to Rooney but did not learn anything to suggest strange occurrences in the building.

40

"What's she like?" asked Kendall.

"She's nice. But guarded. Like she has something to hide. And skittish, like those little brown birds over there." She pointed to a group of wrens on the ground that flitted in unison to the interior of a bush as Jenna and Kendall drew near.

They entered the Necropolis through a white, Gothic archway. The Victorian gingerbread and exposed ribbing above their heads suggested passage through the bleached skeleton of a chapel. To their left sat a small sanctuary covered in ivy, with a Gothic turret capped by a black witch's hat. Sunlight spilled through the trees, creating dappled patterns on the grass and walkway. Black squirrels skittered across the lawn, pausing to eat delicacies or listen to the sound of footsteps and voices, their tails twitching. Pedestals capped by small obelisks rose amid slab tombstones and monument blocks. A few of the obelisks, tinted a soft shade of salmon, caught Kendall's eye, providing relief from so much black and white. He thought of the colorful Guatemalan gravestones he had seen once in a photo, vibrant with shades of turquoise, peach, burgundy, verdigris, and goldenrod, and lamented the unnecessary North American restraint.

Jenna stopped to inspect one tombstone, the words on its face half-buried in lichen. Kendall tried to read the dissolving name, the physical embodiment of a memory gradually being effaced while equally old markers nearby looked as legible as if freshly minted. It hardly seemed fair. But who ever claimed the world was fair? So much seemed arbitrary in what people deemed acceptable or unacceptable. Take a bright orange tombstone, for instance. How would people react if he were to erect one here for his own grave? Would they shake their heads and wag their tongues, perhaps prevent it from being erected, or violently deface it?

He pointed to a salmon-tinted obelisk to their right. "I'm glad to see someone had the sensibility to choose something with a touch of color."

"Yeah, it's otherwise pretty monochromatic here. No surprise." A falling leaf landed at her feet. "Do you think we'll be able to find Monmouth's grave?"

"Well, the picture I found on the Necropolis website will help us narrow down its location by what's around it." He pulled up the photo on his phone, looked around, then pointed toward a far corner. "Over there, I think."

They passed along a shaded stretch of the path. Out of direct sunlight, the air noticeably cooled. Kendall rolled down the sleeves of his sweatshirt. A grandiose monument with a Gothic spire rose majestically beneath a broad oak, prompting his trademark irony. "Such a humble statement."

"What would you want for yourself?"

"Not that, for sure. Something colorful, full of life. The inscription would read: *He was kind to animals and small children yet could spot the difference between a Jimmy Choo and a Miu Miu.*"

"I don't want a tombstone. I want to be cremated. You have to promise me you'll scatter my ashes on Ward's Island. Near that beach we like to go to. And have a big party on the beach afterwards. Unless it's winter. Then you can have the party indoors."

"How considerate."

Jenna jabbed him in the ribs and he shouted "Ow."

They reached their destination and stopped. Kendall pulled out his phone again and held it up, comparing the photo to the scenery. He tried several different angles before he found what he wanted. "There it is."

They approached the marker. The slab had been knocked from its foundation and rested face up. It was unclear how that had been accomplished, but the inscription had also been defaced with several gouges as if by a crowbar or other heavy tool.

"Who would want to do that?" asked Jenna.

"I can imagine an angry relative of one of his victims having done this back in the day, but the break looks relatively fresh." He took a photo of the marker.

Jenna yanked on Kendall's sleeve and lowered her voice. "Don't be obvious or turn around fast, but there's someone—or something—watching us through the bushes. It looks like a satyr, with great big horns." As Kendall swiveled his head, she grabbed his sleeve and jerked him back around to face her. "I said don't be obvious!"

"You expect a casual glance when you describe something out of Greek mythology?"

"I don't know if that's what it is exactly. It's hard to see through the bushes. Oh, it's moving away."

Kendall heard the snap of a twig and guessed the individual was thirty feet away from them. He turned around and glimpsed the backside of the creature as it dropped out of sight where the land descended toward the Don River. The glimpse had been so fleeting he was not certain what he had seen, except for the black horns that twisted into the air in menacing spirals. "What was *that*?"

"I don't know. But it was obviously watching us."

Kendall suddenly remembered what Elliott had told them. He grabbed Jenna's arm. "Oh, no! The goat-headed man—Monmouth's ghost."

"No, that's not... That's impossible." They both looked down at the gravestone, then at one another. "Isn't it?"

Kendall hugged himself. "This is too, too creepy."

"Should we follow him?"

"No!" The force of his response surprised him. "What are you thinking, girl? That's exactly what the crazy people would do in a horror movie. Let's get out of here."

Kendall looked back several times to make sure they weren't being followed. Only once they had passed beyond the gate and onto the street did he relax. He could sense Jenna laboring to come up with an explanation for what they had seen, a nervous energy animating her limbs as she stared into the distance.

"Elliott's the one who told us about the goat-man, right?" she said. "And he told us that Monmouth's grave was in the Necropolis. Maybe he followed us here and is pranking us."

Kendall checked behind them once more as they walked down Winchester Street. "Why would he go to so much trouble to scare us?"

"I haven't worked out that detail yet."

"Was that a mask covering its head?"

"That's what it looked like. With an animal face, not a human face. Two large nostrils at the end of a long, black snout. With widely spaced eyes and stiff ears sticking straight out."

Kendall recalled the goats across the street from the Necropolis at Riverdale Farm. The last time he had visited was on a field trip in elementary school. He had watched the goats grazing in their paddock. They had returned his gaze blithely, mouths moving from side to side as they chewed. A young doe had wandered down to the fence. Kendall stood on the bottom rail of the fence so he could reach over and pet it. The doe seemed harmless, almost cuddly. Then he saw another goat chase a worker across the paddock and butt the man with its head, knocking him off his feet. It had happened so quickly, without provocation. All the kids laughed. The goat turned and trotted away, apparently satisfied with the outcome. Perhaps it was settling an old grudge. Or perhaps it had done it just for sport. Whatever the reason, Kendall's teacher had explained how goats were like any animal: unpredictable. Kendall did not pet any more animals that day.

"I only saw him from the back," he said.

"Then you're lucky. It was freaky-deaky."

The incident haunted Kendall the rest of the day, reminding him of the masks in his nightmare. Not that they looked anything alike, based on Jenna's description. But both conveyed ill-omened intent. Sure enough, sometime after midnight, the nightmare crept in on its little goblin feet. Torchlight. Masked men. The glint of a knife blade. Kendall cried out, a guttural moan that catapulted him out of the dream. He opened his eyes to the pitch black beneath his Blanche Devereaux and used both hands to slip the mask onto his forehead. Seeing the familiar shapes of his bedroom did nothing to diminish the panic still coursing through his veins. The drumming of his heartbeat threatened to burst through his chest. His mind raced, on the verge of losing control. Something pressed down on his chest, keeping him from breathing, and he felt clammy. The panic kept expanding until it crowded out all other thought and feeling. He felt the impulse to flee—to just keep running forever, as if he needed to outrace whatever roiled inside him.

The vision at the Necropolis must have stirred up something. He focused on his breathing, one deep breath in, one deep breath out. He unclenched his fists and pictured a peaceful tropical beach with a warm, lazy sun. That usually worked following his nightmares, something his mother had taught him as a child. But bursts of wind rustling the Jungle disturbed his idyll, and his thoughts kept returning to the fear that he was going crazy. Tree limbs shook and cast ragged shadows that scampered across the bedroom wall. Out in the alley, the hinged lid of a garbage can banged open.

He sat up and turned on the bedside lamp, then rose and went to the window. Clouds scudded across the sky, a giant herd of fluffy sheep fleeing something unseen. Broken twigs littered the patio, and one of his chairs lay on its side. The Chinese lanterns swung wildly with each gust. Then he noticed something standing in the Jungle, almost completely camouflaged in the dark mass of bushes and trees. Its shape suggested the creature with the goat head and spiraling horns, standing perfectly still while everything else shook and shifted in the wind. It was watching him. He blinked hard, uncertain that the image was actually there. It must have been his imagination, because a moment later it stepped back and melted into the foliage. He yanked the curtains closed and backed away from the window.

He dialed his mother's number. Helen answered just before the call forwarded to voicemail, a ripple of worry in her voice. Kendall apologized for calling so late and told her about the suffocating sensation and the overwhelming fear that made him think he was losing his mind. He did not mention the image in the Jungle.

"Ah, is that all? Don't worry. It was a panic attack. We see patients at the clinic with similar complaints. Sometimes they worry they are having a heart attack. Did you also have your nightmare?"

"Yeah. But when I woke up this time, the feeling was different. Much more intense. Even worse than the dream. What was that thing Aunt Abbie used to talk about?"

Helen paused. "Ogun Oru?" Kendall could hear the slight annoyance in her voice, to be forced to talk about superstitions.

"That's it. Ogun Oru, when a demon presses down on the chest of sleepers while trying to steal their breath. That's what it felt like."

"People all over the world have similar myths to explain night terrors: slip-skin hag, nattmara, jinamizi, karabasan. I've heard so many. It's just the way different cultures externalize the same psychological experience. Did you experience any temporary paralysis? No? That's good. That happens to some people coming out of bad dreams. But I promise you, this is nothing to worry about. The feeling is horrible, though, I understand."

"More horrible than anything I can describe."

"I know. That's what I've heard our patients say. You're sensitive and artistic, like Aunt Abbie. And that often brings a special burden, a cross to bear. I can refer you to a counselor. There's also anti-anxiety medication you can take, but I would save that as a last resort."

"I'll think about it. It helps just to talk to you."

"Do you have plans tomorrow evening? Let me take you to dinner."

"Sure. Sounds good."

"I'll come get you at six o'clock after I get off work."

"Thanks, my beautiful mother. See you tomorrow then." Kendall's nerves calmed, and he dispelled the image of the goat-man. It must have been a hallucination in his heightened, panicky state. Even so, he left the light on when he returned to bed.

The Hunger

Jenna

When Jenna was nine, she saw a young woman on the subway with a most unusual purse that comprised a patchwork of faces. Not cute drawings of faces, but panels suggesting the designer had actually flayed human skin and cut it into squares, then stitched the pieces together with bloodied twine. Lips, noses, and closed eyes jutted out slightly, each bas-relief face a different shade of skin. Jenna could not look away, equally fascinated and horrified. The woman noticed Jenna's interest and smiled.

"Did you make that?" asked the ever-intrepid Jenna.

The woman said that she had. Jenna pictured a witch collecting children and making human purses in her gingerbread cottage. Although the thought made her uncomfortable, she asked if she could touch the material. It felt supple like leather. Jenna ran her hand over the stitches and felt the bumpy texture. Up close, she could tell that it was only the illusion of stitching, and the material was one continuous piece, dyed to look like separate components.

In the days that followed, Jenna became obsessed with the memory of the image. She checked out macabre stories from the library. She devoured all the Goosebumps books. She felt like a vampire with an insatiable appetite for blood. One book in particular stayed with her, a book that presented evidence to support the truth behind various myths and legends: the Loch Ness monster, Sasquatch trekking through the mountains of the Pacific Northwest, the man-eating wendigo of Algonquin folklore, the real-life werewolf that stalked a region of France during the seventeen-sixties, poltergeist hauntings that had never been explained. That began her fascination with horror.

While her female classmates wrote sentimental poems or drew glittery unicorns, Jenna drew ghostly figures and monsters. The other girls thought she was weird. So did the boys, but at least they thought the drawings were cool. That was when Jenna experienced firsthand the price for being different. She did not conform to the stereotype of the demure, passive girl. She was an outsider. Not in the way she looked, but in the way she behaved.

Kendall knocked on her door. "Ready to interview some more neighbors?"

"Let's do it."

A red mystic knot decorated the door where Jenna's neighbor lived, hanging just below the peephole: a woven diamond shape of interlocking threads with two tassels dangling from the bottom.

Jenna pressed the buzzer and pointed to the knot. "Chinese good luck symbol." On the other side of the door, they heard pitter-patter and the tinkling of a dog tag. Jenna knocked again when no one answered. The dog barked once. "I guess we'll have to come back later."

As they turned away, a short woman arrived at the top of the stairs carrying two bulging grocery bags, her black hair streaked with gray. Jenna introduced themselves and explained that they were getting to know their neighbors. The woman said her name was Lucy Lee. She set down the bags at the door to retrieve her key, and invited them in.

A Yorkshire terrier danced around their feet as they entered the apartment. "That's Aubergine," Lucy said. "Bergie for short." She opened one of the bags to show six plump eggplants. "The clerk said they were having a special later today. Six for two dollars. But I told him I couldn't come back. So he made a special package for me and gave me the discount anyway. I think I reminded him of his mother." Her eyes twinkled when she said this.

Jenna admired how flawless the eggplant looked, with shiny, dark purple skin, unmarred by any imperfections.

"I used to cut them into circles and fry them," Lucy continued. "Now I bake them in the oven with a little olive oil and salt. Much healthier. I take a fork and make two rows of holes so the oil seeps in. I say, *Okay, now, Mrs. Eggplant, let the oil go deep inside and fill you up with flavor. Don't be shy. That's it.*"

"You talk to your food?" said Jenna.

Lucy put her hand on her chest and feigned disbelief. "Of course. That's how you get the best flavor out of it."

"How do you know it's Mrs. Eggplant and not Mr. Eggplant?" asked Kendall.

"Have you ever seen a rooster lay an egg?" Lucy lifted the bags to set them beside the sink. "I also use eggplant to make a killer vegetarian lasagna. You have to caress the noodles as you lay them out in the pan. *There, that's a good noodle. You look so dainty with your wavy edges.*"

Kendall and Jenna laughed.

48

Lucy put the vegetables away. "I'm telling you, it works."

"I'll try it next time," said Kendall. He pointed to Jenna. "This one, however, doesn't know how to cook."

Lucy wagged her finger. "That is such a shame. Everyone should know how to cook. I'll give you lessons sometime."

"I know how to cook," Jenna protested. "Sort of. I just don't like to."

"Diva, you even have trouble boiling water."

Jenna pretended to pinch him. "Pay no attention to the man behind the screen. Do you have any children, Lucy?"

"No. Never married. I was engaged once, but I broke it off." She pulled out a chair and joined them at the table, feeding a treat to Bergie. "I'll bet your next question is what I do for a living. I teach special needs kids. Mostly autistic. I have to trick them into getting exercise, because they don't like to move around a lot. They say, *I don't want to get up*. But you can't just sit around all day. Otherwise you'll turn into a rooted-in-place potato. So I show them how to baste a chicken." She lifted her arms to demonstrate, as if applying deodorant, then rubbed her neck and shoulders. "I tell them, *Let's baste it together*. And they copy my movements. Then I stand and say, *Okay, now shake it all around to mix the juices*." She stood and shook her butt, turning around in place. Bergie took this as an invitation to jump at Lucy's calves, her tag jingling. "And they get some exercise without even knowing it."

Jenna steered the conversation to life at Covington Terrace, which prompted the usual jokes about Turnbull's neglect of the property. "We've heard rumors that apartment six is haunted," said Jenna. "Have you ever noticed anything strange?"

Lucy rested her hands on the table and leaned forward with a serious expression. She looked first at Jenna, then at Kendall. "Do you know about the *diao si gui*? It's the ghost of a person who hanged himself or herself. They have long, straight hair, and their tongues hang out of their mouths, as much as two feet down to their waists, or longer."

"I don't think the human tongue is even that long," said Kendall.

49

"That's what some people report. Not the one I saw, of course. I agree that's unrealistic. The *diao si gui* appeared one night while I was watching television." Kendall and Jenna leaned in closer as Lucy lowered her voice, pointing across the room. "I was sitting right there, on the couch. I saw it at first out of the corner of my eye. It appeared in that corner there. All pale white, and barefoot, with scraggly black hair hanging down hiding its face, wearing a dirty, torn dress. Slowly it lifted its head. The hair fell to the side, revealing two red eyes like hot coals." Her voice was almost a whisper now. "I was petrified, couldn't move. It glided toward me in fast motion, faster than a cheetah, its arms reaching out toward me, and—BAH!"

She slammed her hands on the table, making Kendall and Jenna jump while Bergie barked. Lucy threw her head back and laughed. "I'm only playing with you. Sorry, I couldn't resist."

"You had me going there for a minute," said Jenna. "Especially since several of our neighbors have reported strange, unexplained sounds."

"I've never heard or seen a ghost in the ten years I've lived here. But this is a lucky apartment—number eight. Maybe the *feng shui* helps protect me, too."

Jenna looked around the room. Dark oak sectional pieces framed a stressed plank coffee table, in the center of which sat a small bamboo plant with entwined stalks in a rock-filled, glass vase. Two rice-paper floor lamps guarded the corners. The room emanated a comfortable, welcoming ambience. "You really believe it works?" she asked.

Lucy thought a moment. "Some of it's mumbo jumbo. Like anything, you can take it too far. But I do believe we are sensitive to our environment. You have to be attentive to order and arrangement so you have a harmonious flow. Like music, no? You can arrange the notes so they create certain kinds of energy in the listener."

"Except that with music, sometimes the point is to arrange the notes precisely to create a sense of disturbance," said Kendall.

Lucy nodded. "True. The point is, the arrangement conveys something emotional, just like the arrangement of items in a room.

50

Here, now, I'm a terrible host. I should offer you some tea." She rose from her chair.

"Should we talk to the tea leaves?" Kendall teased.

"That's really just for cooking. But I'll introduce you." She pulled a box of green jasmine tea from the cupboard. "Jasmine, I'd like you to meet Kendall and Jenna." She displayed the box like a game show model, rotating her body first to Kendall and then to Jenna.

"Nice to meet you, Jasmine," they said in unison.

Lucy busied herself with the tea kettle. "You know, this is the first time I've actually sat down with any of my neighbors."

"I guess we're all too busy with our individual lives to take the time to get to know the people around us," said Jenna.

"Yes, modern life, rush, rush." While waiting for the water to boil, she brought out a traditional ceramic tea set and stuffed the filter with tea leaves. She told them she was raised in Vancouver and came to Toronto because of a job offer. It was here she met her fiancé.

"Do you mind me asking why you decided to break off the engagement?" asked Jenna.

Lucy set the tea service on the table. "Oh, heck, I might as well tell you. I called it off because I fell in love with a woman."

"Why, Lucy Lee!" Kendall exclaimed.

Lucy tittered. "It's true. She was the only woman I've ever been with, but I loved her deeply."

"What happened?" asked Jenna.

"She was here on a student visa and had to go back to Spain when she couldn't get permanent residency. It was 1985, before gay marriage was legal, or we might have considered that. At first, we tried to make the relationship work long distance. But it was too hard to sustain over the long run. She ended up marrying a man and raising a family. We still keep in touch, though. And before you start to feel sorry for me, I have many blessings in my life, and no regrets. I'm grateful I was allowed to experience that kind of passion. Many people do not ever receive such a gift."

51

The kettle whistled, and Lucy poured the water into the ceramic vessel.

"Girl, you are full of surprises," said Kendall.

"That's how you keep the ghosts away. They don't like surprises. They want to be in control and be the ones doing the surprises."

"Wasn't that sort of Sarah Winchester's philosophy?" asked Kendall. "The woman in California who built the crazy mansion with stairways leading to nowhere, doors that open into thin air, maze-like corridors?"

"She believed that would confuse the ghosts so they'd leave her alone," added Jenna.

"In some ways, she must have been a pretty smart cookie," said Lucy. "Crazy, yes, but she had the right idea. Keep your enemies confused and surprised."

Lucy shared more stories about her students. Jenna brought up her own struggles to communicate with her grandmother. Lucy had some ideas, and offered to accompany Jenna on a future visit. "Music and motion," Lucy said. "That's the key. It's not a cure, but it will help you sync up with her soul, share something precious, and find some peace. Choose songs and pieces that she remembers from her youth. It will help both of you feel happier."

Kendall announced that his mother was due shortly, and rose to leave. As he and Jenna paused at the door, thanking Lucy once again for the tea, Jenna reached out to touch the mystic knot. "My grandmother used to have one of these hanging in her living room."

"Do you know what it symbolizes?" asked Lucy.

"I only know it's for good luck."

"It symbolizes the never-ending cycle, the continuous flow of energy, good fortune, longevity. The number eight—the infinity symbol—is woven into the design multiple times." Lucy traced the loops with her finger. "The design has been used for thousands of years. Archaeologists found a version dating back to ancient India, and variations have appeared in numerous cultures. Very auspicious." She pointed her finger at Jenna. "I'll bring you one. Soon. When we have that cooking lesson."

Superstition
Kendall

Helen Akande kissed Kendall and entered the apartment, her thick heels clicking with determination across the hardwood floor. She still wore her nurse's uniform following a day at the clinic. She set her purse down in a corner of the couch and walked to the window that overlooked the Jungle. The setting sun had already plunged the garden into shadow. Kendall turned on a lamp and watched his mother lift part of the curtain to inspect a hole. She let it fall back into place without saying anything.

"I'm going to sew that up," he offered, unprompted.

"The landlord should replace them. They've probably hung here for fifty years."

She asked about Jenna. Kendall described the visit to Happy Gardens and the difficult time Jenna had dealing with her grandmother's dementia. "But Grandma Lily enjoyed my little show lip-synching to Diana Krall."

"Music is good—especially familiar tunes. How is that boy you've been seeing—Robbie?"

Kendall looked down at the floor. "We've broken up."

"Oh, son, I'm sorry to hear that." Her voice still carried the lilt of her Nigerian youth, even after two-and-a-half decades in Toronto. "Just remember, the moon that wanes today will be the full moon tomorrow."

His mother had an inexhaustible supply of proverbs for every occasion, which had always amused Kendall. "How do you manage to stay so optimistic all the time?"

"I've survived. I made it to Canada and have a beautiful life. Besides, I have you. A mother must have hope in the future for her children."

Kendall wanted to ask what she meant by saying she survived, but he knew from experience that she refused to discuss certain things from the past. Instead, he pulled out his drawing of the dress he intended to make for Halloween. "Look, Mom, this is the design I told you about."

Helen studied the drawing, then indicated her approval with a nod of the head. "It shows a lot of skin. That's going to be a big challenge to make. Let alone to wear."

"That's why it will be a *tour de force*."

"How will you manage all that cleavage?"

Kendall explained that he would wear a silicone bodysuit that blended with his real skin. "I want to create the illusion of a real woman this time. When you see me you'll think you have a daughter."

Helen laughed. "That's one of the reasons I love you so much. I get a son *and* a daughter—all for the price of one."

She sat and asked how the podcasts were going. Kendall shared the idea for an episode on the building's haunted past. Helen clucked her tongue. "Doing drag I don't mind. But all this interest in horror and superstition..."

"I think of it as a vaccination. I inoculate myself with horror as a way to tame my fears."

"You don't really think the building is haunted, do you?"

"Mrs. Gupta heard something. And my neighbor across the hall heard footsteps when the apartment above was vacant."

"Oh, son, that's nonsense."

Kendall expected such skepticism. "You're probably right. But it's all in good fun, and should make for an interesting episode." He thought of the goat-man he had seen last night in the Jungle. "How can you be sure ghosts don't exist?"

Helen straightened the collar of her blouse. "It boils down to facts. There is no scientific evidence. I have to look at the situation rationally."

"But Aunt Abbie believes in ghosts."

"My little sister has been high-strung ever since she was a baby. She jumps at her own shadow. Oh, I used to get so angry at her when she filled your head with those stories about witches and bush babies. She's probably the reason you like horror movies and books so much." Helen put her hands on the armchair decisively and announced that it was time to go to dinner, her treat.

On their way out, they encountered Mrs. Gupta bringing a basket of clothes up from the laundry room. Kendall re-introduced them, reminding his mother they had met once before.

Mrs. Gupta addressed Helen. "I'm so fortunate to have Kenny as a neighbor." She had started using that affectionate nickname, which would have annoyed him if anyone else shortened his name but charmed him whenever she said it. "He takes good care of me and looks out for my welfare."

Helen beamed and patted her son's shoulder. "He's always been a good son, so full of compassion."

After they left, Helen leaned toward Kendall and said, "She does not seem like the kind of woman who would imagine noises. I have a nose for these things. There must be a logical explanation for what she heard."

"Let's hope."

In the restaurant, Kendall studied his mother's face while she read over the menu. If there was any trauma over having lost her husband so young, she showed no trace of it. But then, she had always been practical and matter-of-fact. She had been twenty years old when she met Kendall's father at university in Lagos, twenty-two when she gave birth. He had come from Ireland to pursue an interest in West African culture. Kendall had few memories of his early years in Nigeria—certainly not of the big city. He remembered playing dolls with two neighbor girls, and the boys who teased him and threw sticks. That had been after his father died, when Helen returned to her hometown to live with her brother and sister-in-law. Helen preferred not to talk about those days. When Kendall would press her, she would say, "Don't let yesterday use up too much of today." Kendall wrote it off as a painful period—the years following his father's death—that she did not want to dwell on.

Helen closed the menu and set it aside. "Have you had any more panic attacks since last night?"

"No. I think it was just because of the stories about the haunted apartment. Then Jenna and I—" He had not wanted to mention the sighting, but it had already slipped half-way out. "We saw a man wearing a goat mask at the Necropolis." The one sighting was enough to mention. At least Jenna had seen it, too. No way would he tell her about the shadowy image in the Jungle.

"What were you doing at the Necropolis?"

"Trying to find the grave of the man who lived in the haunted apartment."

She flicked open her napkin, not without a touch of impatience, and placed it on her lap. "And why would there be a man wearing a goat mask at the cemetery?"

"We think it was one of our neighbors playing a joke—the same neighbor who told us about the tenant who killed people while thinking he was the incarnation of a goat-man."

"Not a very funny joke, if you ask me."

The waiter appeared, temporarily suspending their conversation. Once they had given him their order, Helen resumed her opinion. "Are you sure it's a good idea to pursue this story if it stirs up nightmares and panic attacks?" Kendall looked sheepishly down at his lap. "Look at me, Kendall. I really want to know what you think."

Kendall twirled a knife on the table. "I can handle it. It's not like I'm in danger or anything." Light from the table's candle reflected off the blade. "Do you remember that bully who used to pick on me in fifth grade?"

"Yes. Brian? Butch?"

"Brock. That was his name. He would follow me home from school every day, calling me names and throwing rocks at me. Then, finally, one day I'd had enough. He said something mean about you. That was the last straw. I turned around and marched up to him and kicked him in the balls, and told him if he ever said anything again I would cut his tongue out with a butcher knife. I can take care of myself, and I have a great role model sitting across the table. So don't worry about me."

Helen sighed. "I know you can take care of yourself, son. But that won't stop me from worrying, just the same."

"Last night was the second time I've had that nightmare in the past week."

Helen chastised him with a stern look. "You didn't mention that before."

"I know. They've been so infrequent the past few years. I thought the gods had finally taken pity and given me a reprieve." He paused for a moment. "Did the nightmares start with those stories Aunt Abbie used to tell me?"

"Oh, that was so long ago, I'm not sure."

"Do you remember how old I was when they started?"

"You've asked me that before. I think you were five. No— four. Around the same time we came to live with Aunt Abbie in Toronto."

"So it could have been because of the stories she told me, right?"

"Yes, it could have. But you would beg her to tell you those stories, jumping up and down until I thought your legs would fall off." She shook her head, then took a sip of water. "So what exactly happens in this dream? You never told me the details, you know. I only knew it was something distressing."

"Just a series of sensations. It's night. I see firelight, men with masks, a knife. I'm tied up and someone wants to hurt me."

Helen's glass of water spilled across the table as she distractedly set it down on the edge of the bread plate. Her face looked stricken, but whether from the mishap or from what he had said, Kendall could not tell. She began dabbing her napkin at the wet spot.

"It's only water, Mom."

She seemed not to hear him, and pressed her napkin into the growing wetness. She looked frantically around the room for the waiter, who hurried over when she caught his eye. He gathered up the ice cubes from the table with a napkin.

"It's no big deal," Kendall tried to reassure her. "Not like you spilled a glass of Chateaux Margaux." He'd hoped the joke would make her smile, but he could see the distress in her eyes. "What is it?"

"Nothing. It's nothing." She straightened her back and winced, as if from the memory of something painful.

Kendall leaned back and regarded her with suspicion. "You're not telling me something."

The waiter brought Helen a fresh napkin. She smiled and thanked him, then gave Kendall a look that he recognized as her end-of-conversation look. "Don't let yesterday use up too much of today."

The Tenant

Rooney

Rooney carried her laundry down to the washroom, quarters jangling in her pocket. She spotted Jenna and Kendall when she reached the entrance and stopped. "Oh. Sorry."

Jenna was folding clothes that she had just removed from the dryer. Kendall sat on the table beside the pile of clothes, his shoulders hunched. "That's okay," said Jenna. "I'm all done."

Rooney hesitated a moment, then approached the washer. The basement's skeletal space, with its exposed beams and ductwork, locked doors, spider webs, and ghosted bicycles sporting deflated tires always made her uneasy. So she was glad for the company. While she transferred her clothes into the washer, no one spoke. She was aware that her intrusion had disturbed their conversation, and felt self-conscious. She dropped a small pod of laundry detergent into the washer and closed the lid.

"How do you like the pods?" asked Jenna, dispelling the deadness that hung in the air.

"They're more convenient. No mess." After arranging the quarters in the slots, she pushed in the lever, and a jet of water reverberated inside the drum.

Kendall swung his legs like a kid. "The only problem is they're more expensive. But I guess the ad campaign was successful since they're so popular."

58

"Rooney knows all about marketing," Jenna announced. "She moved here to study it in college."

"Really? Where did you move from?"

"Ottawa."

Jenna looked at her with surprise. "I thought you came from Barrie."

For a moment, Rooney was confused, but landed cat-like on her feet. "Oh, right. Well, I was born in Ottawa but raised in Barrie." Ottawa sounded more prestigious than Barrie, but consistency was not her strength. She watched Jenna try to assimilate the information. As a distraction, Rooney filled the silence with more words. "I moved here to go to school at George Brown but dropped out after the first year."

Jenna opened her mouth as if about to say something but stopped. Rooney worried that she had made another gaffe. She scrambled to recall what she had told Jenna. Her CV—the one provided to prospective clients on her website—said she received an Ontario College Diploma in marketing. Actually, she dropped out after the first year. Had she admitted to Jenna that she dropped out? She could not remember, but decided to hedge her bets. "I dropped out for a while, then later re-enrolled to complete the program."

Jenna looked away to finish stacking her clothes. Rooney feared that the explanation sounded unconvincing. She was accustomed to such awkward moments and the need for improvisation. So she leaned casually against the washer to signal that she was unconcerned by any discrepancies. "Sometimes I don't like to tell people I have a degree in marketing, because they expect free advice. I'll say I dropped out, so they figure I'm not good enough to ask."

Jenna stopped stacking her clothes and looked straight at Rooney. "That is the craziest thing I've ever heard."

Rooney laughed and pushed herself away from the machine. "Yeah, well, it works."

"How did you like the program?" asked Kendall.

Rooney fabricated a response, dropping the names of the professors she remembered from her one year in the program. She still harbored embarrassment that she never completed what was only a two-year program.

The roar of the water jet stopped, and the washing machine began to churn.

Kendall hopped down from the table as Jenna lifted her basket of clothes, and they said goodbye. Rooney waited until they had climbed the stairs before she returned to her apartment.

When she opened the door, she saw a man standing in her kitchen with his back to her, and almost screamed. But when he turned around, she recognized Wade Turnbull. "Jesus, you scared me."

"I left you a message that I was coming."

"I didn't get any message. When did you call?"

"Earlier."

Rooney was about to check her phone but decided she was just grateful he had finally come to fix the faucet. The cabinet doors were open below the sink, and a toolbox rested by Wade's feet. "Don't let me distract you. I'll just be in my bedroom."

She busied herself posting reviews online, half listening to the squeak of the water line being turned off and the clang of the wrench whenever he laid it on the counter. She logged into her different accounts, one for each persona, and posted ten five-star reviews for a particular client.

Before long, she sensed someone behind her and turned around to see Wade standing in the doorframe, holding the wrench. "The leak is fixed," he said.

She closed the computer lid and stood, thanking him. Stalling to keep him a bit longer, she tilted her head so some of her hair coyly half-covered her face. "So, are we going to get a new tenant?"

"You mean the woman who looked at the apartment last week? No, she decided not to take it."

Rooney tried to hide her pleasure. "Oh, that's too bad. Any other prospects?"

"A few. Someone's coming by in a bit to look."

"Hey, do you want to hang out here until they arrive? I can make some lemonade."

"Sure. Okay."

Rather than move out of the way, he only turned to the side so she had to brush against him as she passed through the doorway. It annoyed her and thrilled her at the same time. She chattered on as she mixed the yellow packet with water in a plastic pitcher. She mentioned the problem with the oven. He turned the temperature knob and, hearing no click, agreed that the thermostat probably needed to be replaced.

The ice cubes in Rooney's glass clinked as she swirled the lemonade. Wade sat in a chair with his hands on his knees, the glass set atop a coaster on the coffee table. He drummed the fingers of one hand. The way the T-shirt draped his torso hinted at the outline of a muscular chest—not a gym-toned body straining against the shirt, but one honed naturally through manual labor. She crossed her legs and sipped the lemonade. The conversation proceeded in fits. She could tell that Wade was not shy, just a man of few words, accustomed to swaying minds not with argument but with the power of his presence. He reminded her of a granite monolith. She shared things about herself, exaggerating that she had a Master's in marketing. She had learned that men like Wade found a well-educated woman extra alluring, as if tempted by what they imagined to be out of their league. Such men liked a challenge.

She was disappointed but not surprised that Wade offered no personal details. She knew his father lived on Ward's Island, because that was where she sent the rent check each month, ever since her lease expired and she went month-to-month. At one time she had imagined she would find a better-maintained building. Paying monthly, rather than supplying a year's worth of post-dated checks in advance as was the custom with a lease, gave her flexibility to leave quickly. But it had not turned out that way. The cheap rent kept her tethered to Covington Terrace as if to a boring boyfriend who nevertheless offered useful perks. When Wade mentioned the ferry, she deduced that he still lived with his father. It was unlikely he would own a separate property there, since homes on the island were extremely difficult to acquire, with a long wait list that dragged on for years. But she was curious why Turnbull did not just let Wade stay in one of the building's apartments, so she asked.

Wade shifted uncomfortably. Probably a sensitive topic. He attempted a smile, but his mouth only turned up slightly at the corners, unable to commit fully. "He's seventy-two and needs me to help take care of him."

Rooney nodded as if in agreement, but she found the response unconvincing, and recognized the equivocation of a fellow evader of the truth. Oddly enough, that made her warm to him. She elicited more information about Wade's background and learned that he worked in construction, that his mother passed away when he was a teenager, and that he liked movies about superheroes. Despite the lack of any common interests, she was won over by a certain confidence in his vocal rhythms, as if he did not need to try hard to impress her (unlike so many other men she had met). The over-eager suitor was always such a turn-off.

His phone rang and he excused himself to answer the call. Rooney heard his half of the conversation, piecing together that the prospective tenant had arrived. Wade ended the call, thanked Rooney for the lemonade, and headed for the door with his tools. As he turned the knob, he said, "Maybe we can hang out together again soon."

So she had enticed him with her flirtations after all. During their conversation, she'd had trouble deciphering his level of interest. He was guarded, like her, holding things back. She responded with a simple, "Sounds good," and reminded him about the oven.

After he left, she stood back from the bay window, trying to be inconspicuous, and watched him greet a young man on the sidewalk. Despite her warming attitude toward Wade, she still seethed over his father's neglectful ways. She yearned to punish the old man and tried to figure out a way to corner the visitor like she had done the previous week. As the two men entered the building, she opened her door and asked if she could tag along to see the apartment. Up close, something about the visitor seemed familiar to her, with his shaved head and nose ring. She wondered where around town she might have seen him. Perhaps behind some counter, making her latte. He displayed a gruff expression that did not invite conversation, so she quashed her curiosity.

After the story she heard from Jenna, she half expected to see old bloodstains on the floor. But nothing about the apartment struck her as unusual. She stood at the window, thinking of the woman who had plunged to the ground below. Could an unseen force really have pushed her? That seemed unlikely. But Rooney felt a shiver, and wondered whether the sensation would have occurred had she not known about the history. She took a few steps back from the window, just in case.

In the kitchen, the man tested the faucet and opened cupboards. Rooney wandered into the bedroom, pulled out her phone, and found the recent call from Wade. It was the only call she had received that morning from an unfamiliar number with a Toronto area code, so it had to have been his. She texted him, pretending to be a prospective tenant, and hoped he would not recognize the number. *Hi, I'm at the front door and wonder if I could see the apartment for rent.*

In the other room, Wade's phone chimed. He excused himself, saying he had another prospect.

After he left, Rooney returned to the main room and said, "I love the view from these rear apartments." The man grunted agreement as he opened the refrigerator. "It's just too bad what happened." She watched him pause, hooked by her bait. "Didn't Wade tell you? About the stories? Oh my God, it's not fair to withhold that information."

She proceeded to tell the gruesome history, embellishing the tale with an additional murder for good measure. For the *coup de grâce*, she revealed that the apartment was haunted.

The man just stared at her, then offered his deadpan response. "In that case, it will be perfect."

The comment shocked her so much that her mouth froze in imitation of a fish gasping for oxygen. She wanted to believe the man was joking, but he offered no reassuring smile. Instead, he returned to inspecting the kitchen. She felt like she had just been slapped.

Without looking at her, he continued talking. "Actually, I'm just going through the motions. I already know this apartment." He walked over to the door and inserted a key into the deadbolt, clicking it open and closed. He held up the key. "I'm not surprised that they never bothered to change the locks."

Rooney remembered. "You used to come by to see your girlfriend. This was her apartment."

He pocketed the key. "You got it."

Rooney suddenly felt embarrassed, fearing that the visitor might think she had made up the story about the murders. "What I told you was true. Did you ever know about that?"

"Nope."

"What about your girlfriend? Why did she move out?"

"She didn't." He stared at Rooney with an intensity that made her shiver. "She disappeared."

Rooney wanted to know more, but her phone buzzed. Wade had texted her back after finding no one at the front door, asking what happened. As she left the apartment, she improvised a response and quickly texted back. *Sorry. Emergency. Had to leave.* Stepping out of the apartment, she encountered Morvena in the hall with her hands on her hips. Neither of them smiled a greeting. She passed Wade on the stairs and said, "Where's the prospective tenant?"

"Oh. She had an emergency and had to leave."

It wasn't until a minute later, entering her apartment, that Rooney realized Wade, without apparently knowing the gender of the prospective tenant, had said *she*.

3

Excerpt from Shockadelica Podcast
Episode 30: Goats and Demons

Jenna: Welcome, ghoulies and goblins. Today we're going to talk about goats and demons.

Kendall: Goats and demons. They go together like cake and ice cream. Or a strapless black cocktail dress and a strand of pearls. Why is that, Jenna?

Jenna: You have to go back almost two thousand years to the early days of Christianity. In Greek mythology, satyrs were half man and half goat. They lived in the woodlands and had lusty, uninhibited natures. To Christians, that kind of lifestyle represented sin. According to the Bible, during the Last Judgment, Christ separates sheep on the right from goats on the left. The sheep represent the souls of the saved, while the goats represent the souls of the damned.

Kendall: That seems unfair to heap all that shame on those innocent goats.

Jenna: You can blame it on Pan. The hooves, pointed ears, and horns of the goat were eventually appropriated into images of Satan because of the association with sinful satyrs like Pan. Now, at that stage, Pan and Satan shared a human face, but with goat-like attributes. The goat-headed image of Satan is a much more recent creation. But it starts in the fourteenth century when the Knights Templar were accused of worshiping a heathen deity called Baphomet. There was no accepted concept of what

65

Baphomet looked like, or even any evidence that such a pagan deity existed. Modern scholars believe the name was a corrupted version of Mahomet, or Mohammed. In other words, Islam. But whatever, Baphomet wasn't goat-headed. Then, during the eighteenth century, folks who wanted to discredit Freemasonry fabricated histories that linked Freemasonry to the Templars, Baphomet, and occult practices. The occultist Eliphas Levi exploited this link in 1856 by reimagining Baphomet as a winged, goat-headed figure with breasts and a pentagram on its forehead.

Kendall: So we have that guy to thank for Satan as a goat.

Jenna: Exactly. But Levi wanted to symbolize the union of opposites: male and female, good and evil, et cetera—not to create an image of Satan. The problem was that, for Christians, the goat and pagan icons were demonic. Aleister Crowley adopted Levi's Baphomet for a twentieth-century reinterpretation of paganism, but the demonic associations were already firmly established for Christians. It's arguable that Crowley deliberately reveled in being controversial by adopting such an image. In any event, it was only a short jump for a group like the Satanic Temple, which openly worships Satan, to commission a statue of Baphomet.

Kendall: That's the same statue that prompted a lawsuit when it was used without permission in *The Chilling Adventures of Sabrina.*

Jenna: And everything from goats to Baphomet have been used to represent Satan in innumerable horror movies to this day.

Kendall: Like the goat in *The Witch.*

Jenna: Or *Drag Me to Hell.*

Kendall: *Paranormal Activity.*

Jenna: Looks like we're stuck with it.

Bewitched, Bothered and Bewildered

Kendall

Morvena intercepted Kendall on his way up from the washroom. He had the distinct impression she had been lying in wait. A white and aqua silk caftan billowed around her body, revealing white leggings that hugged her spidery legs. A pendulous turquoise necklace draped her bosom.

"Love the outfit," said Kendall, resting the empty laundry basket on his hip.

Morvena grabbed the folds of the caftan billowing beside her thighs and fanned out the fabric. "You like it? I wore it for you, darling."

"In that case, *you* need to get out more." He pointed his finger to emphasize *you*. "Where'd you get it?"

"I have my secrets. But come upstairs for cocktails and a cigarette, and I'll tell you."

"You know I don't smoke."

"Alas, that's the problem with the young. You do drink, though." She presented it more as a command than a question, as if daring him to say no.

"Of course."

"Good. Then I shall tell you all about the dress while you wait for your laundry to finish." She led the way up to her apartment, ascending each step with care as she gripped the handrail. "I've been trying to invite you in for a cocktail ever since I moved in two months ago."

"Yes, well, I've been busy."

"Phooey! You just think an old person has nothing interesting to offer. Because you know everything. I was like that once, too. Everybody is when they're young. You'll see that one day."

Kendall was about to protest, then decided it was easier not to contradict her. Instead, he said, "So you used to model? Professionally?"

The question must have pleased her, because she paused on the stairs and turned to face him, her head held erect. "I was in London during the Swinging Sixties, darling. It was the center of the world. I partied with Twiggy." She tilted her head down to look at him on the lower step like a professor about to berate an ignorant student. "You do know who Twiggy is, I trust."

Kendall nodded, well familiar with iconic models.

"Good, because I haven't the energy to educate you on the finer points of life."

They continued into Morvena's apartment. She immediately set about preparing a martini, not bothering to ask him what he preferred. Posters featuring the work of Toulouse-Lautrec and fashion shoots of a model who Kendall assumed to be Morvena covered the walls. In one photo, the model wore white bell-bottom pants, the camera angled up from below to emphasize the length of the legs. She was looking off into the distance, her thick false eyelashes splayed like the petals of a daisy. A silk scarf wound around her head and cascaded down the front of her flowery blouse. In another photo she and a bevy of other models leaned on one another, all dressed in hot pants and go-go boots. He squinted, trying to see the connection between the model and the woman standing at the sink opening a stainless-steel cocktail shaker. "Is that you in the photos?"

"Yes, darling, *c'est moi.*"

"I love this one with the killer boots. Very sexy."

She came to stand beside him and look at the photo, an unlit cigarette in one hand and the shaker in the other. "1968. A fabulous year." She gestured toward another one, the cigarette quivering as she raised her arm. "This layout appeared in *Vogue.*"

"I should get your autograph."

Morvena returned to the kitchen to finish mixing the cocktails. "People think modeling is easy, that all you have to do is stand there and look beautiful. They have no idea."

"It's like drag, in a way. You're presenting a carefully constructed illusion."

"Precisely." She shook the shaker with surprising vigor given her frail arms, then poured out the mixture into two martini glasses. As a finishing touch, she plucked two thin lime wedges from the refrigerator and garnished the rims.

"With a garnish, even. Girl, you don't hold back, do you?"

"Presentation is everything."

Kendall took one of the glasses from her hand and raised it. "I'll drink to that."

They sat. Kendall admired the retro sixties furniture: a plainly upholstered sea-green armchair with a round yellow pillow; a simple oak coffee table, its thin legs angled out and narrowing at the tips; a credenza with similar spindly legs and recessed handles. If Morvena were a piece of furniture, she would have fit right in. "So, about the dress."

"Ah, yes. I found it in a boutique in Kensington Market. Second hand, of course. I could never afford something like this fresh off the rack."

"Don't even get me started on second hand. I know every thrift shop in the city. Emily's Attic, am I right?"

She raised her glass to his correct guess. "Very good."

"You've never thought about making your own dresses?"

She lit her cigarette and blew out a stream of smoke. "God, no. I don't have the patience. And I have no interest in learning a new trade at this point in my life. That outfit I saw you coming home in a few weeks ago—did you make that yourself?" Kendall nodded. "I'm impressed."

"My mother taught me to sew. That's how she earned a living back in Nigeria, before coming to Canada. Then I majored in textile design in college."

"Were you born there, or here?"

"Nigeria. We left when I was four—came to live here with my aunt." The mention of those early years in Nigeria, so clouded in the vaguest of memories, always made him feel he was discussing the life of another child. None of it seemed real, like a dream before his life truly began in Toronto. No one here except his mother knew him from those days—not even Aunt Abbie, who had emigrated the year he was born—and his mother never shared any stories. What little he knew existed as fragments. "What about you?"

Morvena took a long, contemplative drag on her cigarette. "*That* is a complicated story. My mother was French Canadian. She married a Frenchman. I was born in Bordeaux—Paris without the attitude. Then they divorced and she moved with me to London. I spent my youth going back and forth between Québec, England, and France, so I'm a child of many countries."

"Very cosmopolitan."

"Yes. It was delicious. So many options. It's important to have options when you're young."

Kendall sipped his martini. "I guess I don't need to ask if you've ever heard or seen anything odd in the short time you've lived here."

"I hear plenty. It's like living in an arcade."

"But what about anything out of the ordinary?"

"I'll tell you something, darling. I know all about *haunted*. The flat where I lived in London was haunted. Small things, mostly. Chairs would get moved around. My keys would get displaced. In the morning I'd discover that the tea cupboard was open." She took a drag and blew out a long stream of smoke, letting the facts sink in. "So I started leaving a cup of tea out before I went to bed. And you know what? In the morning, I could tell that a bit of the tea had been tasted, because the level of the water was slightly lower. After that, I wasn't bothered by my ghost any longer. But this place? This place isn't haunted."

"What do you think Mrs. Gupta heard?"

"I'm sure it's the same things I hear. Her neighbors. People on the stairs." She crossed her legs and fanned out the fabric of the caftan on the sofa like a peacock. "I hope the person who rented the vacant apartment next door won't be noisy."

"That's the unit that has a haunted history."

Morvena leaned in. "Do tell."

Kendall shared what he had learned from Elliott. At the conclusion of the story, Morvena said, "Well, I suppose we shall know whether it is true before long."

"I'll bet you're glad that unit wasn't vacant when you came looking."

Morvena waved her hand with the cigarette, sending flecks of ash flying. "I know how to get along with ghosts. As long as they don't make a lot of noise."

Kendall chose his next words with care. "Why do you think you're so sensitive to noise?"

Morvena stubbed out her cigarette with the kind of forceful twists one might use on a stubborn screw, then picked up her martini. "You say I'm so sensitive, but to me it's perfectly normal."

"Have you ever tried renting some place with newer construction, like a condo? The concrete walls and floors would insulate you better from the sounds of your neighbors."

"I can't afford those exorbitant rents." She took a sip of her drink, then gestured to the photos on the wall. "Yes, I made good money on some of those shoots. But people assume that just because your face is in a magazine, or your song is on the radio, you have a truckload of money. Nothing could be further from the truth."

"Did you ever do drugs back in the day?"

"You're a cheeky one, aren't you?"

"It's just, you know, the sixties had a certain reputation."

"I tried pot a few times. But my constitution is too sensitive. One puff and I was off in la-la-land. So I was more of an observer than a participant." She started to laugh, but it turned into a coughing fit.

Kendall checked his watch. "Well, my load should be about done. Jenna and I are going to talk to the tenants in the basement, find out if they've had any unusual experiences."

Morvena shook out the last hacks from her cough. "I could not live in a basement apartment. Watching people's ankles march past all day long, so little sunlight. Like being in a grave."

He stood, waiting for Morvena to get up as well. "Being on the top floor, do you feel like you're closer to heaven?"

"If I believed in heaven and hell, I suppose I might." She finished off her drink. "Do you know the parable about the samurai warrior and the Zen master? Then I shall tell you." She motioned for

Kendall to sit back down while she recounted the story. "A tough samurai warrior wanted to know the nature of heaven and hell. He saw a Zen master deep in meditation and approached him, brusquely demanding an answer to his question. The Zen master looked him up and down and said, *Why should I tell a disgusting slob like you something you won't even understand*? The samurai became enraged and raised his sword to chop off the master's head. The master simply looked straight in the samurai's eyes and said, *That is hell*. The samurai froze, understanding that anger had him in his grip, and that hell was not a place but a state of mind, right here on earth. He put down his sword and bowed in gratitude for the insight. The master then said, *And that is heaven*." With the last sentence, Morvena waived her empty glass in the air with a flourish. "I heard that from a boyfriend in the sixties. Everything then was peace and love, flower power, Eastern philosophy, ashrams, the Tao, love beads... Sometimes I wonder what happened to it all. The idealism. The hope. Where did it go?"

Kendall stood mutely. The sixties belonged to a hazy time before he was even born. He knew the decade only from a series of clichés repeated for popular consumption. The same thing would probably happen someday to the decades he was living through. He wondered what it must have been like to have been Morvena, once so swept up in idealism and peace, and now reduced to shouting out windows at the world's noise, trapped in her own version of hell. "It's a beautiful story," Kendall finally muttered.

"Then you must come back sometime, darling. I have plenty more."

The Witch

Jenna

Jenna stood in the mailbox alcove on the first floor. With her finger, she scanned the rows, looking for the names of the basement tenants. The label for apartment nine read *Lilith Adebayo*. The

72

mailbox for apartment ten had no label, and neither did a numberless mailbox beside it, which Jenna presumed was for the landlord.

Kendall came down the steps behind her. "I just had a conversation with Morvena."

"How was it?"

"Not bad. She's actually a kick. No reports of ghosts, though."

Jenna pointed to the mailbox for apartment ten. "No name."

"Maybe it's vacant."

"I don't think so. Turnbull was only showing the apartment upstairs."

"Which has been rented, according to Morvena."

"I thought so. Someone took down the *For Rent* sign."

They trudged down to the basement so Kendall could move his clothes to the dryer, then rang the buzzer on apartment ten. Jenna heard the faint rustle of someone within. She could see light filtering through the peephole, then black as someone stood on the other side, blocking the light. "Hello!" she called out. "We're your neighbors from upstairs." She and Kendall waited for a response, but were met with silence. "I know you're home. We won't take much of your time."

"What do you want?" a nasal voice called through the door.

Jenna leaned into the door as if addressing someone who was hard of hearing. "We just want to introduce ourselves and get to know you. We've been going around to all of our neighbors." When the door did not open, Jenna looked at Kendall with exasperation.

Kendall offered his reassurance. "I promise we're harmless. Well, except my friend here, who is a vampire, but she only goes for new-born babies."

The deadbolt clicked and the door opened a crack. A face with two small, close-set eyes peered out. "You shouldn't joke about such things."

Kendall offered an apology, then introduced himself and Jenna. The man with the suspicious eyes said nothing, studying them.

"Is this a bad time to talk?" asked Jenna.

"No time is a good time," the man croaked. "Now go away, please."

He shut the door. Jenna heard footsteps shuffle deeper into the room, growing fainter. "Well, that went well," she said.

They received a much different reception when they knocked on the door for apartment nine. A wave of sweet scents assailed Jenna's nose as soon as the door opened. The woman introduced herself as Lilith and invited them inside.

"What is that wonderful scent?" asked Jenna.

"Oh, I was burning some incense. A combination of sage, lavender, and frankincense."

Lilith wore her hair short in tight black curls, shaved close to the scalp on the sides. She had a high forehead, an incandescent smile, and the most expressive, luxuriant eyebrows Jenna had ever seen. There was a certain elegance and confidence that flowed through the way she carried herself that Jenna found charming but at the same time made her envious.

A low table covered with a purple cloth squatted in one area of the room. On the table sat two figurines, angular pieces of quartz crystal, several candles, and assorted other items. Bracelets and necklaces in various stages of construction lay scattered on a desk, where a lamp blazed. Lilith must have been in the middle of working on jewelry when they knocked.

"Is that quartz?" asked Kendall, pointing to the center of the table.

Lilith nodded. "Yes. It's good for encouraging clarity of thought and purpose."

Kendall pulled a necklace out from under his shirt, showing a small quartz pendant. "I like to wear it close to my skin."

"That's smart. It draws away negative energy," said Lilith. "There's too much negativity in the world."

"Amen, sister." Kendall tucked his necklace back under his shirt. "I detect an accent. You're not from Canada, are you?"

"No. I was born in Ireland, and came here three years ago. For work."

"I didn't know there were any black people in Ireland."

"Not a lot, but there are some of us, especially in Dublin where I'm from. My father is Nigerian, my mother is Irish."

Kendall clapped his hands with excitement. "So are mine— well, except it's the reverse. Mother, Nigerian; father, Irish. We could be mirror twins!"

"You don't say? Wow. And here we are together at Covington Terrace, of all places. It was meant to be."

"My father passed away, but my mother lives here in Toronto."

"Mine are both back in Dublin."

Kendall linked his arm with Lilith's. "Then I shall be your family away from home. We'll be sisters."

Jenna felt a pinch of jealousy as she watched Lilith place her hand atop Kendall's hand.

"It's a deal," Lilith said. "Please sit. Would you like something to drink?" Jenna declined, but Kendall accepted the offer.

They talked about Lilith's experience growing up in Dublin, favorite places to eat in Cabbagetown, how the weather in Toronto compared to Ireland. Lilith had not heard the rumors about the haunted apartment. Kendall asked if she had ever experienced anything unusual.

"Two years ago. I thought I heard someone crying. Or not really *heard*—more like *sensed*. I sensed someone crying. It went on for several days. I supposed if I had actually heard crying, I would have just assumed it was my upstairs neighbor. But this was something else. A sensation of distress."

"What happened?" asked Jenna.

"It eventually went away. I never heard it again."

Kendall rubbed his chin. "Strange."

"Very. My intuitions are always right. I'm certain I picked up on some vibration of trouble. Something was wrong. But, alas, it remained a mystery."

"Did you ever talk to any of your neighbors about it," asked Jenna, "to see if you could resolve the mystery?"

"I keep to myself for the most part and don't mingle with others. It's my way of avoiding judgmental attitudes."

Jenna noticed that Lilith glanced at the low table as she said this, which drew Jenna's attention to the array of objects. She catalogued the items again, this time with more concentration. Candles. Incense. Crystals. Deity figures. Abalone shell. Amulet. Miniature black cauldron. Then it all came together. Lilith was a witch. Jenna began to feel the same discomfort she felt that day on the subway, staring at the purse that looked like human skin. Lilith certainly was friendly, but the idea of casting spells and calling on strange forces unsettled Jenna. Not that she was afraid. But other incidents bubbled up from the cauldron in her past.

When she was eight, an elderly couple lived at the end of the street in a dilapidated house. The old woman was as mean as a pit bull, and glared at children from her front porch to discourage them from dragging sticks and rulers along the slats of the fence as they walked home from school. She was stocky like a pro wrestler, with short gray hair that hung in bangs. Jenna and her sister Beth had nicknamed her Witch Hazel. Along with other neighborhood kids, they would deliberately try to rouse the woman's ire, challenging one another to greater feats of daring. *Pick a carnation from her garden. Knock on her door and run.* When Beth stepped on a nail and got a staph infection, they were certain Witch Hazel had made it happen with magic.

The problem was that Jenna preferred witchcraft to stay in the realm of fiction, where she could keep it safely at arm's length. It seemed dangerous, like the firecrackers that made such a racket during Chinese New Year and Canada Day. Witch Hazel might have been childish fantasy, but in high school rumors swirled around a Goth girl named Raven who decorated her notebook with pentagrams and carried a deck of tarot cards in her backpack. Raven projected an air of mystery and danger. At first, Jenna sympathized with her as another outsider. She talked to her, just as she had approached the lady on the subway. But unlike the careful artifice of the purse, Jenna found out that Raven's drawings were not make-believe. She was dead serious. After that, Jenna avoided her. It wasn't that Jenna was afraid—just uncomfortable. And that's how she felt sitting in Lilith's apartment.

She looked around the room for additional clues, but other than the altar, everything seemed normal. What did she expect, though? Jars filled with dead man's toes? A steer's skull nailed to a post? An upside-down cross? Perhaps a purse stitched with real human flesh this time, not the clever art piece she had seen on the subway.

Kendall mentioned their experience trying to talk to Lilith's neighbor and asked if she knew anything about him.

"I've seen him maybe a handful of times," she said. "Sometimes I hear him late at night taking his clothes to the laundry room. He tends to do his laundry at the same time, around midnight on Tuesdays. I imagine that's when he least expects to run into any other tenants."

"A recluse," said Jenna.

"That's the impression I get."

Kendall put his finger to his chin. "If that's his routine, I should hold a stakeout and corner him, then force him to talk to me."

"Kendall is relentless," said Jenna. "You'll never meet anyone with such a singular focus."

"I'm sensing Capricorn," said Lilith. "Maybe Aries. But, no, I think Capricorn is more likely."

Kendall threw up his hands in amazement. "Pretty good. My birthday is January fifth." He pointed to the desk scattered with beads, chains, and stones. "You design jewelry?"

"Yes. And I sell it online. Are you familiar with Celtic knots?" She retrieved an object from her work desk. "There are a variety of designs that symbolize different things, but in general the interlocking patterns represent eternity. This triple spiral knot"—she held out a silver pendant comprising three spirals that together formed a triangle—"represents certain threefold aspects of nature, such as water, fire, and earth, and symbolizes oneness of spirit and unity."

"That's similar to the Chinese mystic knot on Lucy's door upstairs," said Jenna.

"This concept occurs in numerous cultures. It possesses a profound power."

Kendall took the pendant from Lilith and held it in his palm. "You're going to turn this into a necklace?"

"Yes."

He handed it back to her. "I'd like to buy it when you're done."

"I'll give it to you as a gift," said Lilith.

The offer made Jenna ill at ease, although she could not articulate why. She experienced a fleeting thought that Lilith planned to place a hex on the object. But that was silly. She saw Kendall beaming and felt another pinch of jealousy.

"We're artistic, too," he said. "I design dresses and textile pieces. Jenna paints and does graphic design."

Lilith grinned. "I sensed that you both had artistic souls. I'm sure we'll get along famously."

Jenna was not so sure of that at all.

A Song for Quiet

Kendall

Apart from the failed attempt to talk to the mystery man in apartment ten, only one tenant interview remained. Yet, standing before apartment six, that interview gave Kendall a profound foreboding. The door was unremarkable, like every other apartment door in the building. The layout, he knew, would be identical to his own, just in reverse. But he could not un-know the awful history of the space within.

The door opened to reveal a thin but tautly muscled man in his late twenties, with a shaved head and a joyless expression, who surveyed them coolly. He wore faded black jeans. Tattoos wound up his forearms and disappeared under the sleeves of his black T-shirt. A necklace with a small silver skull draped his collarbone. Kendall felt a moment of speechlessness. What had he expected? Someone average, undistinguished. Certainly not this. And such a shocking contrast to their warm visit with Lilith.

Jenna took up the slack and introduced themselves as neighbors. The man said his name was Vince Fournier. Kendall tried to peer behind Vince into the apartment. What he expected to find—some mark of the unit's malevolence, perhaps?—he could not say. He saw arrays of boxes, some in piles, others disgorging their guts like cut-open cadavers.

"Do you want to come in?" Vince asked. "Sorry, the room's still a mess."

Kendall was inclined to say no, but Jenna accepted the offer and was already stepping into the room. Kendall hesitated, however, frozen by the man's surly look. He had observed such men before at a distance—bikers, ex-cons, bouncers—but never face to face like this. Under other circumstances, Kendall might have found intriguing the eerie images on the man's arms and the skull necklace. Instead, the way that Vince stared at him made his legs tremble. Kendall was accustomed to being stared at. His effeminacy had drawn attention for years before his flame-orange hair made him stand out in any crowd. Kendall had the feeling that Vince wasn't staring because of the way he looked, but because he *knew* Kendall. Yet Kendall was certain they had never met.

Jenna approached an electronic keyboard set up in one corner. "Oh, you're a musician."

"Yeah. I record music. Under the name the Bone Man."

She hovered over the keyboard but stopped short from touching the keys. "What kind of music?"

"Hard to describe. Dark themes. The occult. Ghosts, vampires, demons. Shit like that."

"Death metal?"

"No. It's not as frenzied. More of a synth influence, with slower beats. If metal is a cave full of bats at sunset, my music would be a black widow spider spinning its web."

"I hope you'll play some songs for us sometime. Kendall and I are into the horror scene. We have a podcast—"

"I know. Shockadelica."

Vince's recognition of their podcast drew a smile from Jenna. Although that seemed to explain why Vince regarded Kendall with familiarity, something else still bothered Kendall like a persistent splinter.

Vince cleared some boxes from the sofa and invited them to sit. Jenna commented on his tattoos. He pointed to the gaunt face of an older man with hollow cheeks and stubble, wearing a plaid cap. "This is Ed Gein. Not many people know the name now, but he was notorious in his day, during the late fifties. He was the original model for *Psycho*, only he was far worse. He made wastebaskets and lampshades out of human skin, capped his bedposts with human skulls. After his mother died, he made a suit out of her body parts so he could literally crawl into her skin." Vince seemed to relish seeing Kendall squirm.

Jenna shuddered. "That is so gruesome. And what about the man with the bushy mustache and bowler hat?"

"That is the incredible H. H. Holmes. Another name overshadowed by more recent serial killers. He confessed to murdering twenty-seven people, but actual estimates range from twenty to two hundred. For the 1893 Chicago World's Fair, he built a hotel with secret rooms and passageways. People checked in but never checked out. He came to Toronto for a while, too, and killed some people here. Rented a house on St. *Vincent* Lane." Vince emphasized his own name and grinned. "That's where he buried a couple of the bodies, in the cellar of the house."

"You're making this up," said Kendall.

"No, it's true. Look it up."

Kendall thought to himself, *Okay, it's been a lovely chat, but we've got to be going.* Yet he knew they had not yet broached the reason for their visit and Jenna would not leave without bringing it up. He decided to facilitate the conversation so they could leave as soon as possible. "Speaking of murders, do you know about the history of this apartment?"

"We're doing research for our podcast," Jenna added. "An upcoming episode will be about our very own haunted Covington Terrace."

Vince crossed his arms and took a moment before answering. "The day I came by to look at the apartment, a girl who lives downstairs tagged along and told me."

"That must have been Rooney," said Jenna. "Did she tell you it was haunted?"

"Uh-huh."

Kendall made a face. "And that didn't discourage you from moving in?"

Vince spread his arms out with his palms up. "I mean, look at me, man. Do you think I'd be bothered by a ghost?"

"You've got a point," said Kendall.

Vince leaned forward. "Besides, I know this apartment. It's where my girlfriend used to live. Before she disappeared."

If Vince was surprised by the sideways glance that Kendall and Jenna gave each other, he did not let on.

After a beat, Jenna said, "What was your girlfriend's name?"

"Alyssa."

"Last name?"

"Blackwood."

She wrote the name down on her pad. "And she just disappeared without a trace?"

"Yeah. Left all of her stuff behind."

There was an awkward moment of silence, then Jenna announced, "Well, if you notice anything strange or see a ghost, let us know. And, hey, maybe we can have you on the podcast sometime to talk about your music."

"That'd be great."

Vince followed them to the door. As they stepped out, Jenna turned around. "Well, welcome to the building. For the second time."

Once they were safely in Jenna's apartment, Kendall said, "I could have kicked you when you invited him on our podcast."

"Why?"

"Something scares me about him. I had a funny feeling the minute he opened the door."

Jenna waved her hand as if shooing a meddlesome fly. "You're too sensitive. He's just into horror, like us."

"No. There's something else. I can't put my finger on it."

"Straight guys always intimidate you."

"Only when they have tattoos of serial killers on their arms."

"You have to admit, the ink work was beautiful. Did you recognize the images from different horror movies? The Nosferatu was killer."

"Mmm. Nice word choice, because you can admire it while he's chopping you up into little bitty pieces."

"We could do an episode just on his tattoos. My dragon tattoo pales in comparison. The one thing I'll admit struck me as strange is when he mentioned his girlfriend used to live here."

"The same girl who Elliott said vanished mysteriously."

"Probably. Let's look up the Bone Man." She pulled up his website on her computer. The first image that appeared was Vince's face painted with black and white makeup to resemble a skull, with black circles around the eyes and on the nose, and the lips painted over like teeth. She perused the song list and selected the song "Box of Bones." An ominous baritone voice rapped out the lyrics.

Do you hear that voice in the wall?
See that shadow at the end of the hall?
Hiding in the closet, or under the bed,
Out in the field where worms feed on the dead?

Scratching at the window, it's something you hear,
A feeling in your skin that tells you I'm near.
Now the adrenaline rush,
The ice-cold touch that you fear so much.

Out of the mist I materialize,
Your worst nightmare, the monster now coming alive.
Feel me behind as you walk alone,
And I find another body for my box of bones.

"Interesting song," she said. "Not exactly reassuring."

"It's creeping me out."

"But don't you think he's just playing a part? I mean, no one who really had a box of bones would sing about it." She looked at Kendall, waiting for his reassurance.

"I don't know, diva. Not an area in which I have any expertise."

Jenna reviewed the results of their interviews, ticking off names on the list. "We've talked to Mrs. Gupta, Elliott, Rooney, Lilith, Lucy, Vince..."

"Morvena," interjected Kendall.

"Morvena. We're still missing the mystery man in apartment ten. And we need to pay a visit to Turnbull on Ward's Island. We can ask him about the mystery man." She bounced the pen between her fingers. "Can I ask you something? What do you think of Rooney?"

"She's okay, I guess. A chatterbox."

Jenna chewed on the end of the pen, thinking. "Something doesn't add up. The things she says about herself keep changing."

"You think she's a chameleon."

"Yeah. Too many inconsistencies." Jenna drew a circle around Lilith's name. "I think Lilith is a witch."

"Oh, goody, my sister is a witch!"

"I don't know, it kind of spooks me. A little too freaky-deaky. Too real."

"So the white guy with the serial killer tattoos is fine, but the black girl with the candle scares you?"

Jenna pushed his shoulder with mock anger. "Shut *up*! Now you make me sound like a racist."

"I'd be more afraid of the man whose girlfriend went missing."

"It's just that witch stuff and spells make me uncomfortable."

Kendall watched as Jenna searched an online database of the *Globe and Mail* newspaper for an article about the 1932 murders at Covington Terrace. Just as Elliott had said, the article she found described Monmouth's journal, his obsession with the goat-man, and how the image "possessed his mind to perpetrate the demonic deed."

"You still think Elliott pranked us at the Necropolis?" asked Kendall.

"It's one possible theory. Easier than believing we were hunted by a ghost."

"But all we have are a handful of suspicious reports from Elliott, and Lilith's claim of picking up on vibrations of sadness."

Jenna typed *Alyssa Blackwood* into the computer. "What about what you saw in the Jungle?"

"Easily dismissed as my imagination." The response sounded unconvincing even as he uttered it.

Jenna scanned the search results. "Nothing comes up on the disappearance of Vince's girlfriend."

"Probably because they never found the body he's got stuffed away somewhere. Maybe he's even got it buried in the Jungle, like the goat-man did."

Jenna closed the computer's lid. "You're being too suspicious. I guess we'll just have to wait to find out more from Turnbull."

Paranormal Activity
Mrs. Gupta

Nobody outside of her Indian friends called Vijayalakshmi Gupta by her first name. For one thing, people unaccustomed to long Indian names had trouble remembering it, and she was too proper to allow any but her confidants to use an affectionate abbreviation. But she also carried herself with a dignity that automatically commanded deference, hence most people knew her as Mrs. Gupta. You became aware of your choice of words and tone of voice in her presence, such was the effect she had on people. Her impeccable English and Oxford pedigree made you self-conscious of your shortcomings, and you found yourself using uncommon words like "happenstance" and "hooligan" in an effort to impress her.

Mrs. Gupta had wedded her husband through an arranged marriage, but those who knew the couple before Vikram passed away vouched that they never had seen a happier couple. The pair had downsized once their children graduated from college, and while the Guptas possessed the means to afford greater luxury, they had led frugal lives, which is how they ended up at Covington Terrace. As a bonus, the building's name reminded Mrs. Gupta of her days in England.

Returning home with a pull-cart of groceries, Mrs. Gupta paused at the bottom of the steps in order to summon the strength to conquer the climb. Just then, the front door opened. Kendall and Jenna emerged, laughing. As soon as they spotted her, they scampered down to help, each taking one of the bags from the cart and muttering, "What good timing." Mrs. Gupta expressed her gratitude and followed them, the wheels banging against each step.

She slotted the key into the lock and swung open the door of her apartment. Kendall and Jenna moved past her, but she stopped in her tracks, her mouth agape. Every cupboard door in the kitchen stood ajar. Kendall stared at the cupboards as he set his bag on the table, then at Mrs. Gupta. She felt as if she had been caught naked.

"I don't know what could have happened. I certainly did not leave them like this when I left." She shut each cupboard.

"Is anything of value missing?" Kendall asked, steadying one of the bags that had started to fall over. Mrs. Gupta looked around the room, then said that everything seemed to be in its place. She was grateful when he offered to help put away the groceries, because the open cupboards had rattled her and she did not want to be left alone just yet. Kendall transported items from the bag to the counter, pausing to study jars and packages of unfamiliar products.

"Do you like Indian cuisine?" she asked. "You should let me cook for you both sometime."

Kendall grew enthused. "We could each bring a dish. I can make one of my mom's traditional Nigerian dishes."

Jenna scolded him. "You know I don't cook."

"You can buy something, diva."

Mrs. Gupta slotted a bottle of garam masala into the cupboard. "Then it's settled. We'll consult our calendars and pick a date."

When the last item had been put away, she asked if, just to be safe, they would check her bedroom and closets.

"All clear," Kendall announced after the inspection. He also checked the windows, which were securely shut. If someone had entered the apartment, the person certainly had not come in through there. Kendall suggested she might have accidentally left the apartment door unlocked. He opened the door, turning the knob from the outside. "Just as I suspected. You should keep the doorknob locked as well as the deadbolt. It's possible you thought you locked the deadbolt but didn't. See?" He twisted the knob. "I always keep both locked. The last thing I want is a strange man coming through my door."

Jenna crossed her arms. "Oh, really? You could have fooled me."

"I'll get you for that later."

Mrs. Gupta thanked them once again. After they left, she made sure to lock the deadbolt and the doorknob. She called her daughter Sirisha to find out if she might have come by the apartment unannounced and left the cupboards open. The idea seemed far-fetched, but she hoped her daughter would confess, and then she could put the unsettled feeling out of mind. Maybe Sirisha had popped by after work, let herself in when no one answered the door, and went looking for something—a snack, or ingredients with which to make dinner. It seemed ridiculous—and, not surprisingly, when she answered the phone, Sirisha explained that she was still at the office, working late again. She reminded her mother about the episode with the voice in the wall, and floated the idea of coming to stay with her in her condo for a few weeks.

"No, I'm fine here," said Mrs. Gupta, who did not want to be a nuisance in her daughter's life, and prided herself on her independence.

"Well, think about it if anything else happens."

Mrs. Gupta heated some leftovers and sat down to watch television. She thought of what a friend had said a few days earlier, that perhaps Vikram's *bhoot* has returned, since the apartment was where his stroke had happened. *The bhoot always returns to the scene of death,* the friend had said. Mrs. Gupta was not superstitious, and had dismissed the suggestion. Even if it were true, Vikram would never have behaved so irresponsibly, doing things to frighten her.

The hours ticked by, and she changed into her pajamas. This was her favorite time of day, when she could relax with a good book. She sat upright in bed with the reading lamp on, absorbed in her latest acquisition from the library, *I Dined with Satan.* The book's subject amused her, despite being based on a purportedly true account of a Satanic cult. Yes, she knew people could behave with evil intent, but she was disinclined to put much stock in Christian concepts of the devil.

The pages flipped past. She raised her reading glasses to rub her eyes, feeling sleep start to descend. During this brief pause, however, she became aware of something amiss in the room. The closet door stood slightly ajar. She never left the door open, and it distracted her to see the black vertical line of the gap like some disorderly pile of books sitting askew. She sighed and rose from the bed, slipping her feet into her house slippers. She shuffled across the floor and shut the door, pressing her palm against the wood to confirm its closure.

Once back in bed, she resumed reading, anticipating another ten minutes before she would turn out the light. She followed the light footsteps of her upstairs neighbor moving across the room and heard the faint sound of a drawer opening. Then more footsteps retreating toward the bathroom, followed by the sound of the pipes. She heard the little dog scamper across the floor, and realized she had read the last two sentences without paying attention. She started the paragraph anew.

The water stopped, leaving a blissful silence. But Mrs. Gupta started, noticing that the closet door had again opened a couple of inches. She had not heard it open—the sound, if it had made any, must have been masked by the running water. She blamed the issue on the vagaries of the old building, something to which she had become resigned. That a door would not stay shut did not surprise her in the least. In the back of her mind, though, recalling the incident from two weeks ago when the walls had breathed, she felt uneasy.

She went to the door and again closed it, but this time she moved a small wooden chair in front of the door to keep it in place. Tomorrow she would complain to Turnbull. Perhaps his son could check the hinges. Well, it would probably take him weeks to get around to it. She would call her own son instead.

She managed to finish several more pages before her eyelids grew heavy. She placed the bookmark in the crease, set the book on her nightstand, and was reaching for the reading lamp when she heard the doorknob unlatch and the chair scrape a few inches across the floor. Instead of staying in the room to investigate, she collected her keys and scurried next door, hoping Kendall would be home.

"It's Mrs. Gupta," she called through the door. "I hope it's not too late, but I require a favor, please." She looked nervously down the hallway, half expecting a ghost to be following her. When the door swung open, she repressed the urge to take refuge in his apartment. "There is something amiss with my closet door. It keeps opening of its own accord, even when blocked."

Kendall stood with his hand still on the knob of the open door. "Is this related to what you experienced last week?"

Mrs. Gupta took a deep breath. "I don't know. I was just too nervous to investigate alone. Something isn't right."

There was a rustling on the stairs, then Morvena's voice calling out, "Hello? Hello? What's going on?"

That broke the tension, and Kendall and Mrs. Gupta both chuckled. She turned around and saw Morvena standing midway up the flight of stairs at the landing with her hands on her hips. "It's nothing," said Mrs. Gupta. "I just need a favor."

Kendall stepped into the hall, closing the door behind him after unlocking the knob. "Let's go to your apartment and check together."

Frowning, Morvena watched them cross the corridor. Mrs. Gupta heard the stairs squeak as Morvena descended from her perch.

Mrs. Gupta gasped as she and Kendall entered the bedroom. The door had been shut and the chair moved back to its place. "It was open slightly when I left." She placed her hand on her breast to settle her racing heart as Kendall reached for the doorknob. He hesitated, his eyes on Mrs. Gupta. She did not know what she expected might come rushing out—a person, a ghost, a monster?—but she dared not imagine. Her hand curled to grip the folds in her robe. He yanked the door open and jumped to the side.

The closet looked undisturbed, clothes hanging in tidy rows on the rods, blankets stacked on the shelves above them, shoes lined up in place. She realized she had been holding her breath, and exhaled as she released her grip on the robe. Kendall flicked on the closet light. Mrs. Gupta did not see any shoes attached to legs, which gave her enough confidence to step into the closet and brush her hand through the clothes. "I don't understand. I'm certain the door kept opening. You must think I'm mad, especially after what happened before."

"Not at all. I can think of plenty of times I've been frightened to death. Just today, I was scared to check my bank balance."

Mrs. Gupta emitted a gentle laugh. "You always make me feel better, Kenny. I've been at wit's end ever since Vikram passed away."

"I never would have guessed. You always seem so—heroic. So resolute."

"That's kind of you to say so. But on the inside, I feel much more vulnerable." She picked up a framed photograph of her and Vikram posing with Niagara Falls in the background. "And now I fear my nerves are getting the better of me."

"Now, now. Don't be so hard on yourself. You have every right to feel vulnerable."

She replaced the photograph. "I just wish I could explain what happened. Something forced the door open and pushed the chair across the floor."

"Maybe it was a gust of wind."

"I would have an easier time believing it was a ghost than a gust of wind that came from inside the closet."

Kendall nodded. "I see your point."

When they walked into the living room, they saw Morvena standing at the threshold. Her presence rankled Mrs. Gupta, who worried that Morvena might have overheard their conversation. Adopting a more formal tone, she asked, "Can I help you?"

Morvena offered a haughty smile. "I heard you discussing ghosts. Do you think your apartment is haunted?"

Kendall jumped in before Mrs. Gupta could respond. "Might be. And you know what they say, ghosts never stay put, they wander all over a building." He swept his hand through the air with exaggerated flair and lobbed an additional dig. "And if you think the building is noisy now, just wait until the poltergeists start partying."

Morvena made a face and shuffled back upstairs. Mrs. Gupta placed her hand on Kendall's arm. "Thank you. For everything."

"No problem. Like I said, any time you need something, just knock."

4

Excerpt from Shockadelica Podcast
Episode 40: A Literary Hoax

Jenna: There's a huge controversy in the publishing world at the moment over a book published as a real-life account that turned out to be fictitious.

Kendall: We're talking about *I Dined with Satan*, by Anne Montgomery.

Jenna: Which turned out to be a pseudonym for Marvin Gumbal. It really bothers me that he passed himself off as a female author just to get more attention for the book. I mean, I have no problem with pseudonyms, but in his case he decided it would get more publicity if it was written by a woman. It would make it more salacious.

Kendall: But it was just an invented persona. We all invent personas. Drag is nothing but inventing personas. Well, more than "nothing but," but you get my drift.

Jenna: But wouldn't you feel cheated if a man in drag won the Miss Universe pageant, when everyone believed they were looking at a woman?

Kendall: Gender, dress—it's all an illusion anyway. I don't see what the big deal is.

Jenna: Well, okay. But what about the fact Gumbal presented fictional events about a Satanic cult as if they actually happened? Everyone was up in arms, adding their two cents on social media. The police even launched an investigation into child sacrifices that he described. And it was just a hoax, to sell books.

Kendall: And it worked. That's because people *want* to believe that stuff. Conspiracy theories are the crack cocaine of the Internet.

Jenna: But doesn't it bother you that you were duped?

Kendall: On the one hand, yes. No one likes to feel gullible. On the other hand, it did make a fabulous story.

Night Things

Kendall

The nightmare clawed its way out of the recesses of his mind, intruding in its usual fashion. Firelight reflected on shrouded figures that twirled as he stood there restrained. The blade of a fearfully long machete flashed. Kendall woke in a panic. But this time, he sensed the presence of someone else and heard the sound of something shifting on the other side of the room. He tried to raise his hand to slip off the sleep mask, but he could not move, nor could he open his mouth to scream. Even the smallest gesture took immense willpower, as he imagined gravity would feel like on Jupiter, exerting a pull too strong for his muscles to overcome.

This was the full manifestation of Ogun Oru in all its awful power. What were the other terms his mother had mentioned? Slip-skin hag. Nattmara. It did indeed feel like a demon was riding his chest, its weight pressing down on his lungs, its claw hands holding back his arms. Restraining him just as in his dream, only he was certain he was awake.

A floorboard groaned as the thing came closer. It approached with slow steps, as if nervous about waking him. Beneath his sleep mask, with his eyes wide open, Kendall's world remained pitch black. The thing paused by the side of the bed. Kendall tried to will his limbs to move but felt only frustration and terror.

The thing bent over him. He could hear its guttural breathing, close to his ear, and could smell its stale breath. Something touched his throat. The sensation was enough to unleash the beginning of a sound that struggled to escape from deep within his vocal cords. He managed to let out a low moan, but the effort took every ounce of energy. His finger jerked, then he was able to move his hand. The paralysis thawed, and he ripped off his sleep mask, afraid of what he might see yet desperate to move. Throwing back the covers, he leaped out of bed, landing on the opposite side from where the thing had been standing. In his peripheral vision he spotted a headless body standing against the wall. His heart thumped with even greater terror than the impulse that had catapulted him from the bed. But then he realized it was only his dressmaker dummy, and relaxed.

Nothing in the room seemed out of the ordinary. There stood the dresser, topped with wig stands that now reminded him of decapitated heads. A vanity next to the dresser. Beside the bed, a nightstand with a lamp. His sewing machine and stand. No evidence of the thing that had stood over him.

He turned on the light, but his reassurance was broken when he noticed the closet door stood half-way open. He approached it with trepidation and pulled the door all the way open. Nothing hiding there. Just clothes hanging from the metal rod, a neat row of shoes along the floor, a box with yearbooks and other mementoes.

He surveyed the rest of the apartment, checked the door to make sure it was still locked. Everything was in order. If not for the open closet door, he might have been able to convince himself he had hallucinated the experience in tandem with his sleep paralysis. He had not actually *seen* anything, after all. Yet the experience had seemed so real. He had never left the closet door open before, but he could not remember for certain whether he had shut it before bed.

Kendall's hands still trembled as he sat at the kitchen table, waiting for water to boil so he could have a cup of tea. The sleep paralysis had been a new development, and that worried him. Rain beaded on the window. Usually the sound of rain at night soothed him, but the patter sounded like taunts. He gently drummed on the table. Ogun Oru. *Nocturnal warfare*—that's what Aunt Abbie had said, translating the Yoruban phrase that suggested a war waged by witches and demonic spirits of the night. He heard his mother's retort: "We came here to escape such superstitions."

He looked up *sleep paralysis* on his phone and found a website that described the experience of being conscious but unable to move, occurring between the stages of sleep and wakefulness, sometimes accompanied by the feeling of pressure or the sensation of choking. The description also noted that one may hallucinate during an episode and see or sense things that are not there.

The explanation captured his experience with textbook precision, so he began to calm down. Then he thought about the closet door. If Mrs. Gupta had not experienced something similar, he would not have given the matter a second thought. The tea kettle whistled, interrupting his tumble down the rabbit hole of fear. He was just scaring himself with talk about ghosts, murders, goat-men, and closet doors that would not stay shut.

He waited for the tea to steep. In the quiet of the night, the noises of the building asserted their presence: clicks, groans, squeaks, knocks. He had never noticed before just how many different sounds emerged from the walls, floors, and ceilings. It reminded him of a hobbled old man with stiff limbs and labored breath. So it was easy to imagine the sounds coming from something alive. Or from something that had once been alive.

Tomorrow, he and Jenna were going to the islands. With luck, Arthur Turnbull would be able to lead them closer to either the truth or the fiction about their ghost. Kendall hoped it would be the latter.

House of Leaves

Jenna

Sunday turned out to be one of those days in autumn's seesaw when nature tossed out a bone to those reluctant to see the summer depart. Although their ultimate destination was Turnbull's home on Ward's Island, Jenna suggested she and Kendall take the long way around and head first to Centre Island. The long walk would provide the opportunity to enjoy the pleasant day and drop by the beach they loved one last time before the onslaught of winter. The warm weather had drawn out a large number of city dwellers who waited in line for the ferry on one of the last weekends to enjoy the Centreville amusement rides before they shut down for the season.

The short ferry ride took them across the inner harbor. Behind the ferry, the skyline, punctuated by the CN Tower's exclamation point, grew smaller. As they stood on the upper deck, the breeze streaming through the open windows, Jenna could sense Kendall's distraction, and asked him what could be wrong on such a beautiful day.

"I had my nightmare and another panic attack last night. And this time, it was accompanied by sleep paralysis."

"Oh, I'm sorry to hear that."

"It's okay. They were classic symptoms, nothing to worry about." He picked at a scab on his hand and looked into the distance.

Jenna grabbed his jaw and turned his head to face her. "No, I can tell when something is bothering you."

He told her about Mrs. Gupta's closet that kept opening, the hallucination that accompanied his sleep paralysis, and his own experience with an open closet door. "I know each thing on its own has a logical explanation, but they keep accumulating, and now it nags at me."

"We don't have to keep pursuing this. We can spend the day at the beach without ever going to see Turnbull, then go home and forget about it." She slapped his hand. "Stop picking at your scab."

"Yes, mother." He slipped his hands into his pockets. "I'm not so sure that if we stop investigating this story crazy things will stop happening. It might be better to pursue it to the end."

"And what if it's a—dead end?"

Kendall rolled his eyes. "Ha. Ha. Ha. Very funny. Don't give up your day job."

"Okay. Just promise me if things get too intense you'll let me know."

Kendall drew back in mock dismay. "Too intense for La Chandelle? Why, child, I am known across the land as the personification of Intensity herself. Here, how about this?" He adopted the expression of a Japanese oni demon, eyes bugged out, eyebrows tensed, mouth agape in a grim rictus.

Jenna laughed. "Can't you ever be serious?"

"I thought I was giving you No Laughing Matter realness."

After disembarking, they strolled along Centre Island's main path. The laughter of tiny voices drifted over from the children's amusement rides. They passed a lagoon flanked by weeping willows and a cafe with a roof in the shape of an unfolding umbrella. Ducks dotted the water, and kayakers paddled by in bright red kayaks. An arched bridge took them over one of the canals. A short time later they found their favorite beach and sat down in the shade of a tree for a picnic. The turquoise water of the lake lapped at the shore. In the distance, they could see the headlands of New York State, appearing even closer than usual in the crystalline air.

"Did you ever notice that the Toronto Islands are laid out like a giant scythe sweeping the water of Lake Ontario into the harbor?" asked Kendall. He pulled up a map on his phone. "See? Ward's Island stretches out along the lake like the back edge of the scythe, ending with the handle at Hanlan's Point and Billy Bishop Airport. And at the tip of the scythe are the cluster of cottages where Turnbull lives."

"You've been watching too much horror," she said. Kendall positioned his phone to snap a picture of Jenna, but she held up her hand. "Don't."

"I'm *not* ready for my close-up, Mr. DeMille," Kendall teased in a husky voice.

Jenna sighed wearily, shook back her hair, and smiled without enthusiasm. "Go ahead, then."

The phone made the sound of a camera shutter. "I don't know why you're always so shy about getting your picture taken."

"Maybe I'm worried the camera will steal my soul." Kendall picked up a fistful of sand and threw it at her. She held up her hands and turned away, even though it was a futile gesture to block the sand. "If you can't play nice, you'll have to leave the playground."

Kendall plopped a grape in his mouth. "Have you decided yet what you're going as for Halloween?"

"You know I always wait until the last minute."

"I know. Just checking. It will be hard to top when you dressed as a map of Canada."

"That's why I wait until the last minute. Too much pressure. That way I can always blame any failure on not having enough time." She picked up a fallen twig and began making designs in the sand. "Have you changed your mind about interviewing the Bone Man for Shockadelica? It would make a great Halloween podcast."

"He scares me too much. Too intense."

"I thought *you* were the personification of Intensity."

Kendall picked up another fistful of sand, but changed his mind and let it fall through his fingers. "Okay. You get points for that one." He leaned back on his elbows and looked out over the water. "Seriously, though, I don't think I'm ready to sit down with him again for a *tête-à-tête*."

After finishing lunch, they strolled along the boardwalk, moving to single file to let a cyclist pass whenever they heard the *ching-ching* of a bicycle bell. Soon all the concessions would shutter for the winter. The thought made Jenna a little melancholy, picturing the boarded-up windows, the bare branches, the amusement rides standing still under a dusting of snow. Endings always made her sad. Maybe that was why she always picked up a new book the moment she finished one.

Eventually the lake fell away and they entered a quaint residential area. Jenna pulled up Turnbull's address on her phone. Bungalows and cottages clustered close together in the warren of narrow paths. Picket fences lined the walk, with trellis gates leading into gardens that still hinted at their summer lushness. Many of the houses were almost buried in greenery, but that would change by November. The small scale of everything, the closeness of nature, made it seem like a wooded fairyland. To Jenna it looked like paradise. A few people had already put up Halloween decorations: fat pumpkins, a gangly paper skeleton in the front window, a ghost hanging from a tree limb and blowing in the light breeze.

Turnbull's house sat at the fringe of the community, apart from its neighbors. While some of the houses had been renovated and updated, his looked much the same as it must have looked when it was built in the nineteen-thirties. The clapboard siding had not been painted in a long time. Dead leaves gathered on the roof. Above the front door, punctuating the roof line, a solitary second-story window squinted like a pirate's one good eye.

Jenna stared at the cottage. "Definitely a Turnbull house. I can see the family resemblance."

A frail man in his early seventies, with bushy white eyebrows and a thick shock of white hair, answered the door. Jenna repressed the urge to whisper to Kendall that Andy Warhol was still alive. The man nodded when she asked if he was Arthur Turnbull. She explained that they were tenants who had heard stories about the apartment building, and they wanted to interview him as background for their podcast.

"It's a podcast on horror stories and such," added Kendall.

Jenna feared that Turnbull would turn them away as he eyed Kendall's orange hair, but instead he said, "Then you'll probably appreciate my collection."

They stepped into the dusky interior. Bands of light peeked between the slats of the half-closed blinds, dust motes dancing in the beams that angled toward the floor. Turnbull walked around the room turning on Tiffany lamps. Curios too numerous to count crowded the room, leaving no space or wall uncovered. In her quick sweep of the room, Jenna noticed a shrunken head, Indonesian demon masks, a bird skull, a necklace beaded with tiny carved skulls, Victorian dolls, Egyptian statuettes of Horus, and maquettes of the skeleton warriors from Harryhausen's film *Jason and the Argonauts*. And that was just a fraction of the collection.

Turnbull dropped a quarter into an antique mechanical diorama that was displayed on a table. Garishly painted clowns began moving with jerky motions, striking other clowns or pretending to juggle. One clown lifted his hat to reveal a miniature clown standing on his head. Another skated in circles on a small track. Jenna squatted to inspect the figure up close. Each time it circled back around, its rictus leered at her.

"This is remarkable," she said. "I've never seen anything like this."

"Penny arcades used to be filled with such delights a hundred years ago." Turnbull approached a glass-enclosed box with a uniformed wooden figure standing in a courtyard near two Gothic doors. A sign above the case spelled out *Execution*. The quarter made a series of plunks as it dropped into the slot. Jenna watched the two doors slowly open to reveal a figure with its head positioned in a noose. A trap door opened, and the noose stretched taut as the figure dropped into the void. The figure jerked for a moment from the force of the drop, eerily realistic, then stilled.

"How long have you been collecting all of this?" she asked.

Turnbull picked up a display with the wings of a death's head moth splayed out, the upper wings mottled with black, sepia, tan, and a rusty brown, the lower wings a vivid golden yellow, and on the back of its head the semblance of a skull. "*Archerontia atropos*. A quite beautiful creature, but it makes a sharp, mouse-like squeaking that unnerves most people." He put the display back down. "It was my very first object. I've been collecting since I was a boy. So this"—he swept his arm through the air—"represents a lifetime of effort." He motioned for the two visitors to sit. "I've always felt like I was of a different era. My taste in music, books, movies... I have no interest in the modern world." He cranked up an old Victrola and placed the thick tonearm onto the vinyl record's first groove. Clicks and hiss filled the room, followed by a tinny voice that Turnbull identified as Jimmie Rodgers. Turnbull settled into an overstuffed armchair, crossed his legs, and set his intertwined fingers across his lap. "So. Ask away."

Turnbull answered their questions, explaining that Covington Terrace had been in his wife's family for several generations. When her parents died, the property passed into her hands. Because of their faith, Turnbull had consented to a Catholic wedding. He was not the least bit religious and would not have minded if they had been married in a barn. His father-in-law employed him to manage the building. Turnbull used to handle most of the maintenance himself, and taught the trade to his son Wade.

"It was such a tragedy when my wife Emma died, leaving me to raise a fourteen-year-old boy. She'll be gone nineteen years this November." The record came to its end, and Turnbull rose to place the tonearm back in its cradle.

"Do you know anything about the history of the property?" asked Jenna. "The tenants who lived there, any unusual stories?"

Turnbull stood at the Victrola, his back to Kendall and Jenna, and took his time before responding. He slipped the record back in its sleeve. "I take it you are referring to certain incidents that occurred decades ago."

Kendall glanced at Jenna and raised his eyebrows. "Well, we *have* heard some rumors."

Turnbull picked up an object next to the Victrola, a wooden viewfinder at one end connected by a length of wood to twin photographic prints at the other end. He held it aloft by a spindle attached to the underside. "You probably don't know what this is. It's called a stereoscope. It was a form of amusement long before the advent of movies or radio. When you look through this part, the photographs on the other end merge to create a realistic, three-dimensional image. But notice the photograph." He brought the device over to Kendall and Jenna. "It's titled *The Ghost in the Stereoscope*, from"—he peered at the back of the stereoscopic card—"around 1856. See the two terrified men sitting at the table, and the ghostly woman with the raised, skeletal hand? It's not a real photograph, of course. Several negatives were manipulated and combined to produce the spooky image. There are countless such examples. Many people were fooled by this so-called evidence of ghosts."

"And the hauntings at Covington Terrace?" asked Jenna.

"The people who claim to have heard or seen something are like our Victorian friends looking through the stereoscope."

"But why is it so hard to keep apartment six rented?" asked Kendall.

Turnbull set the stereoscope down. "I do find the stories entertaining. After all, look around you. But I know every square inch of that building. I spent countless hours there for forty years, making repairs, maintaining the premises, helping tenants... Until ten years ago when it became too difficult for me and I turned over most of the tasks to Wade. I had a tenant who lived in that apartment for fourteen years, never once complained to me about a ghost."

"But other people haven't stayed long in the apartment," countered Jenna.

"Some tenants stay for many years. Others move on quickly, get married, buy homes. Rental units are always in flux in a city like Toronto."

Jenna looked down at her notes. "Do you know what happened to the tenant who disappeared two years ago—Alyssa Blackwood?"

"No. She just vanished. Left everything behind." Turnbull picked up an elongated glass skull with large occipital lobes. Jenna imagined he was about to launch into a soliloquy from *Hamlet*. "This is from *Indiana Jones and the Kingdom of the Crystal Skull*."

A rustling in the other room drew Jenna's attention. She turned and saw Wade emerge into the vestibule, apparently on his way out the door.

"It's two of our tenants," Turnbull announced. "Jenna and..."

"Kendall."

Wade nodded a greeting in their direction. "I'm on my way into town to pick up a few things. I'll be back later tonight."

Turnbull held up the skull. "This was one of Wade's favorite items—wasn't it, Wade?—I think because he had seen it on the big screen." The announcement seemed to spark a memory for Turnbull. Wade did not wait around and walked out—probably had heard such stories a dozen times, thought Jenna, as Turnbull launched into his reminiscence. "Like Wade, I was raised on Ward's Island. But unlike me, he didn't get to benefit from the world that once existed here. When I was a child in the fifties, we had a movie theatre, a bowling alley, stores, hotels, dance halls. Grand Victorian summer homes lined the boardwalk along Lake Ontario. Then the city tore it all down. Even tried to evict the people who lived here. The city wanted to turn all of the islands into a park. But we fought back. Our families wanted to stay, even with the inconvenience of having to take the ferry to do our shopping. But we're a close-knit community here. Survivors, that's what we are."

"There's one more thing we wanted to ask you," said Jenna. "The tenant in apartment ten, in the basement. We tried to talk to him, but he shooed us away. Who is he?"

"Oh, you mean Marvin. He's lived there about twenty years, I believe. Never had any problems with him."

Jenna was about to comment on his odd behavior, then looked around the room and reconsidered. Kendall, however, plunged right in.

"He's a little strange, isn't he?"

Jenna repressed the urge to kick him.

Turnbull mulled over the question. "He keeps to himself. I really know little about him. Never gave me any trouble." He steepled his hands and rested his chin on the tip of his fingers. "Been at least ten years since I've seen him—perhaps even longer."

Kendall pressed further. "You haven't noticed anything noteworthy about him in all that time?"

An antique mechanical clock chimed the hour. Small doors opened, and a wooden grim reaper rotated out on a mechanical wheel. The conversation halted as they waited for the figure to complete its circuit and return to its housing. Noticing their interest, Turnbull grew animated. "Nineteenth-century Black Forest clock. Look at the words on the carved scroll: *Alle sind mein*. Everyone is mine. To remind us where we all are headed. Eventually." He held up his finger. "And any moment—ah."

Another clock chimed from its perch in another part of the room. Turnbull rose and approached an ornate gold mantel clock. "The so-called death clock. Such clocks got that name because the makers eventually succumbed to poisoning from mercury fumes, the process they used to gild these bronze timepieces. Ormolu—that was the name of the technique." He said the word again, softer— *ormolu*—and traced his finger over a reclining robed skeleton. "Seventeenth-century France. Very unusual, this one, with the memento mori touch."

"I guess they're both pretty valuable," said Kendall.

102

Turnbull nodded. "The entire collection is priceless. They are like my children." He turned to face his visitors. "I set both clocks ahead of the hour, which means you have ten minutes to catch the ferry. A little trick I've used for years so I wouldn't miss it. Otherwise you'll need to wait another hour."

It was clear to Jenna that no response to Kendall's question would be forthcoming.

Walking the short distance to the ferry, she and Kendall shared their impressions of the collection and what they learned about Covington Terrace.

"Freaky-deaky," she said. "And no luck confirming our ghost."

"Unless he's lying, and trying to downplay the rumors so tenants aren't discouraged from wanting to live there."

Jenna looked at her watch. "I've got to stop by the store to pick up something to bring tonight to Mrs. Gupta's. Are you making something?"

"Yep. My mother's traditional stew."

Jenna spotted Wade on the ferry and decided to take advantage of the opportunity to get his perspective on Covington Terrace. He stood on the upper deck, looking across the water to the docklands. She sidled up to him and started out with an innocent question to get the conversation going: how did he like living on Ward's Island?

He shrugged. "It's fine. Quiet."

"Your dad has quite an unusual collection."

"Yeah. Keeps growing."

She tried to find a way to segue to her real question. "Kendall and I have a horror podcast, so we were intrigued by all the memorabilia. It must have been interesting growing up around all that stuff."

Wade rested his forearms on the railing and leaned forward. "I guess so." He picked at a strip of peeling paint, then stepped back from the railing and stretched his arms. His T-shirt lifted up, revealing a taut stomach and a pale band of skin between his belt and navel. A dark thatch of hair climbed like ivy out of his groin. He

103

looked at Jenna and caught her looking at his stomach. Their eyes met, and she felt herself blush as she looked away.

Her next question spilled out in a self-conscious rush. "Um, for our podcast, we're—uh—planning a story on Covington Terrace and, you know, its supposedly haunted history." She laughed, but it came out robotic. "Do you know anything about the rumors about apartment six?"

Wade kept staring at Jenna. It seemed to her a minute passed before he responded, although it must have been no more than five seconds. "Yeah, I've heard the rumors. But that's all they are. No ghosts." He turned back toward the harbor. "Does that disappoint you?"

"Not me," said Kendall. "I'm sort of relieved."

The ferry drew close to the waterfront dock. Passengers began standing and moving toward the exit.

Sensing the opportunity coming to an end, Jenna posed her question again. "So you've never heard about anything strange happening?"

"Like what?"

"Voices in the walls, strange presences"—she looked at Kendall as she said *presences*—"footsteps when the apartment was vacant... You know, things that people might attribute to ghosts."

Wade grabbed his empty grocery bags from the bench. "Look, it's an old building. Old buildings make strange noises. That's all it is." He gave a tight smile and headed toward the exit.

Thriller

Rooney

Rooney was getting ready for her date with Wade. Not a date, exactly. More like a casual get-together. She had suggested going out for coffee when he called, something that did not involve committing to an entire evening together, so they picked a Sunday afternoon. Although she looked forward to seeing him, she did not feel the tingling sense of excitement she sometimes felt with other men. The reason? She was not yet sure how she felt about him. She considered the possibility that she was using him for the benefits he offered as the landlord's son. But that seemed too cynical as the only reason, even for her. He intrigued her—that much she knew. She pondered all of this as she tidied up the apartment.

She sniffed as she opened the cabinet beneath the sink. The trash was starting to smell. Rooney hated taking out the trash. It entailed walking out the back door, down several steps, then walking through the backyard garden and into the alley where the garbage bins stood beneath a sheltered enclosure—one bin for regular trash and one for recycling. She tied up the garbage bag and started her trek to the bins.

As she crossed the garden, she saw the new tenant with the shaved head returning from his trash trip. Despite his intimidating demeanor, she smiled as they passed one another. A moment later, from behind her, she heard his voice call out.

"Hey, you're the girl from the day I looked at the apartment— the one who told me about the ghosts."

He introduced himself. She told him her name was Rooney. The day was warm and he wore only a black T-shirt and jeans. Macabre tattoos covered both arms: skulls, a demon with horns, grim faces. She tried not to stare.

"I'm still waiting to see the ghost you promised," he said.

Rooney laughed uncomfortably. She wondered if he had been exposed yet to Morvena's fits. "You might have more luck being haunted by a certain ghost in the flesh in the apartment next to you. Have you had any trouble yet with the old lady?"

"You mean the one who invited me in for cocktails? No. Why?"

The trash bag was getting heavy, so she set it at her feet. "She pounds on the floor if she hears me sneeze. It's so aggravating."

"I know what you mean. The neighbor where I used to live complained about my music. I tried to be respectful by recording during the day, but he still got pissed off. That's one of the reasons I moved."

She took in his intense look, the shaved head, the tattoos. "I'd be too scared to complain to you."

Vince looked down at his arms. "Yeah, it does have certain advantages sometimes."

She picked up her trash bag. "Well, I should go ahead and throw this in the bin so I can get ready to go out. Nice talking to you."

In fact, that last statement stretched the truth. Everything about him intimidated her. When he had been around visiting his girlfriend, the tattoos had always been covered up. Thank God Wade did not have grim tattoos covering his biceps and forearms. That would be a deal breaker. Imagine staring at a skull whenever they made love. Ugh!

The bottles in her trash bag rang out when the bag hit the bottom of the near-empty bin, making her jump.

Walking back to the building, she spotted Kendall standing at his bedroom window. He struggled to raise the bottom half, which stuck for a few moments before it jerked up, allowing him to lean out. "I swear, this raggedy-ass place…"

Rooney laughed. "I know, right?"

"Do you have a moment to stop by?"

Inside his apartment, something was cooking. Rooney smelled the fragrance of curry, thyme, onions, garlic.

Kendall shut the door behind her. "I heard you talking with the Bone Man—that's the name he uses for his music. Did you know his girlfriend used to live here but disappeared?"

"I just thought she moved out, but, yeah, I remember seeing him before."

"Do you think it's strange that he moved here after she went missing?"

Rooney scanned his face for a motive. The question itself betrayed that Kendall must have been uncomfortable, so she decided to be honest. "Yeah. It struck me as a bit odd."

"That's what I thought, too. Did you know her?"

"No, we never actually met. I saw her a few times in the hall and said hello—sometimes she was with him—but that was about it. I didn't even know what apartment she lived in."

Kendall scrolled through his phone until he found the album cover featuring the Bone Man's photo with the skull face. "That's him."

Rooney leaned over to look at the screen, sweeping strands of her hair behind her ear. "Wow."

"You know Jenna and I are into horror, right? Well, the Bone Man is maybe just a bit too close to the real deal for me."

"Not someone you'd want to meet alone in a dark alley?"

"Not even in a well-lit alley. There's a mystery here, and maybe we can get to the bottom of it. So if you learn anything worth sharing, let me know."

Rooney agreed, then returned to her apartment. Kendall's concern about the vanished girlfriend had invaded her thoughts, though, and she found it difficult to concentrate on what to wear for her get-together. She slipped on a long-sleeved, wine-red dress that wrapped in a low V across her cleavage, then changed her mind. They were just getting together for coffee, after all. She needed to find a balance between something provocative and something casual. She settled on snug jeans, a black knit sweater with loose elbow-length sleeves, and black strappy sandals with a stacked heel and gold accents. A necklace with a silver and gold pendant completed the outfit. She bunched her hair and arranged it to cascade over her right shoulder, then applied plum-colored lipstick. She looked at herself in the bathroom mirror, struck a coy pose, and judged the look to be a success. Wade would definitely be enticed. She no longer remembered what she had been obsessing about fifteen minutes earlier.

When Wade arrived, he suggested a cafe franchise spot nearby on Parliament Street. Rooney would have preferred one of the independent coffee shops, but she was content to defer to his choice at this stage. She knew such deference made men like Wade feel more secure.

They walked together down the street, Rooney taking short, cloppy steps in her heels to keep up as Wade took long strides with his hands in his pockets. "On Monday it will officially be fall," she said. "You know, the Equinox."

"Uh-huh. Soon it will be time to turn on the boiler."

The day's warmth made her think of summer, but she could already feel the air cooling as evening approached, a sure reminder that this was fall. Rooney said she loved this time of year the best, even though spring was actually her favorite season. Just a little white lie, to keep the conversation flowing. She asked him how he got into construction. *Through my dad.* What was it like growing up on Ward's Island? *Everybody knows everybody.* Any brothers or sisters? *No.* Short answers. Conversation would definitely be a challenge with this one.

Sitting with their beverages, Rooney studied his thick hands that were wrapped around the paper cup. She imagined all the tools those hands had worked with: hammers, screwdrivers, wrenches, power drills. She resisted the temptation to ask him about his past girlfriends. Too soon, although she was dying with curiosity. In fact, she was curious to know everything about this man of few words. She said something that made him smile, revealing his dimples. She gazed at his cleft chin. These etchings in his face appealed to her. She asked about the scar near his right eye.

"Oh, that. Just a childhood injury."

She wanted to reach out and touch it, as she would caress a wounded bird. He looked back at her intently. She was the first one to break the stare and look away. She took a sip of her latte to hide the fact that she was blushing.

He asked her what she did professionally. She explained that she promoted people's products online, posting reviews and testimonials. *And you can make a living doing that?* She assured him that was the case. She described her work process, omitting the fact that she commented on items she never used and places she never visited. He mentioned that he had ordered the part for the oven— being an old oven, naturally, the parts were hard to find.

108

They talked about favorite movies, music, Internet videos. She showed him some funny videos featuring cats, including her favorite one where a mischievous cat knocked a line of small stuffed animals off a shelf. They found a common interest in electronic dance music, though neither professed to understand the proliferation of sub-genres. Wade said he'd like to be a deejay, spinning records at a club and watching people lose themselves in the dance. The pulse of the music appealed to him, the way it took over every nerve in your body. She nodded with fervor, because she loved how the music made her feel sexy and alive, how it made her forget her many personas so she could let loose and be herself. But she didn't say all that to him.

She noticed he had warmed up to the conversation, and the words now came more easily. She revised her assessment of the get-together from six out of ten to eight. All at once, she was curious to know the taste of his lips. She liked staring into his blue eyes with the long lashes. *Wade.* She said the name to herself as she listened to him. It made her think of wading into the blue waters of Lake Ontario on a hot summer day, naked, the water rising above her knees, then up her thighs as she walked farther out, then covering her hips and groin, lapping gently until she slowly lowered her upper body, feeling the liquid creep up over her nipples, forming a caressing ring around her neck, then her entire torso submerged, her eyes closed, her head sinking beneath the surface as the water kissed her lips, her nose, her eyelids.

She did not consider herself a gold-digger, but the benefits of dating the landlord's son did not escape her. Priority attention when repairs were needed. Perhaps a break in the rent. And some day he would inherit the property, so he represented a good investment. All in all, not a bad bargain. She expected he would ask to see her again, maybe for dinner and a movie. And he did, right after tilting back his head to drain his cup in one final gulp. They set a date for Friday. She felt in control, pleased with her powers of seduction.

The afternoon with Wade had put Rooney in a good mood. After they had parted and she was back in her apartment, she felt motivated to tackle the semi-annual rearrangement of her closet, moving summer wear to the back and bringing forward winter coats and boots. She pulled out plastic crates that had been stacked in the back of the closet and emptied the contents on her bed. A jumble of boots stared back at her: fur-lined red boots that just covered the ankle, calf-high black slip-ons with a block heel, sexy mahogany high-heeled boots with dainty buckles.

She removed a crate from the closet shelf—a crate filled with sweaters and pullovers—but lost her grip. It fell to the hardwood floor with a loud crash. Within seconds, she heard Morvena above pounding on the floor. A few flecks of ceiling paint snowed down. Rooney detested this woman and her intolerance for noise. "It was just a little accident!" she yelled at the ceiling. "Lighten up, for God's sake."

She gathered the contents that had spilled on the floor and placed them on the bed alongside the boots. She would replace the shorts and camisoles in her dresser with the heavy sweaters and pullovers. The shorts and camisoles would go into the crate and onto the shelf. As she performed the switch, she seethed. Ever since Morvena moved in two months ago, Rooney had become stressed out by the constant complaints. She was not used to being intimidated to the point of being afraid to use the bathroom during the night. She filled up the crate, held it chest high, then deliberately let it drop to the floor. Morvena paced above, the floorboards creaking, but Rooney was almost disappointed when no pounding ensued.

She stuffed the crate back on the shelf, then stood back to look at her array of summer shoes displayed in shoe racks along the floor. Despite the apartment's many drawbacks, she adored the large walk-in closet—its most redeeming feature. The place where she previously lived had a standard closet that was inadequate for her needs. And those needs were not just a matter of personal taste, since she required different outfits for her promotional personas. She even deducted the cost as a business expense on her tax return, as they were essential parts of her livelihood.

As she stood with her hands on her hips, feeling grateful for the magnificent closet, she noticed the small square door at the back.

She had noticed it before, of course, but for the first time, perhaps prompted by recent events, she felt curious. The door reminded her of something out of Alice in Wonderland. It had no knob, just an indentation where you would insert your fingers and pull, like the cover to a utility box. The dimensions were large enough to crawl through. But why would someone need to access the space beyond? As she knelt before the door and pulled it open, she thought of a similar trap door in the ceiling of her previous apartment, and how she never once thought to open it. Such complacency about her environment no longer seemed acceptable. Not since talk of voices in the walls and ghosts.

The interior was dark, but she could make out a space about two feet wide that separated her unit from Elliott's apartment. Horizontal slats comprised the walls, with narrow gaps between slats—apparently a type of old construction she had never seen before. She stuck her head into the space and shined the flashlight app from her phone in both directions. To her right, the light illuminated bathroom pipes and, farther on, a low-ceilinged space that she realized must be beneath the mid-point landing of the stairs. To her left, she saw a ladder built into the wall. The ladder ascended through a hole in the ceiling to the second floor, and descended to the basement through a similar hole.

Undaunted by the musty odor and cobwebs, she crawled through the door and stood. The corridor felt claustrophobic, walls pressing in on both sides. A thrill raced through her body as she realized that she could move between floors unseen. She had discovered the perfect vehicle for bringing the building's haunted reputation to life. A new plan began to form. She would haunt Morvena and scare the woman into moving. She could already taste the sweetness of revenge. Not tonight, but soon. First, she needed to finish her task laying out her autumn and winter wardrobe. But she could hardly contain her glee.

The Feast of the Goat

Mrs. Gupta

Mrs. Gupta stood over the stove preparing chicken biryani. The fragrance of cardamom, coriander, nutmeg, mint, and other spices suffused the kitchen. A side dish of raita, plastic wrap pulled tightly across the lip of the bowl, chilled in the refrigerator. The rice simmered on the counter in a rice cooker.

She set down the wooden spoon to answer the knock at the door. Kendall stood at the threshold gripping the handles of a large pot. At his side, Jenna held a small box. They exchanged greetings and joined Mrs. Gupta in the kitchen while she finished cooking.

"I hope you haven't had any more unnerving experiences," said Jenna.

The griddle sizzled as Mrs. Gupta laid out the skewers of marinated chicken. "Unfortunately, I have. The other night."

"I told Jenna about the closet," said Kendall.

"It gave me quite a fright. The door kept opening, just a few inches. That's never happened before." The memory of the incident made her shiver.

"I remember once when I was a girl, my parents rented a cabin on Lake Simcoe," said Jenna. "The stairs to the second story had a door that sat on the first step instead of the floor. If you tried to leave the door open without securing it to the wall, it would slowly swing shut, like it was guided by an invisible hand. Freaked me out."

Kendall inspected a glass case displaying blue-and-white porcelain dishes. "You collect these?"

"I used to. I stopped once we moved here. There simply isn't enough room."

"This plate is beautiful—the one with the fountain, and the castle, and all the floral swirls around the edge. It's so intricate."

"Yes. Vintage Crown Staffordshire bone china. An amazing level of artistry."

"We both attended OCAD," explained Jenna. "So we appreciate craftsmanship."

"We met in the material art and design program," added Kendall. "Jenna commented on my unusual outfit, and we started hanging out together. I continued to work with textiles, while Jenna switched majors to study graphic design."

"Do you know the Gardiner Museum?" asked Mrs. Gupta. "Across the Street from the Royal Ontario Museum?" Her two guests shook their heads. "I'm surprised you've never been, given your interests. They have a marvelous collection of ceramics. In the late seventeenth century, imported porcelain from China and Japan created feverish interest in Europe. It took a long time for the Europeans to imitate the quality produced in Asia, but eventually they achieved masterful results. The Gardiner has fine work from Asia, Europe, and the Americas. That's how I became interested in collecting. It all started by visiting the Gardiner. I prefer designs that hew close to the original Chinese technique, just the simplicity of using blue as decoration. But other styles can be quite colorful." She set out the raita on the table. "How are you coming along with your podcast? Have you spoken to all of the other tenants?"

"Everyone except the mystery man who lives in apartment ten," said Kendall. "He refused to talk to us."

Mrs. Gupta admitted she had never seen the occupant of apartment ten. It amazed her to think she could live in a building for five years and never cross paths with someone. The person might as well have been a ghost. "Does anyone else have stories of strange experiences like mine?"

"Only Elliott," said Jenna. "He's heard footsteps when the apartment above was vacant."

"I tend to believe him," said Kendall. "He seems pretty sensible—not the kind who is prone to superstitions."

"I think he finds the prospect of a ghost rather amusing, not something to be frightened about," added Jenna. The two of them launched into a run-down of the other tenants.

"Lilith—who lives below you—takes ghosts more seriously," said Kendall. "She's very intuitive and attuned to the supernatural."

"Rooney says she's not afraid of ghosts, but I don't believe her. There's something evasive about her. She's like a slippery eel that you can't quite get a handle on."

"The new tenant who moved into the supposedly haunted apartment—"

"—Vince—"

"—scares me a bit. Rough-looking. Watches you like he's trying to burrow into your soul."

"Kendall is exaggerating. He's not that bad. He writes music."

"As an alter ego named the Bone Man."

Mrs. Gupta flinched at the name.

"Have you met Lucy?" asked Jenna.

"Yes—the woman with the little dog. She's quite lovely. I hear the dog scurrying across the floor."

"Lucy has a mischievous sense of humor," added Kendall.

"And then there's Morvena." Jenna paused. All three of them looked at one another and burst out laughing.

"I don't wish to be judgmental," said Mrs. Gupta, "but she *is* a handful."

"Yes, but she's rather entertaining when she's not shouting in the hallways," said Kendall. "A bundle of exaggerated gestures and drama. Put her onstage at Dante's and you'd swear she was a drag queen."

Jenna asked if Mrs. Gupta had known either of the young women who had lived in apartment six prior to Vince.

"No. We never spoke, except perhaps a smile in passing."

"Did you know about the disappearance?" asked Jenna.

She vaguely remembered the police coming to question her. But she had nothing to tell them, and their visit had been no longer than perhaps two minutes. Now, the memory made her uneasy, reminding her of the threatening words she had heard coming from the wall just over two weeks earlier. She was glad she had never mentioned the visit from the police to her daughter. That would be one more piece of evidence for Sirisha to insist on moving temporarily to the waterfront condo. She still resisted the idea, even after the incident with the closet. Why had Vikram left her to face this situation alone? The transition to life after Vikram had been difficult, certainly, but she had managed it without falling to pieces. She had never been especially religious, but she believed in reincarnation, the role of karma in human affairs, and the need to accept what happens in life with a certain amount of detachment. Above all, she was practical.

At dinner, she laughed over Kendall's stories about certain performances at Dante's—especially about one drag queen named Rainbeau ("That's B-E-A-U, but it wasn't pretty," said Kendall) who grimaced as she performed her lip-synch, waving streamers that had the unfortunate effect of tangling her up like a mummy and tripping her just as she reached the song's climax. Before long, Mrs. Gupta had completely forgotten her worry about recent events. Jenna and Kendall insisted on doing the dishes before they left, despite her protestations.

Mrs. Gupta stared into the mirror as she brushed her teeth, enjoying the licorice taste of the Vicco toothpaste. It reminded her of childhood, and her mother's insistence on Ayurvedic approaches to health. A renewed need for such childhood comforts had resurfaced ever since Vikram passed away. Comforts such as recreating her mother's favorite dishes. Or buying a sari on a whim. She had not owned one in decades, yet there she was stopping in that shop, letting the saleswoman remind her how to drape it. Funny how the mind worked.

She rinsed her mouth, then smiled broadly for the mirror, checking for any remaining particles of food.

Out of the corner of her eye, she saw a figure walk past the bathroom door, heading toward the bedroom. She had only the vaguest impression that it was a man, dressed in dark, drab colors, with something on his head. Something with horns. Yet she knew no one else could be in the apartment. Ever since Kendall told her about the doorknob, she had made sure to keep it as well as the deadbolt locked as a double precaution. She tiptoed to the threshold where she could see the apartment door. The deadbolt was clearly in the locked position. She glanced toward the dark interior of the bedroom, but could not convince herself to investigate.

She slipped as quietly as she could into the living room, then noticed an empty spot in the glass case of Staffordshire porcelain. For a split second she pondered whether Kendall or Jenna might have taken the plate. But no, that was preposterous. No one had been trying to conceal a plate when they left.

She heard a floorboard creak in the bedroom. That was enough to propel her out the door and down the hall to Kendall's apartment. No one answered when she knocked. She kept looking down the hall, waiting for something to emerge from her apartment, pursuing her. She knocked again, more insistently. Perhaps he was upstairs in Jenna's apartment. What would she do if whatever she had seen in her apartment suddenly appeared and cornered her in the hall, no Kenny coming to her aid? She stepped across the hall to try to rouse Elliott, and was relieved when he finally answered her knock. She explained that she had seen something. "It may have just been a trick of the light, but I would appreciate it if you could check my apartment."

Elliott looked under the bed, peered in the closet, tested the windows. There was nowhere someone could have hidden or entered the apartment. She mentioned that one of her Staffordshire plates was missing.

"I'm certain I haven't misplaced it. Kendall and Jenna were just over here for dinner, and he was admiring the very plate that is missing. I know what you must be thinking—that I'm one of those women with overactive imaginations who are susceptible to superstition. But I've been a sensible person my entire life. Rational, even-tempered."

"Mrs. Gupta, I don't think there's anything the matter with you at all. I believe the building may actually be haunted."

Mrs. Gupta hugged herself. "Doors opening on their own accord. Noises in the wall. Fleeting figures and missing objects. This is all becoming a bit much for me. I may take up my daughter on her offer to stay with her for a while, where I'll feel safer."

"Well, I've been here fifteen years, and nothing's happened to me yet."

"You're a man. Not a woman living alone."

Elliott nodded. "Yeah, I get it."

She thanked him for checking out the apartment. After he left, she went over to the glass case, wondering why that particular piece was missing. Almost as if someone, or something, had been listening to them.

5

Excerpt from Shockadelica Podcast
Episode 36: Humor in Horror
Guest: Screenwriter Gabe Muñoz

Kendall: What is your opinion about humor in horror? I'm not talking about satire, or horror comedies—

Jenna: Like *Hocus Pocus*.

Kendall: —but where the fear is lightened with something humorous. For example, De Palma's version of *Carrie* is great in many ways, but I always thought the shifts in tone with the funny music were too jarring and ruined the mood.

Gabe: I know what you're saying, although that didn't bother me. But, yeah, it can be done well or it can be cheesy. Rodriguez pulls it off well in *From Dusk to Dawn*.

Jenna: Partly because he's having fun with the pulp genre.

Gabe: Right. There are some fun sarcastic exchanges between Vincent Price and his wife in *The House on Haunted Hill*. In that case, it advances the plot by showing the bitterness in their relationship.

Jenna: But does the humor detract from the horror? Dilute it?

Gabe: No, I don't think so. Humor and horror are twins. One of the reasons we like horror is because it provides an emotional release. It's like a roller coaster. Humor is one way to relieve the tension. You know, like how you laugh after you've been scared out of your pants by something at a haunted attraction. It doesn't detract from your experience—it enhances it.

Jenna: But can you take it too far?
Gabe: Uh, maybe. I can't think of an example off the top of my
          head.
Kendall: And then we have horror movies that are unintentionally
          funny.
Gabe: That's a whole nother story.

The Night Visitor

Kendall

Kendall set the basket of laundry atop the dryer and sighed. The tedium of another washday. *If I live until I'm eighty,* he calculated, *that means I can look forward to about 2,700 more wash days.* The washer's lid rang out its metallic clang as he let it fall against the control console at the back. He began sorting clothes, stuffing dark items into the bin and setting lighter colors aside.

His mind wandered to the dress he had started making. Five weeks remained until Halloween—plenty of time to complete his creation, despite its complicated design. He had started to appliqué coiling silver filigrees to a body-hugging, sheer base that let skin peek through on the thigh, side, and stomach. Spikey silver flames shot up and over the breasts. Long silver tendrils would dangle down to the calf and swirl around his legs with each step. It was sensuous, sexy, and over the top, appropriate only for a starlet on the red carpet—or a drag queen.

The reverie ended once he heard the click of the coin mechanism and the water pouring into the bin. He gathered the laundry basket in one arm and turned around. Since he had not heard anybody descend the stairs, he was startled to see a figure standing in the doorway.

"You're new here, aren't you?" said the stranger.

"Relatively new. I've been here about nine months. I don't think I've seen you around before, either."

"No. We wouldn't have met before. Many years ago I used to live in this building. At the moment, you could say I'm just visiting."

"Visiting who?"

The figure stepped into the room and waved his hand with a flourish that to Kendall seemed deliberately fey. "Friends."

"Friends," Kendall repeated, running through the list of names in his mind now that he had met (if only briefly) all of the residents. "Anyone I know?"

The stranger moved closer and leaned against the dryer. He had hazel eyes flecked with gold that almost seemed to glow, and wavy, thick black hair. He wore a T-shirt with a galloping horse in silhouette across the chest. "No, I don't suppose you would know them." He picked up a discarded fabric softener sheet lying on the table beside the dryer and held it up to his nose. "*Meadow fresh*, I believe. Although it really smells nothing like a meadow at all, if you ask me." He winked and let the sheet drop back to the table.

"What's your name?"

The stranger hopped up to sit on the dryer. "Guess. What do I look like?"

Kendall scrunched his mouth to the side, studying the stranger. The accent reminded him of Lilith. "Not a Bruno." The stranger shook his head. "Definitely not Emilio or Sanjay... What about Lucas?"

The stranger spread his arms and bowed his head. "Then you can call me Lucas."

"But I take it that's not really your name?"

Lucas—or maybe not-Lucas—laughed. He propped his elbow on the dryer's coin arm and leaned forward to rest his chin in the palm of his hand, flirtatiously drawing closer to Kendall. "It's always more interesting when you don't know someone's name, or all the baggage of their past. They can be whoever you want them to be."

This time it was Kendall who laughed. "And who do you want *me* to be?"

Lucas shrugged. "The kind of guy who's not afraid to talk to someone who may or may not be named Lucas."

121

The washing machine kicked into its wash cycle. "You said you used to live here?"

Lucas sat up straight. "I did, at one time."

"So... Did you ever hear about any ghosts, especially in apartment six?"

"There are ghosts all around us."

"But did you ever see any here?"

Lucas looked away from Kendall, studying another part of the room. Kendall turned to follow his gaze, then turned back when he saw nothing in particular.

"Maybe," said Lucas.

"That's not a helpful answer. Is it yes or no?"

"Which would you prefer?"

Kendall rolled his eyes. "I can see I'm not going to be able to get a straight answer out of you—no pun intended."

Lucas let out a laugh that sounded like a whinny. "Why are you so keen to know?"

"Well, some strange things have been happening lately. I've talked to everyone in the building except the guy in apartment ten." He gestured beyond the laundry room, guessing that Lucas might be one of the mystery tenant's little tricks. "If he's one of your friends, perhaps you could convince him to talk to me."

"You have greater things to worry about than ghosts, Kendall Akande."

Kendall slammed the laundry basket onto the table. "Hey, wait a minute! How do you know my name?"

Lucas smiled. "You do that horror podcast, Shockadelica."

"That's not fair. You didn't tell me you knew who I was. And what do you mean, I have greater things to worry about?"

Lucas hopped down from the dryer. "Listen. Samhain is coming. Here in North America you call it Halloween. Give me the dress you designed, and you will remain safe."

Kendall narrowed his eyes. "Bitch, you've got to be kidding."

"Call it a kind of sacrifice."

"A sacrifice for what? How do you even know what I was planning to wear? If Jenna told you something, I will kill her."

"You don't have to give it to me now. Just let me have it before Halloween."

Kendall grabbed the laundry basket and held it so tightly that the plastic cut into his side. "If you think I am going to abandon my outfit to some crazy-ass stranger, you're even crazier than I thought."

"Suit yourself. You still have time to think it over." Lucas spread his fingers and looked down to admire his nails. They were painted a dark cherry that verged on black. "I love this color. *Bruised velvet*. It should go nicely with the dress, don't you think?"

"What makes you think you deserve to wear my creation? If you can even fit into it."

"Ouch. That was cold. Well, it's your choice. Completely. I'm not going to force you to do anything against your will."

"I don't get it. You come popping up out of nowhere, acting all cute and flirty, then you say I'm supposed to give you the dress I've spent weeks designing. And I don't even know you. What is this all about?"

Lucas dropped the playful smile he had dangled during their conversation and grabbed Kendall by the arms. "It's no joke, my friend. This is how you can protect yourself from certain dark forces that are out there. You've encountered these forces long ago, in your past. They are coming again, as they are wont to do."

"*Wont to do*? You sound like a character out of a nineteenth-century novel."

Lucas released his grip. "Well, old habits die hard."

"Jenna put you up to this, didn't she? As a joke."

"Would it were true."

Kendall emitted a groan of frustration and stomped out of the room. As he reached the stairs, he noticed the laundry room had become quiet. The mechanical agitation of the washer had stopped, and everything was perfectly still. His first inclination was that Lucas had mischievously pressed the pause button. But when Kendall returned to the washroom, Lucas had vanished. Even as he called out Lucas' name, he realized the futility of doing so. He looked around the hallway, carefully noting the various doors: the two apartments, the locked doors of the boiler room and supply closets, and the door that led up the steps to the backyard Jungle. It was inconceivable that Lucas could have slipped away through any of those doors in the short time it had taken Kendall to walk to the stairs. Kendall passed through the washroom into the storage locker area. Lucas was not hiding in there. And without any other way in or out, he could not have slipped away through that space.

The washer still sat silent. Kendall now worried that it had broken down. He put down the basket and opened the washer lid, expecting to find a tub full of water. But the wet clothes lay plastered together along the sides of the drum, suggesting the washer had completed its cycle. He extracted a black T-shirt and sniffed it, surprised that it smelled clean. Improbably, thirty minutes must have passed in the blink of an eye. He shrugged and began transferring the clothes to the dryer.

Jenna appeared in the doorway. "Are you still doing laundry? I've been waiting for two hours. I started to come down the stairs at one point but figured whoever you were talking to was doing a load, too."

"You couldn't have been waiting that long. I thought I'd only been here ten minutes max, but it was just one thirty-minute wash cycle."

"No, it's almost ten o'clock. You left me at eight to start a load."

"Is this part of your trick, along with that guy you sent down to talk to me?"

"What guy?"

"That cute guy with the dark hair, who talks funny and said I had to give him my Halloween dress."

"I have no idea what you're talking about." Kendall stared into her eyes, expecting her to break into a big grin since she was terrible at keeping a straight face or fibbing, but she just gave her head a little shake. "What?"

"This is really weird." Kendall recounted his conversation with the stranger as he transferred items into the dryer. The more he described it, the odder the experience sounded.

"Well, there's one way to find out the truth. We can go door to door until we find him and his friends."

"Unless someone wants to keep me in the dark." He started the dryer. "The thing is, I haven't told anybody but you and my mom about my dress idea." He gestured toward the washer. "Are you going to do a load?"

"It's getting late. I'll just wait until tomorrow."

Together they climbed the stairs, Kendall mulling over possible explanations for the strange visit. "There's only one queen I can think of who might want to sabotage my Halloween plans. Tipsy Hedrin."

Jenna scoffed. "You two have a friendly rivalry. I don't think she would stoop to such a desperate measure."

"True. But she might do it as a joke, just to see how far she could push it."

"Then you should ask her. But that still leaves you with the question: how would she know what you planned to make?"

They reached the first floor and paused before returning to their respective apartments. "It would be easy to guess that I was designing my own dress. That's an obvious conclusion. But I think I will pay Tipsy a little visit."

"You still planning to intercept our mystery tenant when he does his laundry tonight?"

"Absolutely. Are you sure you don't want to wait up with me?"

Jenna headed up the stairs. "No thanks. That's past my bedtime on a weeknight. You can give me the full report tomorrow."

Kendall spent the next forty-five minutes working on his dress as he waited for his clothes to dry. He kept trying to explain the strange visit, but like trying to explain the vision at the Necropolis, nothing quite made sense. Lucas vanishing suddenly. Two hours passing in what seemed like no more than thirty minutes. The enigmatic warning. His intuition told him that, somehow, everything was connected. Ghosts. Goat-men. Lucas. Exactly how they were connected—ah, that was the mystery.

The timer on his cell phone tapped out its woodpecker reminder. He trudged back down to the laundry room, folded his clothes, and stacked them in the basket. Then he sat down, waiting for the mystery tenant while he busied himself reading social media posts and news reports on his phone.

He checked his watch. Eleven thirty-five. Any time now, if Lilith was accurate.

He heard footsteps on the stairs and worried that another resident was coming to do laundry, which might upset his plan. When no one entered the washroom, however, he got up to investigate and stood just inside the doorway, peering out as unobtrusively as possible. Across the hallway, the Bone Man (Kendall had taken to calling Vince by his musician moniker) stood before a locked door with his hand on the knob. Kendall watched him slip a credit card into the crack between the door and the frame, right next to the doorknob, and wiggle the card back and forth a few times. The door popped open, and the Bone Man stepped inside.

From his position, Kendall could not see into the room. He considered creeping across the hall to peek inside and see what compelled the Bone Man to break into it, but he was too afraid of how the Bone Man would react if caught in the act. Kendall closed the laundry room door halfway so he would not be seen, then stood behind it spying through the crack. A minute later, the Bone Man emerged and closed the door. He stood in the hallway, facing the back door as if pondering something. Then he slowly headed toward the back door, examining the wall as he walked. He passed out of Kendall's field of vision. Kendall heard the footsteps pause at the end of the corridor. Perhaps a minute of silence passed. Then the footsteps started anew, moving decisively down the corridor. Kendall jumped back to his chair and pretended to be absorbed in his phone in case the Bone Man popped in. But instead the footsteps retreated up the stairs, gradually dying away.

When he felt comfortable that the Bone Man would not return, Kendall crept across the hall. The door was still unlocked, so he opened it and flicked on the light switch. He found a supply room filled with gardening tools, plastic pots, and several dusty old bags of mulch. From the condition of the Jungle, it was clear the tools had not been touched in quite a long time. He struggled to imagine why the Bone Man would want to break into this room.

He checked his watch: ten minutes to midnight. After he had returned to the laundry room, he heard a door open down the hall, and a moment later Lilith appeared.

"I thought I'd come out to see how it's going," she said.

"You're sure he always does his laundry at this time?"

"Like clockwork, every Tuesday. Well, almost like clockwork. Sometime between eleven-thirty and midnight. I hear him leave his apartment, then come back a few minutes later after the washer has been loaded."

Kendall patted the chair beside him, and Lilith came over to sit. "Jenna thinks you're a witch." He expected Lilith to laugh, but she looked down at her lap.

"It's complicated. I don't call myself that. Not that I'm ashamed of what I am. But there's a lot of baggage associated with the term. A lot of prejudice. People treat you differently once they find out. Besides, I don't follow any particular witch tradition. I practice my own blend of different traditions, but focused on goddess spirituality, being positive, respecting others, and respecting the earth."

"Do you do spells?"

"Yes. For the purpose of creating positive energy in my life."

Kendall tried to imagine Lilith casting spells. The image that popped into his mind was Hermione Granger brandishing her wand at Hogwarts. Lilith had the same self-assured presence of mind, giving the impression that nothing could unnerve her. But the picture of her turning adversaries into mice was surely wrong.

As if reading his mind, Lilith continued. "It's not what you think. In stories and movies—even the most sympathetic ones—we are capable of fantastic feats of magick. But it's really just another spiritual practice. A way to lead a mindful, ethical life. Just like

127

Christianity, Buddhism, Islam, Judaism... What is prayer, after all,
but a form of magickal thinking?"

"I hadn't thought of it that way. It sounds perfectly sensible to
me." Kendall remembered Lucas. "Do you have an Irish friend
visiting you, by any chance?"

"No. Why?"

"A stranger was snooping about earlier. He knew me and what
I was designing for Halloween. I think he was Irish. Very cute. He
claimed to be visiting someone in the building."

Kendall heard a door open down the hall. Lilith put her finger
up to her lips. A moment later Marvin appeared carrying a laundry
basket filled with clothes. His bald head merged with his neck to
create a single block, the chin vanishing into flesh.

"Oh, I didn't know the machines were in use," he said, turning
to leave.

"We're done," said Kendall. "We were just talking."

"I'll come back later."

"That's silly," said Lilith. "Here, we'll get out of your way."
She winked at Kendall. The two of them left the room, Kendall's
laundry basket in his arms. At the door to her apartment, Lilith
whispered, "Go back in there. I'll leave you two be. Good luck."

Marvin was busy loading the washer, placing the items with
meticulous care inside the drum. Kendall cleared his throat. "I don't
believe we completed our introductions. My name is Kendall.
Kendall Akande."

Marvin whirled around, his tiny, pale blue eyes brimming with
worry. "Yes, I remember you. You came to my door with that young
woman."

"And you are?"

"Uh, Malcolm."

"Malcolm? Hmm. Turnbull said your name was Marvin."

Marvin reddened into a cherry. "Malcolm is one of my *noms
de plume*."

"You're a writer?"

Marvin turned back to the task of filling the washer. "Yes."

"Anything I might have read?"

"Oh, I don't think you'd know it. The title is *How to Mind Your Own Business*."

"Excuse me?"

"I think you heard me."

Kendall marched over to the washer and slammed down the lid. "Listen, Miss Thing. I don't know who you think you are, but no one—and I mean no one—gets away with treating me with disrespect. I'm just trying to have a friendly conversation. There's no need to behave like a thug. I talked to your little trick earlier."

"I don't know what you're talking about."

"The cute young guy with the green eyes and the Irish accent?"

Marvin avoided looking at Kendall. "That doesn't sound like anybody I know. Can I get back to my laundry, please?" Kendall stepped away from the washer, and Marvin lifted the lid to resume his task. "I'm just a very private person."

Kendall tried not to sound too sarcastic. "Oh, really?"

"It's difficult for me to trust people after the way I've been treated. So I prefer to stay under the radar."

"Actually, I understand. I used to be treated badly. Then one day I woke up and said, fuck it. I don't have to tolerate that crap from anybody. And *voilà!*" He swept out his arm to indicate his presence. "No flying under the radar for me."

Marvin retrieved several quarters from a red coin purse, still avoiding Kendall's gaze, and slipped them into the slots of the washer. "I applaud your self-confidence. And I apologize for being rude. But I hope you'll respect my privacy."

"Of course. But all the mystery just makes you more intriguing."

Marvin at last looked Kendall directly in the eye. "You know, Mr. Akande, people are mean and cruel. There is something in human nature that is evil and rotting. It's not something that can be cut out, as with a surgical procedure. It's bred in the bone. That's the reason I keep to myself. And with that, sir, good night."

Marvin stomped out of the room and shut his apartment door with a thump. Kendall felt deflated from his failure to learn much more about Marvin than he already knew: the man was secretive. Probably closeted, too. Well, at least now he knew that Marvin was a writer. And he knew how he and Jenna could finally get into the boiler room to see what Elliott referred to as the "surprise."

Signal to Noise

Jenna

Jenna listened as Kendall replayed his encounter with Marvin from the previous night, and how Vince had used a credit card to open one of the supply rooms.

"What was he looking for?" she asked.

"I have no idea. Then he walked slowly down the corridor to the back door, but I couldn't see what he was doing. I told you there was something odd about him. Anyway, now we have a way into the boiler room." He pulled out his library card and waved it in the air.

"This actually works?"

"Yes," he said as they went down to the basement. "Another reason to make sure you always keep your deadbolt locked. Even when you're home."

He looked around to make sure they were alone, then slipped the library card into the crevice of the boiler room door. Jenna watched him slide the card down until it made contact with the latch bolt. He wiggled the card. The technique did not work as easily as he had recounted, and he had to try several times until the door clicked open.

A massive red capsule perched on supports at the rear of the room, its color dulled with age and mottled by dirt and patches of rust. It sat silent for now, a hibernating dragon. Gauges, pipes, hoses and cast-iron hand wheels adorned the capsule, giving it the look of something in a mad scientist's laboratory. Its ancient appearance did not surprise Jenna. She suspected that Turnbull kept it operating with duct tape and glue. But what surprised her were the images sketched and painted on the cinderblock wall beside the boiler: heads of goats with great, curling black horns. Some of the heads sat atop male bodies to create a human-animal hybrid. Others were disembodied. One portrayed a complete goat, recumbent with its hooves drawn up beneath the body.

"It's the creature from the Necropolis," she whispered.

Kendall took out his phone and snapped several photos. "An unusual place for an art gallery."

Jenna examined the images up close. Some had been sketched in charcoal and looked rather faded, suggesting that they had been drawn decades ago. Others had been painted with delicate black brushstrokes, but the room's rigorous climate had started to take a toll on those images as well. All seemed to have been made by the same hand, clearly that of a skillful artist. She imagined the red boiler during winter, rumbling away, spitting out heat into the narrow room. A version of hell.

"How'd you get in here?"

The voice made Jenna jump. She whirled around to see Vince standing at the threshold. "Oh, the door was unlocked and we were just curious." She walked over to the boiler, trying to mask her guilt. "So this is where we get our heat from. I've always wondered what one of these things looked like. Very steampunk."

Kendall pointed to the goat images. "We never expected to find something like that in here. I wonder who made them."

"They have a real artistic flair," said Jenna, hoping a barrage of talk would distract Vince from their trespassing. "You can tell by how realistic the images are."

Vince nodded, but did not move any closer. "Yeah. I've seen them before."

Jenna snatched a glance at Kendall. "How?"

A mischievous grin bloomed on Vince's face. "Just like you. I found the door unlocked one day." He pointed toward one drawing at the far end of the series, probably a late addition after the artist had refined his or her renditions. "I especially like that one. It's the most ominous looking."

"I can't help but think the drawings are related to Monmouth's obsession, or maybe his ghost," said Jenna.

131

Vince crossed his arms. "How do you figure?"

"Didn't Rooney tell you? About how the occupant of your apartment became obsessed with the figure of a goat-headed man that inspired him to murder?"

"And how the ghost of a goat-headed man supposedly pushed another occupant out the window?" added Kendall.

"She left out those details." Vince walked over to the last image in the series and studied it intently. "I want to make sure I remember this in case I run into the ghost."

The comment sounded sarcastic to Jenna. "You don't believe in the ghost, do you?"

Vince took a deep breath. "I wouldn't say that. I like to keep an open mind. I just think a ghost might not be what you should worry about."

Jenna knew this comment would set off alarm bells for Kendall. Sure enough, he pulled on her arm and moved toward the door, saying, "Well, we should be going. Lots to do this evening still."

Jenna put her finger to her lips after they left the room, and they climbed the stairs in silence. Safely within the walls of Kendall's apartment, she let go a flood of opinions about what they had seen, about Vince's statements, about the growing mystery.

"Now do you see what I meant that first time we talked to him?" asked Kendall.

"Okay, so maybe you were on to something. I don't know what to make of it all, though. Surely he can't be responsible for what Mrs. Gupta experienced. He wasn't even living here at the time."

"It doesn't make sense, I know." Kendall ran his hand over his hair. "But what was he doing prowling around the basement last night, breaking into the supply closet? And why had he broken into the boiler room before?"

"He's not the only one behaving strangely. Let's not forget about your encounter last night with Marvin." Jenna and Kendall stared at each other, neither speaking. She was stumped. Clearly Kendall felt the same. All they had was a growing list of questions.

132

She was the first to break the stare, and looked out the window. The threads in their mystery seemed as tangled as the growth in the Jungle. "I guess we aren't going to solve anything right now. Shout if you have any revelations."

Back in her apartment, Jenna turned on the television. There was time for an episode of *The Chilling Adventures of Sabrina* before bedtime. She had promised herself she would not binge watch the series about the teenage witch, something she had a tendency to do with other programs. She wanted to make the enjoyment last, stretch it out over a couple of weeks. Whenever she found something she liked a lot, she had a tendency to dive in obsessively: working with acrylic paint for the first time; reading every novel in succession when she discovered a new favorite horror author. She wondered if Lucy's cooking lessons would result in a refrigerator stuffed with platters of coq au vin, chicken parmigiana, enchiladas verdes, and other dishes too numerous to eat.

Halfway through the episode, Jenna heard a voice call out from down the hall, the unmistakable smoky voice of Morvena: "Hello? Hello? What's going on?" At first, Jenna decided to ignore her, but the complaint persisted. "This has got to stop!" Morvena shouted to no one in particular.

Jenna opened her door and peeked out. Morvena stood in the doorframe of her apartment, hands on her hips, hair toweled up in a turban and her face swathed in cold cream with a Kabuki grimace. Her shoulders hunched forward in accusation, but once she spotted Jenna, she straightened her spine with newfound hope. "Did you hear it, too?"

"Hear what?"

"The pounding on the wall. I must speak to the new tenant."

Despite her insistent tone, Morvena made no effort to move. Vince probably intimidated even her. "Do you want to knock on his door together?" asked Jenna.

"Yes, darling, that would be good of you."

They knocked on the door once, then a second time when they received no response. Footsteps stirred within. A few moments later, Vince opened the door.

Morvena had been perched right up close to the door until it opened. Seeing his austere expression with the bold dashes of his eyebrows slicing across his brow, she stepped back and clutched at her robe. "The banging on the wall must stop."

Vince looked her up and down. "What banging?"

"The noise you're making in there."

"I don't know what you heard, but it couldn't have been me. I'm working on some songs with my headphones on."

Morvena grabbed the lapel of her robe more tightly, the veins bulging in her papery thin hands. "Your bedroom is right next to mine, is it not? You were pounding on the wall just now."

"I wasn't even *in* the bedroom."

"It had to have been you. I heard you say *Let me in, let me in.* Perhaps you were singing one of your songs."

Vince stared at her coldly. "I don't have any song that goes like that. But tell you what. Why don't you go back to your bedroom. We'll do a little experiment. Jenna can come with me. I'll pound on the wall and say those exact words, and we'll see if it matches what you heard."

Jenna followed him into his apartment. How different the space looked from the day it had been piled with boxes. She recognized a poster on one wall with the front and back of the Black Sabbath album *Sabbath Bloody Sabbath.* In a second poster she recognized the black figure of Baphomet, the goat-headed deity, set against a red background with a pentagram on its chest. On a side table, she noticed a lamp with a stack of skulls supporting the shade. The computer screen on his cluttered work desk glowed with music tracks and the image of a mixing board. The headphones lay on top of a pile of papers. She figured he had been telling the truth that the noise Morvena heard could not have been him.

In the bedroom, she spotted a poster of the Sedlec ossuary in Czechoslovakia, where monks had made artistic sculptures out of human bones and skulls. As much as Jenna liked horror, she could not imagine surrounding herself with the gallery of macabre images in Vince's apartment.

Vince waited a bit, allowing time for Morvena to reach her bedroom. He pounded his fist on the wall and in a loud voice said, "Let me in, Let me in." Seeing him recreate the incident, Jenna had to admit, it seemed ridiculous that he would have had any reason to do that.

They regrouped in the hallway.

"It wasn't the same," said Morvena with disappointment. "It was much louder before. I was sitting at my vanity when I heard it. It almost startled me right out of my chair. Are you sure you tried hard enough?"

"It was pretty forceful," said Jenna.

Morvena patted her towel turban, which had started to unravel. "You're both looking at me like I imagined it."

"On the contrary," Jenna said, "you're not the first person to have heard something strange, you know. Remember when Mrs. Gupta complained about noises coming from the walls?"

"Maybe it came from downstairs," suggested Vince.

"Yeah, I'm really curious now," said Jenna. "Shall we go down and ask Rooney about it?"

The trio trudged downstairs to Rooney's apartment. Jenna heard the television faintly in the background.

When Rooney answered the door, Morvena ran through the complaint once again. Rooney said she had been watching television for the last hour. She had not heard any noises.

"Maybe what you heard came from the TV," suggested Jenna.

Morvena shook her heard. "No. It came right from the wall, loud and distinct. I'm quite sure of that."

The source of the strange pounding would not be solved. Jenna suspected that Morvena still blamed Vince. Of course, that was simpler than accepting that a ghost had made the sound. Jenna did not know what to believe. It had been easier to dismiss the issue when only Mrs. Gupta reported strange sounds.

Morvena and Vince returned upstairs, but instead of following them, Jenna went to Kendall's door and knocked.

"What's up, diva?" he asked.

Jenna slipped into his apartment and plopped down on the sofa. "Morvena heard something in the walls, similar to what Mrs. Gupta heard."

"Oh, no. You don't really think the place is haunted, do you?"

"I don't know what to believe. She thinks Vince made the noise, but I'm convinced he didn't."

Kendall leaned against the cushy arm of the sofa. "Well, we know that Morvena exaggerates every sound. She'd complain if she heard a pin drop."

"True. But she also heard someone say *Let me in*."

Kendall sang the hook from the Friendly Fires song "Heaven Let Me In," threw his hands in the air, and moved his upper body to a silent dance beat.

Jenna laughed. "Stop it. I'm trying to be serious."

"Well, things are definitely getting interesting."

"Let's look at it logically. Why would Vince have pounded on the bedroom wall and then lied about it?"

"Hmm. Maybe he's trying to drive her mad so she'll move."

"But why?"

"Because she's ultra-sensitive and drives everybody crazy."

"Well, if anyone has a reason to want her to move, it would be Rooney."

"Could Rooney have made the sound?"

"That's the problem. It wasn't her, either. Assuming she's telling the truth." Jenna clasped her hands behind her head and leaned back, looking up at the ceiling. "Which brings us back to the ghost."

"Or to Morvena's overly sensitive imagination."

"Except that we now have two separate reports of voices in the walls."

"Maybe it was the power of suggestion. Once Morvena heard about Mrs. Gupta's experience, she was primed to interpret her own experience in a similar way."

"You know what this reminds me of?" She turned to see an expectant look on Kendall's face as he waited for her to elucidate.

"The part in a horror movie where someone comes up with a ridiculous explanation to discount the reality of the haunting."

"So are you ready to admit we have a real ghost?"

Jenna stood and headed toward the door. "Not yet. But I may be getting close. Sleep tight, and don't let the freaky-deakies bite."

Anxious to resume watching *Sabrina*, she settled in on her sofa, reclining against the armrest with her legs scrunched into a tight chevron. Just as she reached the episode's climax, her doorbell buzzed. She rolled her eyes at the second interruption of the night. It had to be either Kendall with a tidbit of gossip that could not wait or Morvena with another complaint. Was her television too loud? She cringed at the prospect of Morvena appearing at her door with her hands on her hips.

But it was Lucy who stood at the door, looking quite upset.

"Sorry to disturb you, Jenna, but I heard something in the walls."

"Oh, I'm so sorry. I'll turn the TV down."

A tremor ran through Lucy's sigh. "No, no, it's not that. I was in my bedroom and I heard scratching, then heavy breathing, then a voice that said *I'm watching you, and I'm going to enjoy watching you die.*"

White Is for Witching

Kendall

Kendall pulled out his key as he approached the front door of Covington Terrace. Just as he reached the front step, the door swung open to reveal Mrs. Gupta and her daughter, both carrying suitcases.

"Going on a trip?" asked Kendall.

"No, Kenny, I'm going to stay with my daughter for a while, down near the waterfront. Sirisha has been trying to convince me for weeks. The incident last Sunday after our dinner was the final straw."

"What incident?"

Mrs. Gupta set her suitcase down and told him about the missing Staffordshire plate that he had admired. Then she glanced at Sirisha and reluctantly added, "And I saw a figure out of the corner of my eye."

"Mom! You didn't tell me that part," said Sirisha.

"I know. I didn't want to worry you even more." She looked directly at Kendall. "He looked like he had something covering his head—some kind of mask with horns." She gently laughed. "It must have been my imagination after hearing you and Jenna talk about the..." She let the sentence die.

Kendall noticed Sirisha rolling her eyes and felt compelled to come to Mrs. Gupta's defense. "Jenna and I have seen him, too. Once at the Necropolis. Then I saw him again one night standing in the backyard."

"Oh, Kenny, please be careful. I'm worried about you both."

"We're tough. Besides, it's only a ghost, right—the ghost of William Monmouth? What harm can a ghost do?" He said this as much to reassure himself as to reassure Mrs. Gupta. "Well, take care. We'll miss you."

"I'll be back eventually. Once things have settled down."

Kendall watched them walk down the street to Sirisha's car. Farther down the street, he spotted Lilith returning home with a shopping bag. Under her lavender dress she wore black leggings with a silver ankle bracelet on one leg and short black boots. An open black coat, cinched at the waist, fell to her knees. She returned Kendall's wave.

"You look very chic," said Kendall as she drew closer.

"Thank you. I've been shopping." She held up a small bag with the name *The Marvelous Shop*.

"Do you always dress so fine to do your shopping?"

Lilith laughed. "It helps me send out positive energy."

They entered the building, the massive oak-frame door groaning on its hinges.

"So what did you buy?"

Lilith opened the bag, letting Kendall peer inside. "Candles, stones, some essential oils—from my favorite shop."

"Witch stuff?" he asked. Lilith nodded. "How did you get interested in becoming a witch?"

"I was always fascinated by witches and magick as a girl. Maybe that's not so unusual, I don't know. But as a teenager, I became disillusioned with organized religion. There was so much disrespect for the feminine in traditional thinking. It seemed out of balance to me. I discovered spiritual beliefs that venerated the female aspect of the divine. Goddess religions. There was just a lot more respect for nature, for the environment, for equality in how we treat one another. And no chauvinistic insistence that everyone must conform to one way of thinking. That fluidity—the permission to fashion my own practice—appealed to me." Lilith asked if he had a moment, and invited him down to her apartment to look at her altar. "If you're interested, I'll tell you a little more about what I do."

In her apartment, she described the symbolism of the different objects, what various herbs were good for, the meaning behind the goddess figurines. "This is Brigid. She is a Celtic goddess, associated with spring, re-birth, healing, and craftsmanship."

"Would that include dress-making?"

"I don't see why not."

"Then I like her. She could be my patron deity." Kendall pointed to the African statue. "And who is that?"

"Oshun, the Yoruba goddess of water, pleasure, sexuality, fertility, beauty, and love. I like being syncretic: a little Africa, a little Europe, a little Asia... At heart, most spiritual traditions are about how to lead an ethical, compassionate life. This is no different."

"You don't try to put hexes on people?"

Lilith looked shocked. "Absolutely not! That goes against everything I believe in. I won't say there aren't some witches out there who do that, but I believe what you put out into the universe is what comes back to you. Putting out negative energy is way too dangerous. Have you heard of the Rule of Three?" Kendall shook his head. "It means that if you harm someone or something, it will come back to you threefold. A form of karma, basically."

Kendall wandered around the living room, inspecting her books and other objects. "How do you like living in a basement apartment?"

"I like the feeling of being close to the earth."

He opened a book on spells that had an artfully drawn cover. "My aunt used to scare me when I was a kid—she was the superstitious one in the family—and say the *aje* would come to get me if I misbehaved."

"The witch is often used as a bogey-man. In Yoruban culture, anyone can have *aje*, or divine witchcraft power, and it can be used for good or for ill. There are even festivals to appease those who have *aje* so that they might work positive magick for the benefit of society as a whole."

"What about ghosts? Do you believe they exist?"

"I think so. I think there are some spirits that linger, for whatever reason. If you're worried about your apartment being haunted, we can do a cleansing ritual with sage."

Kendall riffled through the pages absent-mindedly. "I've had a recurring nightmare since I was a kid. And lately I've been waking up with panic attacks. The other night I was even paralyzed for a short time, and felt another presence in the room."

"Did you see anything?"

"Well, I wear a sleep mask, so I couldn't take it off. It was more a feeling. And I could smell him. Or it."

Lilith nodded. "A cleansing spell. Definitely."

"You think it will help?"

"I do."

Kendall replaced the book. "Well, it couldn't hurt."

Up in his apartment, Lilith opened all the windows and doors, then went from room to room ringing a handheld bell. She set a white candle on the table and lit it. With the candle's flame, she lit a bundle of sage and wafted its smoke toward her, up and over her body. She instructed Kendall to do the same, then moved around the apartment carrying the sage, ensuring that the smoke seeped into every corner.

Jenna appeared at the open door of the apartment, standing with her arms crossed. "Is this a closed party, or can anyone come in?"

Kendall ran over, grabbed her wrist, and pulled her in. "We're doing a cleansing ceremony."

The shrill blast of the smoke alarm shattered the peaceful mood. Kendall fanned the smoke detector with a dish towel. "Just a little extra touch to blast away the bad energy."

Lilith spirited the smoking sage away from the vicinity of the alarm. "Some smoke detectors are more sensitive than others. Next time we can try burning sage incense."

Morvena appeared in the doorway just as the alarm fell silent. She put her hands on her hips and surveyed the room. A silk bandana was wrapped around her hair, the ends flaring gracefully over her left shoulder.

"Come on in," said Kendall. "We're doing a ceremony to cleanse the room of negative energy."

Morvena sniffed the air. "Does it work?"

"I hope so."

Lilith crushed the ends of the sage into a small dish, extinguishing the embers. "It's a sacred ritual in many cultures to restore balance."

Morvena leaned forward, listening with interest. "Perhaps we could perform a ceremony in my apartment. I've experienced some—shall we say, *unpleasant*—nocturnal incidents recently."

"Like the noises you heard a few nights ago?" asked Jenna.

"Yes, and it's gotten worse. Last night, a voice in the wall said, *I'm coming to get you.* Then it snickered like a ten-year-old girl."

"I'd be happy to do a ceremony," said Lilith.

"That would be marvelous. And then I can serve us cocktails."

Kendall closed up his apartment and followed the three women upstairs. Morvena provided a dissertation on the kinds of incense she used to buy back in the Swinging Sixties. "Ah, how we loved patchouli. And frangipani. Such an intoxicating scent, from the plumeria flower. In Polynesia, you wear the plumeria over your right ear to indicate you are looking for a relationship." She touched the lobe of her right ear. "And over your left ear to indicate you are taken. Darling, I switched sides so often the men could scarcely keep up."

Lilith repeated the ritual with the sage. Upon seeing the smoking embers, Morvena lit a cigarette. The smoke from the sage and the cigarette mingled in the air. Lilith pointed out that many First Nations people and Native Americans used ceremonial tobacco for cleansing rituals.

"Well, I can tell you that commercial tobacco is not adequate to the task of banishing bad energy," said Morvena, waving her cigarette through the air. "Otherwise the voices in the wall would have left already." The ceremony ended, and Morvena mixed cocktails. "Just my way of saying thank you."

Kendall could tell Morvena was thrilled to have a house full of guests. She infused each gesture with extra flair.

"Now, Kendall, have you settled on your Halloween outfit yet?" she asked.

"Yes, but I'm keeping it a secret. You'll have to wait for the big reveal on October thirty-first."

"I'm certain it will be magnificent. The *ne plus ultra*. Can you give us one tiny clue?"

"It will dazzle you so much you'll need sunglasses."

"Ah. What color?"

"Silver. And you won't get another word out of me."

"I don't have the right skin tone to carry off silver," she said, fingering the turquoise pendant around her neck. "Not an entire dress, that is. You will be stunning in silver, darling."

"He's making it himself, you know," said Jenna. "Entirely his own design."

Morvena raised her glass in a toast. "*Il est très talentueux.* A very talented young man."

It took barely a nudge from Kendall to convince Morvena to share stories from her modeling days. And she seemed to have an endless supply. She told about the time she modeled on a yacht in the Adriatic and the engine broke down, leaving them adrift. "There we were, facing Scylla on one side and Charybdis on the other." She told about meeting Andy Warhol. "Fascinating man, but such a dreadful entourage." The ash on her cigarette lengthened and drooped, but she had an instinctive sense of just how long she could wait before tapping it on the edge of the ashtray.

They drained their glasses and announced it was time to go. Lilith offered to do another cleansing if needed, and headed down the stairs. Morvena pulled Kendall's arm to keep him back as Jenna waited in the hall. "Is Lilith a—you know?"

"A witch?" asked Kendall.

"Well, yes."

"You should ask her," he replied, not wanting to out her. "I know she follows a spiritual practice that blends a variety of traditions."

The sound of muffled music emanated from the Bone Man's apartment. Morvena leaned out, peered down the hall, and made a face. "A witch doesn't bother me. But him..." She poked her finger toward the end of the hall.

Kendall could hear singing and strained to make out the words. *See the beast within, hunting like a raptor. It's the beast within—that's the part I'm after.*

Morvena shook her head. "Dreadful."

Inside Jenna's apartment, Kendall could no longer hear the music, but he kept imagining what it would be like with the Bone Man directly across the hall, always dreading to open the door the same time he emerged from his apartment—his harsh expression, the awkward moment where you have to think of something to say, walking down the stairs together (God forbid). "I'm glad I'm not the one who lives across the hall from the Bone Man."

"He doesn't make a lot of noise. You can tell how quiet it is compared to out in the hall," said Jenna.

"It's not the noise I'm talking about. It's his whole person. I had a talk with Rooney the other day. She thinks it's odd, too, that he moved in here after his girlfriend disappeared."

"Honestly, Kendall, I think you're exaggerating the menace. It's just an image, for his music."

"But what about his behavior in the basement the other night? And why would he want to live here?"

"So, what, then? He offed his girlfriend so he could have her apartment?" Jenna laughed. "That sounds like the plot from a bad horror movie. And we've seen plenty of them. What I'm more concerned about is the fact that now we have three different people who've heard voices in the walls."

Kendall crossed his arms. "I think all of these strange incidents are connected. We just don't know yet how. Where's Jessica Fletcher when you need her?"

"Well, she isn't real. And this is not a mystery that can be neatly wrapped up in a half-hour episode from *Murder She Wrote*. That's the problem." Jenna poked him in his belly button. "Don't stress out trying to solve this. I'm sure everything will sort itself out eventually."

The Haunting

Rooney

Rooney sat on her couch, flipping through the channels. Images flew by with snatches of dialog, a kaleidoscope that barely registered on her retinas. One hand gripped the remote, the other a mug of hot cocoa. Her knees were bent, and the soles of her feet, covered in thick pink socks, perched on the edge of the coffee table. She was not yet tired but wished it were bedtime already, because the television bored her, and she was anxious to commence her nightly "haunting" of Morvena.

A news channel flashed past, and a reporter saying "Cabbagetown" arrested her attention. The arm holding the remote froze, then dropped to the couch as she recognized the houses in her neighborhood. The reporter described the murder of a Syrian family. A father, mother, and two children. A brutal slaying, the reported called it. But no suspects yet.

Rooney's cell phone rang. She saw Wade's name and put aside the remote as she prepared the girlish voice she always used with the men she dated. "Hi."

"Hi. What are you doing?"

"Just watching the news until it's time for bed. A family was murdered near here. Have you heard about it?"

"No."

"What are you up to?"

"Nothing much. I was just thinking about you."

"Aw, that's so sweet." Her cooing sounded like doves.

They talked a bit, though the specifics washed over Rooney like the bits of images that flashed by on the screen, making no particular impression. It had been a week since their first get-together, two nights since they went to dinner and a movie. She could not yet make up her mind how she felt about him. He was not particularly sensitive or passionate. And they had little in common. *Benefits*, she reminded herself. *Remember the benefits.*

Rooney filled the air with chatter to make up for Wade's lapses into silence. She was good at improvisation. She put down her mug and picked up the remote, flipping through the channels again, then glanced at the clock. She grew bored with their conversation and gently brought it to an end.

She rinsed out the mug while the television droned in the background, some sitcom with a laugh track. She double-checked all the stove dials to make sure nothing remained on, which reminded her that she was still waiting for Wade to fix the oven thermostat. That, in turn, reminded her that tomorrow she would need to mail Turnbull the October rent check.

It was time to scare Morvena again—her nightly ritual for the past week, except Friday, when she had gone out with Wade. She opened the access door and crawled through, holding her cell phone, which she had muted so it wouldn't ring while she was performing her stunt. By now she knew her way around the space by heart, but she pointed the light from the phone down the narrow corridor between the walls. The passage was just wide enough that her shoulders brushed each wall. Tonight she had brought a small rubber ball with her. She giggled as she mentally rehashed her plan one more time. She would open the access door in Morvena's apartment, enter the closet, and bounce the ball into the bedroom with a loud thump, then go back into the wall to hide. She also had a creepy clown doll that she would set in the closet for Morvena to find. The look on Morvena's face would be priceless—too bad Rooney would not actually be able to see her reaction.

Once she had climbed the ladder to the second floor, she aimed the beam from her phone toward the floor to light her way. The first thing she noticed were the pair of shoes that should not have been there. Then she noticed a dark shape rising out of the shoes that blocked her way. The last thing she noticed, in the second before the creature lashed out and knocked the phone out of her hand, was a hallucinatory image that stunned her in disbelief. A goat head perched on the shoulders of the shape—a head with twisting horns that stabbed toward the ceiling.

The creature clamped a hand over her mouth. She felt the blade of a knife at her throat. She knew that trying to make noise could be fatal, but even still she started to moan. The hand clamped down more tightly as the creature pushed her against the wall and pressed close to her body. The thought that this could not possibly be happening kept racing through her mind. The knife blade vanished, but a moment later she felt a sharp pinch in the side of her neck and a cold liquid entered her body. She writhed, but the creature held her tight. She suspected she had only a few minutes of consciousness left, her only window of opportunity to fight back. She dropped the bag holding the ball and clown doll and pounded the creature's head with her fist. The creature pushed her to the floor with a loud thump, and her head banged from the force of the hand pressed over her mouth. The creature pinned her arms down with its knees. Her shoulders hurt, wedged between the walls. She hoped the noise of their struggle would rouse Morvena. *Oh please oh please oh please hear this,* she silently recited.

She could feel her cell phone resting near her thigh, its hard plastic case digging into her side while some of the light shined up along the wall and illuminating the ceiling. There was just enough light that she could make out the goat face hovering over her. The long black snout, the wide-set eyes, the curving horns that glistened in the light. She tried to touch the cell phone. It was ludicrous to imagine that she could grab the phone and somehow press the emergency dial function. But she tried anyway.

She heard Morvena in the hallway: "Hello? Hello? What's going on?" Rooney could move her hand just enough to pound a fist against the wall. She didn't care if the creature slit her throat or not, fearing that something horrific awaited her anyway if she gave in. Morvena shouted, "This has got to stop!" The knife returned to her throat, but the creature made no move to kill her. Clearly it did not want to harm her. At least not yet. It shifted its knees to better immobilize her arms, and waited for the drug to take effect.

The cell phone light shut off. She heard the creature as it made a grunting noise, deep in its throat, and felt the knees digging into her upper arms. She imagined it was saving her for something more terrifying than death. Some long, drawn-out torture, perhaps. She began to cry, and soon everything around her dissolved into a darkness even more absolute than the darkness of the space between the walls.

6

Excerpt from Shockadelica Podcast
Episode 33: Witches in Fiction and Film

Jenna: I did some research for this episode and learned some
           interesting facts. Witches, of course, have been portrayed
           in negative terms for the most part throughout history.
           They're usually dangerous, which reflects patriarchal
           societies' fear of feminine power. Going back to Homer,
           you have the beautiful but dangerous seductress Circe,
           who turns Odysseus' crew into pigs. He's able to free his
           men but decides to stay with Circe on her island for a
           year.

Kendall: Hmm.

Jenna: Then you have the bad witch in fairy tales, and the three
           witches in *Macbeth*.

Kendall: *Double, double, toil and trouble, fire burn and cauldron
           bubble.*

Jenna: In literature from the eighteen and nineteenth centuries,
           witches are invariably evil and portrayed as a threat—no
           surprise. But something interesting happens around the
           turn of the century. We start seeing the image of the
           witch as a vehicle for female liberation. In 1895, Mary
           Chavelita Dunne wrote a short story under the
           pseudonym George Egerton about an unhappily married
           woman who uses witchcraft to express her need for
           independence and strength. Five years later, Frank L.
           Baum published *The Wonderful Wizard of Oz*, where

good witches are associated with the north and south while the bad witches are from the east and west.

Kendall: And then that dichotomy gets turned on its head when *Wicked* came up with a backstory to explain how prejudice against her green skin turned Elphaba into the Wicked Witch of the West. God, I love that musical.

Jenna: The nineteen-twenties saw a flowering of feminist portrayals of powerful women who were witches—interestingly, around the same time when women get the right to vote. The first was Stella Benson's *Living Alone* in 1919, which featured a heroine who was a witch. But there were a bunch of other novels, too. The movies, though, took longer to catch up. *The Wizard of Oz* came out in 1938, with Glinda the Good Witch.

Kendall: Toto, I've a feeling we're not in Kansas anymore.

Jenna: Exactly. The landscape for what it means to be a witch starts to change. *I Married a Witch* came out in 1942, based on the novel *The Passionate Witch* by Thorne Smith, which also was the inspiration for the sixties TV sitcom *Bewitched.* So now there is the potential to treat witches as a bit of playful fun instead of purely malevolent—even though they might have dangerous adversaries in the witch world.

Kendall: Like the movie *Bell, Book and Candle.* And children's books like *Harry Potter* and *The Worst Witch.*

Jenna: It's interesting that we have this paradox: we're fascinated by witches yet afraid of them. I certainly feel that impulse myself.

Kendall: It's the same old story. People either don't understand or are taught to fear those who are different from whatever society and religion define as normal. Like how LGBTQ people are treated.

Jenna: Or any group that society defines as "the other."

Hereditary

Kendall

The shallow stage at Dante's stood two feet off the floor—just high enough that a girl, if she wanted to look ladylike, had to ascend using the three steps on the side rather than from the front edge of the stage. You could catch a glimpse of yourself performing in the mirror above the bar that faced the stage—a helpful advantage, but one that also tempted disaster—which is what happened once to a beleaguered drag queen named Dirt Reynolds, who spent too long admiring herself and tumbled into the audience. Magenta, lavender, and cerulean lighting illuminated the vicinity of the stage and the banner that stretched across the back advertising a brand of vodka.

Kendall spotted the evening's emcee, a six-foot-two drag queen called Tipsy Hedrin, standing beside the bar holding a martini and talking to a good-looking young man. Tipsy wrapped her glitter-studded sapphire lips around the straw and took a genteel sip of her martini. Heels and a blue beehive wig exaggerated her height, giving the appearance of an Olympic deity towering over the mortals around her. Below the neon-blue plastic miniskirt, her legs seemed to go on for miles before ending in blue velvet platform heels.

"There is something distinctly familiar about you," said Kendall. "What do they call it when you experience something you've seen before?"

Tipsy twirled around, struck a pose like Karen Black from *Come Back to the Five and Dime, Jimmy Dean, Jimmy Dean*, and with exaggerated French pronunciation said, "*Déjà vu.*"

They burst into laughter and greeted one another with air kisses.

"You look like a giant Smurf," said Kendall.

"Bitch."

"No, I mean that in a good way. A deliciously sexy Smurf."

"I don't know whether I should kiss you or kick you."

"Maybe both," said Tipsy's friend.

151

Tipsy raised her glass to the comment. "Kendall has always been talented at lacing compliments with vitriol, like a splash of gasoline in a cocktail. Oh, let me introduce my new friend. This is Travis. Travis, this is Kendall—otherwise known as La Chandelle."

They exchanged greetings, then Kendall turned back to Tipsy. "When do you go on?"

She held up Travis' arm and checked his watch. "We have ten minutes. Or in drag time, thirty seconds."

"I see some new girls in tonight's lineup."

"Yes. That one over there"—Tipsy gestured across the bar to a compact queen dressed as a ragged version of Miley Cyrus—"calls herself Uranus Moons."

Kendall frowned. "I think she needs to take a wrecking ball to that name."

"And that look. But, hey, we all can't start out fabulous."

"Are you ready for Halloween?"

"Girl, I've been ready for months. You?"

"Yeah, I've almost finished the dress. It will be sensational. Jenna and my mom are the only ones who know what I'm planning. The funny thing is, some guy came up to me in our building and talked like he knew exactly what I was going to wear. He said I should give him the dress as a sacrifice. And he knew my name. Really young, dark hair, green eyes, cute, with an Irish accent. Any chance you had something to do with it?"

"*Moi*? Definitely not. But it looks like it got under your skin. I wish I *had* thought of it. Are you and Robbie still an item?"

"No. He broke up with me a few weeks ago."

"Good—I mean, not good. But at least I don't have to worry about telling you he's been cheating on you. I've seen him around lately flirting with buff guys."

Kendall spotted Robbie entering the bar, dressed in black pants, a black jacket, and a white baseball cap turned backwards. "Speak of the devil." Kendall watched him scanning the bar, then turned away, hoping not to draw Robbie's attention. But a moment later, Kendall felt an annoying tap on his shoulder, and rolled his eyes for Tipsy's benefit.

152

"Hey, Kendall." Robbie nodded toward the others.

Kendall offered a perfunctory *hey* in response and the fakest smile he could muster. Robbie spread his arms as if about to hug him, but Kendall held up his beer and took a sip to discourage the gesture.

Robbie shifted uncomfortably and dropped his arms. "You're not performing tonight?"

Kendall looked down at his street clothes. "Oh, you figured that out on your own, did you, genius?"

"Just trying to make conversation." He turned to Tipsy. "You're the emcee tonight?"

"That's right."

Kendall noticed Robbie stealing glances at Travis. His anger began bubbling—not so much because he felt slighted, but because Robbie's intent disrespected Tipsy. "Isn't there anyone else here you can pester? Or have you already worked your way through all the other men in the room?"

"Okay, you're still a little bitter. I get it." Robbie reached around and squeezed Kendall's butt.

Kendall grabbed Robbie's wrist and removed the hand from his backside. "You know what your problem is, Robbie? You want it, but without any of the responsibility. I'm good enough for you in bed, but not good enough for you in front of your friends."

"Cat fight," Tipsy purred before wrapping her lips around her straw.

Robbie jerked free from Kendall's grip. "I should have known better than try to be nice to a second-rate drag queen."

Tipsy tottered on her heels. "Oh, no, she didn't!"

Kendall smirked. "My poor, dear Robbie, you don't even know that second rate is twice as good as you deserve." He flicked his wrist and turned his back on Robbie in order to perform a ritual that he and Tipsy had developed, intertwining their arms like a young couple making a toast. But instead of a toast, they both snapped their fingers, then unlocked elbows and did a sideways fist bump—the "homo fist bump," Tipsy always called it, "because it has a tad more delicacy." Robbie stood dumbly for a moment before sauntering away.

"You may not be on stage tonight, honey," said Tipsy, "but that was a star performance." One of the bartenders motioned to her. "Speaking of which, it's time to start the show."

Kendall lingered for a while, but Robbie's presence buzzed like a pesky mosquito. He could even pick out Robbie's laughter in the crowd. Twenty minutes were enough to challenge his patience, and he grabbed his coat to leave.

While he waited at a corner for the light to change, a motorcycle rolled up slowly on his left. The engine idled with a threatening rumble. Out of the corner of his eye he saw the driver turn to look at him, and felt a wave of apprehension. He scanned the intersection for his best escape route and pretended not to notice the driver. The distorted orb of the streetlight reflected across the helmet's curved surface. A hand reached up to lift the visor.

"Hey."

Kendall turned toward the vaguely familiar voice and recognized the guy who may or may not have been named Lucas. "Hey."

"I want to show you something." Lucas tilted his head toward the back of the bike. "Hop on."

"Show me what?"

"You'll see." He patted the seat behind him with a leather-gloved hand.

"Uh, I don't have a helmet."

"We're not going far. You won't need one."

"I don't even know you, Lucas. Or whoever you are."

Lucas caressed the seat. "You know you're curious. Come on."

Kendall looked down the street. "You promise it's not far?"

"Absolutely."

Kendall almost lost his footing swinging his leg over the bike, but grabbed Lucas' arms to steady himself. "I've never ridden on a motorcycle before." The bike bounced slightly as he jostled into the seat and wrapped his arms around Lucas' waist. Lucas told him to rest his feet on the pegs sticking out from the bike. The light changed, and the bike lurched forward with a roar. "Oh, shit," Kendall said, squeezing Lucas hard as they raced along the streets. "Slow down!"

Lucas ignored him. At first, afraid to witness the wild ride, Kendall pressed his cheek into Lucas' back and shut his eyes, but the jacket's cold leather slapped him away. He opened his eyes and watched over Lucas' shoulder as lamp posts and street signs zoomed past. Lucas accelerated to rush through a yellow light. They flew past a police car. Kendall turned back to see the blue and red lights start to flash. "Cops!" he shouted in Lucas' ear over the roar of the engine. Lucas shouted something in response, but it was swallowed by the wind.

The wailing siren pursued them for blocks. Kendall thought, *The last thing I need is a ticket for not wearing a helmet. What was I thinking?* With his orange hair, he knew he stood out like a torch.

Kendall felt certain they would get stuck at the light at busy Spadina Avenue, but the light held. Lucas turned left onto Spadina and narrowly missed an oncoming car that blared its horn. He turned right into Graffiti Alley, an urban canyon of colorful murals. Kendall felt his heart pumping as fast as the engine's pistons. Images raced by in a blur of color. He saw an enormous devil's head, flames licking around the collar, and a spiky tag in bands of aqua, midnight blue, and pale yellow. They passed through a sort of tunnel where one building extended out over the alley. Water splashed as they rode through a puddle, and a trio of teenagers admiring the graffiti jumped out of their way. At the next alley, where an underwater seascape covered an entire building, Lucas swung the bike to the left. Kendall hoped the tight turn would slow down the police car.

A couple of turns later they were heading down Portland Street. Kendall looked back, and in the distance saw the police car still pursuing them. He felt certain this would not end well. Where the street ended, Lucas slowed, then looked to the left and right. Without waiting for the light to change, they crossed the street and navigated up the curb's accessibility ramp, then proceeded over the pedestrian bridge that traversed the railroad tracks. Kendall suspected it was illegal to drive a motorcycle over the bridge. How many traffic laws had they broken? Enough to land in jail, without a doubt. A guy on a bicycle stopped to stare at them in surprise.

Moments later they were at the waterfront. Lucas slowed to a more reasonable speed, and they headed down one of the quays adjacent to a small marina. A phalanx of sugar maples lined the way, just starting to drop their golden-brown leaves. A cold wind blew off of Lake Ontario, churning the black water. To Kendall's left, the CN Tower pierced the night above the city's skyscrapers, patterns of color shooting up its sides. To his right, the derelict Canada Malting Company factory stood sequestered behind a fence topped with barbed wire. A quintet of concrete silos, pocked as if shell-shocked by artillery, loomed into the night. At the end of the walkway, Lucas rolled to a stop and turned off the engine and headlamp as a plane prepared to touch down just across the channel at Billy Bishop Airport.

"You are one crazy fucker," Kendall said as he withdrew his grip. He jumped off the seat, anxious to feel his feet back on the ground. To his right, he saw a concourse of grass between the factory's edge and the water. Four thin, gaunt figures stood on the lawn, each imbued with a yellowish-green glaze. The one in the front, closest to Kendall, stood slightly larger than an actual person, its bony arms reaching skyward and face grimacing in anguish. In the center, a contorted figure sprawled on a circular slab. "What is this place?"

Lucas removed his helmet and ran his hand through his hair. "Ireland Park. It commemorates some forty thousand emigrants who fled the Great Famine and arrived in Toronto in 1847. At the far end—see that broken wall of Kilkenny limestone?—that's dedicated to over one thousand who died in the process. Come. I'll show you."

They followed a walkway beside the water and arrived at the wall, which had been constructed with slabs of blue-black limestone stacked together in broad columns, the edges of the slabs forming an irregular surface. Lights embedded in the ground shone upward in the narrow gaps between columns. Once they got up close, Kendall could see names engraved inside the gaps. Margaret Conn. Susan

Bailey. Mary Gallagher. Frederick Fox. Martin Carlow. Kendall shivered in the cold wind.

Lucas reached into one of the gaps and ran his hand over the names. "Many of the immigrants died of typhus, either during the journey across the Atlantic or after arriving. The boats were known as coffin ships. Not everyone in the city welcomed the immigrants with open arms, of course. The usual story. They were called ignorant, vicious, lazy, improvident, unthankful..." He grabbed Kendall's hand and directed it over the engravings. Kendall felt the indentations of the letters, the smoothness of the stone where it had been polished in preparation for the engraving. Lucas entered the narrow passage, pulling Kendall behind him. When they emerged on the other side of the wall, he said, "Passing through that constricted space with the names is a bit like passing with them on their journey, no? You can almost feel their spirits and what they endured."

"I take it you're Irish?"

"Yes."

"I am, too, on my father's side. But I really know nothing about that side of the family. He died when I was—"

Lucas finished the sentence. "—a wee lad. That's what we would have said back home."

"A wee lad." Kendall chuckled. "Yes. But how did you know?"

"Just a guess. That's what usually follows *but he died when I was...*"

"My mother brought me to Toronto after he died. That's when she changed my last name to her family name—she was a modern woman and kept her last name when she married. She thought it would be easier in Canada if we had the same last name instead of my dad's name." Kendall felt the rough surface of the exterior wall, so different from the smooth surface inside the gaps. "Why do you drive like a maniac?"

Lucas shrugged. "I've never had a ticket or an accident."

"That's hard to believe." He stuffed his hands deep in his pockets. "So tell me, who are you, really?"

157

"My name is Cian. It means *ancient* in Irish. Or maybe Ciarán, which means *little dark-haired one*."

"Which is it, Cian or Ciarán?"

Lucas winked. "Or maybe Lucas."

"Why so mysterious? You know more about me than I know about you, starting with my actual name."

"True, true. I make it my business to know things."

"No one in the building claims to know you. You weren't really visiting friends that day, were you?"

"I'm your friend, but you don't yet know it."

Kendall turned away and shook his head. "Talking to you is like talking in riddles."

Lucas placed his hand on Kendall's shoulder and gently turned him back around. "Now, now, Kendall, don't be so petulant. I want to help you, but you've got to do something for me in return."

"I know. The dress."

"And the shoes."

"Buy why? I've been planning this outfit and working on it for weeks, and I've got to outdo Tipsy Hedrin."

"My, my, a tad competitive, aren't we?"

Kendall looked out toward the harbor. "Did you really live once in Covington Terrace?"

"In a manner of speaking."

"Which apartment?"

"Yours. There was a man who lived there. An artist. He was Irish."

"Is that the connection—why you picked me?"

"Part of the reason."

Kendall eyed him warily. "So where do you live now?"

Lucas swung his arm in an arc. "Here. There. I move around a lot."

"I just don't feel I can trust you."

Lucas backed up in mock dismay. "I'm shocked you would think that."

"Yeah, well, put yourself in my shoes."

"Okay, then." Lucas waited for Kendall to make a move, then held out his hands in supplication. "Well, take them off."

"What? I didn't mean it literally."

"How else am I supposed to put myself in your shoes?"

"Stop being so dense. It's a metaphor."

"But maybe there's truth in the gesture. Go on, take them off. Just let me slip them on, see if it makes a difference."

"You're serious."

"Would I be codding you?"

Kendall started to bend down, but hesitated. "You speak differently from anyone I know. Like you're from another time and place." He proceeded to untie his sneakers. The ground felt cold through his socks, and he balanced the sole of one foot atop the other foot.

Lucas removed his boots and put on the sneakers, then stood with a look of exaggerated contemplation. "Yes, I think I understand what you mean." He laughed, grabbed his boots, and ran past Kendall around the far end of the wall.

"You fucker!" shouted Kendall, chasing after him.

When Kendall emerged on the other side of the wall, however, Lucas was nowhere in sight. "Lucas!" he called. "Lucas!" Vanished into thin air, just like the other night. Kendall looked for the motorcycle at the far end of the lawn, but it had vanished as well. He hobbled toward the placard at the front of the park, cursing. As he got closer, he noticed his shoes sitting atop a large, flat rock. He sat down to put them on, wondering at the strangeness of it all. How could Lucas have disappeared in the blink of an eye and managed to leave the sneakers on this rock? He could not think of any explanation that fit his rational understanding of reality. He drew his coat tight against the wind and walked back toward the street to catch the streetcar home.

The Omen

Jenna

Jenna opened her door to find Lucy holding up a box filled with the ingredients needed to make eggplant lasagna.

"Cooking lesson," Lucy chimed. She marched in with Bergie trailing and set the box on the kitchen counter. "Everyone should know how to cook—man, woman, gender fluid, doesn't matter."

"I usually just buy prepared food or take-out."

"Too expensive." Lucy unloaded the box, spreading the items out on the counter. "With this dish you'll be able to eat all week for seven, eight dollars. Unless you eat like a horse." She eyed Jenna's petite frame. "No, I doubt you eat like a horse."

Lucy commandeered the kitchen, giving out instructions to Jenna while Bergie laid on the floor and watched. "Preheat the oven. Get a baking dish. What, you don't have a baking dish? I thought not." She pulled out a pan from the bottom of the box along with a peeler, which she held up for Jenna to inspect. "Do you know what this is?"

"Yeah. It's a peeler."

"You'll need to get one eventually. Our eggplant today doesn't have a tough skin, so we don't need to peel it. But sometimes you may want to do it."

She demonstrated with her hand to cut lengthwise and handed the eggplant to Jenna, watching her position the knife. "No, too thick. That's better." Lucy curled Jenna's fingers under, protecting them from the blade. When the second eggplant had been sliced, she announced, "Okay, now we've got to sweet talk the eggplant. Don't be shy."

"I don't know what to say."

"Talk to it like a lover."

Jenna blushed, but tried out some phrases as she laid the slices in the pan and drizzled them with olive oil and salt. "There, sweetie. That's a good boy." She laughed, but Lucy nodded and waved her hand to continue. "Oh, you are so tender. You must be the tenderest eggplant I've ever touched. Just look at that gorgeous color. Mmm."

"See, you're a natural."

While the eggplant baked, they prepared the tomato sauce and put a pot of water on the stove to boil. Jenna asked about Lucy's love affair with another woman.

"She was from Spain. I learned to speak Spanish because of her. That started my passion for languages. I went to live in Montreal for a couple of years to improve my French. Oh, turn down the heat a bit, the sauce is bubbling too much." Lucy said she would have liked a long-term relationship. Man or woman, it didn't matter. She didn't miss having kids, though, because her students at school were like her kids. And she had Bergie. "Thank you for allowing me to bring Bergie over with me."

"No worries. She's awfully well-behaved."

Bergie must have sensed they were talking about her, because she started to wag her tail.

Lucy pulled a mystic knot out of the box. "This is for you. Hang it on the wall for protection and good luck. We both need it after what I heard the other night."

"Have you heard any more noises since then?"

"No, thank goodness. No more voices. But if it gets worse, I may leave like Mrs. Gupta. And I won't come back."

"What about your lease? I know I can't afford to break the lease. And it's so hard to find affordable apartments." Jenna had felt so lucky when she found Covington Terrace, and grateful when her best friend moved in downstairs. She shuddered at the thought of moving to the suburbs like her sister Beth had been forced to do because of spiraling rents.

"I'll worry about that if the time comes."

They assembled the lasagna and waited for it to bake. When it was done, they put a slice in a plastic container to take to Lily, deposited Bergie back in Lucy's apartment, and hopped in Lucy's car. Lucy entered the address for Happy Gardens into the GPS, and they headed across town.

161

They found Lily sitting at the fake bus stop. Jenna and Lucy sat down on either side of her. "LaoLao, do you know who I am? I'm Jenna. Nancy's daughter."

"Don't be ridiculous. Nancy is only five years old. Why are you trying to trick me?"

"She's not trying to trick you," said Lucy. "She was just trying to make a joke. Ha-ha. See, isn't that funny? To imagine Nancy could have a child."

Lily regarded her with uncertainty. "Do you know my daughter?"

Lucy leaned forward to catch Jenna's eye. "Uh, all of our children play together. Isn't that right, Jenna?"

Lily brightened. "Oh, you must be Esme."

"Okay—Esme."

Lily patted Lucy's lap. "You are so kind to watch my girl for me."

Jenna stood and held out her hand. "Would you like for us to walk you home?"

Lily looked up in a moment of confusion, then held out her hand so Jenna could help her to her feet. With baby steps, both women escorted Lily to the porch. Although only a short distance from the bus stop, the effort took several minutes. Lily collapsed into her rocking chair with exhaustion and closed her eyes. Jenna sat beside her, holding her hand, while Lucy leaned against the railing. Lily remained like that, as if asleep, for a good ten minutes, her shoulders slowly rising with each breath.

"How often is she like this?" Lucy half-whispered.

"More often than not these days."

"It's really hard, isn't it?"

Jenna nodded, struggling to hold back a tear.

Mrs. Shin shuffled by and called out "Oh." Jenna greeted her and introduced Lucy. When it was clear that Lily remained asleep, Mrs. Shin bowed and continued down the street with her hands clasped behind her back.

"She can't say words," Jenna explained. "A stroke, I think. She's more lucid than LaoLao, but it's hard to tell."

A woman in a wheelchair rolled past in slow motion, clearly distraught. "I said a naughty word, I said a naughty word, and now I'm going to hell." She paused in front of the porch to regain her strength, but seemed oblivious to their presence only a few feet away. "Oh my, I know I'm going to hell." She wrung her hands, her shoulders hunched forward.

Jenna and Lucy looked at one another and began to giggle.

"I'm sorry," said Jenna. "It's not funny, but... To be so distraught over a curse word." The woman rolled on using her feet and hands, her progress painstakingly slow. "If this is what waits for me in the future, please just shoot me when the time comes."

"I'll get there long before you, so better not count on me to come to the rescue," said Lucy. Lily started to stir. "The thing is, if this happens to us, I hope we're fortunate to have someone compassionate enough to sit with us like this, even if we don't remember who they are."

Lily opened her eyes. "I had such a beautiful dream. I became a great tree, so many leaves and branches stretching into the sky, and roots sinking into the earth. Each leaf was someone. You were a leaf, Esme. And you were a leaf, young lady, even though I don't know who you are. Mrs. Shin was a leaf. A young black man with orange hair was a leaf. Nancy, too. And the woman who brings my medicine. You were all part of me."

"That *is* beautiful," said Jenna. "Did it make you happy?"

"Yes, it did. Very happy."

They went inside to serve Lily the lasagna, which the insulated bag had kept warm. Lily took a few bites, then said she was full. Lucy began singing an old pop song in Mandarin about the origins of China, a song that Jenna had not heard since she was a little girl, when Lily would play her favorite cassette on the tape deck. What had ever happened to all of those cassette tapes Jenna once owned? Vanished, along with that past spent with Lily. Jenna had assumed those cassettes would last forever, that nothing would ever change to displace them, just as she had assumed Lily would always remain the same.

163

The song's dignified rhythm flowed deep and wide, reminding Jenna of the stories Lily used to tell about the Yangtze River. Jenna understood none of the lyrics of the song except one: Himalaya. Lucy drew out the penultimate syllable in a spiraling melisma that coiled around Jenna's memory as if afraid to let go. Lily smiled, silently mouthing the words.

It was time to take Lily to the Music Garden. This had been Lucy's suggestion when Jenna told her how much Lily used to enjoy classical music. It would be a more ambitious outing than wheeling Lily around the block, which Jenna did on occasion. They helped Lily into the front seat of Lucy's car, then folded up the wheelchair and stowed it in the trunk.

At the waterfront, Jenna wheeled Lucy down the promenade toward the Music Garden. Not certain how much Lily knew about the origins of the little park, Lucy explained that cellist Yo-Yo Ma designed the garden in collaboration with landscape designer Julie Moir Messervy to represent Bach's Suite No. 1 in G Major for unaccompanied cello. Lily sat with her hands folded in her lap, a shawl wrapped around her shoulders. She did not seem to be listening, but instead gazed out at the sailboats docked in the marina. Their masts undulated with the flow of wind and water, making a sound like tinkling cymbals.

Lucy led them to the starting point of the Prelude. She scrolled through her phone until she found a recording of the suite by Yo-Yo Ma. The Prelude unfolded, a gently coursing river. Lucy pointed out the granite boulders along the path, meant to evoke a stream bed with low-lying plants along its bank, and the line of hackberry trees, whose straight trunks and regular spacing suggested measures of music. Jenna wheeled Lily through the landscape. As the climax drew near, tension building with a chromatic ascension alternating with a repeated bass note, Lily's hands began to flutter in her lap.

They entered the filigree curves of the Allemande in tandem with the second movement. The music flowed much like the Prelude, but the figurations were different—gentler, more introspective, the tonality wandering farther afield.

164

The Allemande ended by the time they ascended the path of the Courante. As soon as the lively tune started, Lily began conducting the air. Jenna remembered that it had been a favorite of hers. The path spiraled through a meadow of wildflowers. Birds flitted in the bushes, seeking seeds and insects, seeming to hop in time with the exuberant music. Lily pointed to the birds and laughed. At the top of the hillock, in the center of the spiral, a maypole pointed skyward, with sculpted iron ribbons unfurled in imitation of blowing in the breeze. They paused a moment to look out at the harbor before descending the other arm of the spiral.

The Sarabande path coiled in on itself to represent a fiddlehead fern. The wheels crunched on the gravel as Jenna pushed the wheelchair toward the center. The gravel slowed their progress, but the path was short so she did not have far to push Lily. The Sarabande's slow, stately rhythms evoked in Jenna the feeling of a vanished past. She pictured the ghosts of dancers from long ago, bending their knees with a flourish of the hands and moving around one another in ritual courtship. Lily, too, grew subdued. Jenna wondered what she was remembering.

After leaving the Sarabande, they ascended another hillock to a circular pavilion with a dome of metal ribs open to the sky. They entered the pavilion to the graceful lilt of the Menuet. Jenna pointed to the metalwork treble clefs and sixteenth notes hanging from the dome. A woman with a purple smock stood before an easel on the perimeter of the pavilion, facing the parterre between the pavilion and a small grassy amphitheater. The artist had filled her painting with the heads of an audience listening to a cellist, who was seated beneath the weeping willow at the base of the amphitheater. Jenna bent close to Lily's ear to tell her to look and pointed toward the painting. The woman turned around, drawn by the music and voices, and smiled.

"That's the final movement—the Gigue," said Lucy, gesturing toward the amphitheater. A jaunty country dance started, and Lucy put her hands on her hips and kicked her legs out in imitation of a jig. She twirled around and almost lost her footing, which made Lily and Jenna laugh.

All at once, Lily blurted out, "I see her. Ma."

For a moment, Jenna thought her grandmother meant Yo-Yo Ma, despite the feminine pronoun. Then she realized who Lily meant. Jenna felt the impulse to contradict her and point out that her mother had been dead for two decades. Instead, she squatted next to the wheelchair. "Where? Show me where."

Lily pointed to the front of the amphitheater, where flagstones set into the grass indicated a stage. "There. She is standing there, but she is worried. She is telling you be careful." The fronds of the weeping willow rustled in a sudden breeze.

"Careful about what?"

"Big... Big..." Lily's hands balled into fists as she struggled to articulate the word. "Dragon. Pig. Rooster. Snake."

"The signs of the zodiac," Lucy said.

Lily nodded, then clutched Jenna's arm. "It is coming. Be careful."

Lucy offered additional zodiac signs. "Tiger? Ox? Monkey?" After each one, Lily shook her head. "Goat?"

"Yes. Yes. That's it."

A chill spasmed across Jenna's skin, and she shot to her feet. It was too close to be a coincidence. Her rational mind struggled for an explanation, just as she had the day she and Kendall had seen the goat-man at the Necropolis. Lucy must have noticed Jenna's discomfort, because she said, "Jenna, are you all right?"

Jenna nodded, although she felt far from okay. Street sounds filled the silence as the gigue ended. A dog barked. A driver honked his horn. A streetcar passed by with the heavy *clack-clack* of its wheels. Yet everything sounded filtered and distant. "I didn't tell you this before, but the ghost in our building? It's the ghost of a goat-man."

Lucy said nothing at first. Then she smiled. "I get it. You're joking. You're getting back at me for the joke I played on you and Kendall with the *diao si gui*."

"I wish I were. The goat image is what inspired him to commit the—you know." She did not want to say the rest of the sentence and spook Lily. She rested her hand on Lily's shoulder. "Is Ma still there?"

"No. Gone now."

Jenna gripped the handles and maneuvered the wheelchair around to return to Lucy's car. They rode back to Happy Gardens without talking. Jenna was content to let Chinese pop songs from the radio fill the dead air. Only after they had dropped off Lily and headed back to Covington Terrace did Lucy venture any conversation.

"That was your great-grandmother that Lily saw, right?"

"Yes."

"Her spirit is watching out for you."

Jenna sighed and looked out the window. "I wish I could believe that. It would be so much easier."

Lucy patted Jenna's leg. "Don't let it worry you. You know that the eighth sign of the zodiac, *yang*, means both goat and sheep. The interpretation depends on the region or country. Your grandmother could have meant sheep."

"That would be reassuring if we hadn't been plagued by images of goat-men." For the first time, Jenna felt rattled. Kendall's panic attacks began to seem like a reasonable reaction to a threat that was growing more real each time they turned around. But real in what way? What did they have to fear about a ghost? She shook off her concern, telling herself to snap out of it.

The sun had begun to slip low on the horizon by the time they arrived at Covington Terrace. Jenna thanked Lucy again.

"No problem," said Lucy as Bergie danced around her feet.

The darkening apartment made Jenna feel melancholy, augmenting the bittersweet mood from her visit with Lily. Nonetheless, she realized Lucy had helped make the visit successful, if only because it had made Lily happy. She began preparing a list of music to play on her next visit, trying to distract herself from thinking about the ominous warning.

She heard a knock on her door, and tip-toed across the room in case she decided to pretend she was not home. The unusual sight through the peephole of Arthur Turnbull so surprised her that she opened the door to find out what unusual circumstances brought him to the property.

Turnbull wasted no time with niceties and launched his question. "Have you seen Rooney Xavier?"

"No, not recently."

"Can you remember the last time you saw her?"

Jenna thought for a moment. "I guess about two weeks ago. Why?"

Turnbull clutched his hands with worry. "She's late with her rent and won't return my calls. I entered her apartment, just a moment ago, and nothing looks amiss. But no sign of her."

He asked if Jenna knew any of Rooney's friends, but Jenna shook her head. "I didn't know her well at all. Have you checked with Morvena? If anyone has heard Rooney moving about in the apartment, it would be her."

Knocking on Morvena's door, they heard the sounds of shuffling, then Morvena swung open the door with a look of delight. "What a pleasant surprise. Won't you come in for cocktails and a cigarette?"

Turnbull declined, but Morvena insisted, opening the door wider. If they wanted to know something, they would have to comply. Jenna remarked on the showroom tidiness of the apartment as they entered.

"One must always be ready for guests. I used to have people dropping by at all hours when I lived in London. So I learned to always be prepared. And that includes a well-stocked bar." She retrieved the cocktail shaker from the liquor dolly. "Ah, such heady days. Now, not so much. Sit."

Turnbull looked as if he were about to say something in resistance, then some magnetic force folded his legs and he collapsed onto the edge of the sofa. Jenna sat beside him and rubbed her hands over the sofa's fabric. "I love this sofa. So elegant."

"*Divan*, dear. Not sofa. And certainly not couch. Oh, I know most people think they all mean the same thing, but divan has so much more…class, *n'est-ce pas*? And what is life without a little class? What can I serve you two?"

Jenna and Turnbull both declined. Morvena shrugged and continued to mix herself a martini.

Turnbull cleared his throat. "What I came to ask you about is, have you seen Rooney recently or heard her in her apartment?"

"Let me see. There have been so many noises, it's hard to pinpoint." She shot a look of remonstrance at Turnbull. "I heard her a couple of weeks ago, rummaging around in her closet and dropping things. It's been quiet during the past week. I thought perhaps she'd gone on vacation."

"When was the last time you saw her?" asked Jenna.

"Oh, that was not quite two weeks ago." She looked at Jenna. "The night we confronted her about noises in the wall."

Jenna pondered the response, then furrowed her brow. "The reason we're asking is because no one has seen Rooney, she hasn't paid her rent, and she won't answer her phone."

"Oh, my. Does she have an emergency contact?"

"Yes, it's listed on her original lease," said Turnbull. "I've already called and left a message. But after what happened before..." He looked nervously at Jenna. "I fear the worst."

His phone rang. He stood and walked over to the bay window to take the call, speaking in a low voice. Morvena looked at Jenna and raised her thinly penciled eyebrows.

"This isn't the first disappearance," Jenna explained.

Turnbull ended his call. "It's the police. Rooney's been reported missing and they want to access the apartment. They're on their way over."

Jenna followed Turnbull down to Rooney's apartment, Morvena trailing with cocktail in hand. The police arrived five minutes later and queried the three of them. Morvena repeated what she had told Jenna and Turnbull. A policewoman took notes while her partner looked through each of the rooms. Dishes had been washed and put away. The refrigerator was stocked with food, including half a carton of milk, but a loaf of bread on the counter had started to turn moldy. The bed had been made, yielding no clue about the last time it had been slept in. Her purse and laptop sat on the kitchen table, untouched. Only her cell phone appeared to be missing. Jenna worried that she might have ended up in the hospital, but the policewoman said they had already checked with all of the hospitals. It was as if she had just decided to walk away, leaving everything behind.

After the police left, Turnbull sighed. "Well, I suppose I should start the eviction process now. It will take roughly seventy-five days, like before."

"You don't think she's coming back." Jenna stated it more as a fact than a question.

"No. Just like two years ago, with the woman in apartment six." He clutched his hands as a tic tugged at the corner of his eye. "This is not a good sign. Not a good sign at all."

Sisters of the Moon
Kendall

The shop occupied the ground floor of a two-story brick building, set far enough back from the curb to allow room for a small courtyard with tables and chairs in front of the picture window. Above the window and door, a purple sign with white lettering read *The Marvelous Shop*. Inside the front door, a central table displaying a variety of occult supplies greeted visitors: hand-made sachets of herbs and plants; polished gemstones of citrine, hematite, garnet, and tourmaline; bundles of incense; diffusers, censors, and cauldrons; crystals of amethyst and quartz. Each sachet charmed the eye with its particular colored netting that represented the items it held and their purpose. The arrangement reminded Kendall of an artist's palette.

Lilith held up one of the sachets, a mixture of herbs and essential oils. "*Flames of Passion*. You can burn it like incense to create a sensual atmosphere or carry it like a charm. I like to mix my own, but this is handy if you don't have the inclination or time."

Kendall pointed to a small bowl filled with polished aventurine, its color a deep cobalt blue. "What's that for?"

170

Lilith placed one in his palm and closed his fist. "Self-discipline and inner strength. It helps you make clear decisions, and facilitates psychic awareness. Can you feel anything?"

Kendall looked down at his fist, then slowly opened his fingers like a flower blooming. "I'm not sure. Maybe."

"Let me buy it for you. It also helps protect against harm." As the clerk rang up the purchase, Lilith continued. "I've had an uneasy feeling lately. Remember when I told you about the sensation of someone in distress I had two years ago? Someone crying? It's come back. I started feeling it even before I found out Rooney was missing. With the other odd things you've told me about, I sense something dangerous is brewing. All of us need as much protection as we can muster."

Through a doorway at the back of the shop, a gallery had been set up with folding chairs. A placard on an easel at the entrance read, *The Origins of Anti-Witch Hysteria and Modern Day Witch Hunts— A Discussion with Historian Beverly Sanderson.*

They took their seats in the gallery. About twenty people wandered in for the session, most of them women. They looked no different than an audience one might find at the University of Toronto waiting for a lecturer to speak on symbolism in paintings of the Italian Renaissance. Kendall surreptitiously studied each person for signs that they dabbled in the occult. He had a fleeting thought that Lilith had brought him to a witch's Sabbath, and he would be the sacrificial victim. Then he felt stupid, and criticized himself for doing the very thing he knew people did the first time they found themselves in a room full of gay men and women.

"Is everyone here a witch?" Kendall whispered.

"Not necessarily. These people have a range of interests: healing arts, meditation, alternative spirituality, and for some, yes, magick and witchcraft. But it's much more fluid and individual than the labels that society wants to impose on it. Which is why I thought you'd be interested in this lecture."

A large woman with short brown hair and ruddy cheeks entered the room, escorting a tall, older woman in a gauzy, cream-colored linen dress with turquoise floral patterns stitched into the collar and cuffs. The hem swished around her ankles as she walked. A puffy cascade of graying hair fell to her shoulders. Kendall pictured her as a woodland nymph with a wreath in her hair.

The room quieted. The woman with ruddy cheeks thanked everyone for coming, then introduced the other woman as Dr. Beverly Sanderson. Kendall only half-listened to the biographical details that followed, intrigued by Dr. Sanderson's necklace with its unusual pendant, a jade-colored twist that bent back on itself like a Moebius strip or the scientific symbol for infinity.

Dr. Sanderson spread some notes out on the lectern, but rather than remain tethered to the post, she began moving around the front of the room as she spoke. "We often think of witch trials as medieval. But they were really a product of the Renaissance and social stresses brought on by the Protestant Reformation. In essence, you can consider them a response to the societal disruptions of early modernity. There were certainly instances of heretical activities involving accusations of sorcery before the fifteenth century, but not to the extent of the obsessive concerns that arose during the fourteen-hundreds and plagued European and North American societies for the next three centuries."

As she paced, Dr. Sanderson described two notorious witchcraft trials during the fifteenth century which resulted in hundreds of the accused being put to the stake. The first big trials started in 1428 in Valais, France, and spread to German-speaking regions over the next eight years. The second took place between 1459 and 1460 in Arras, France.

"The Dominican monk Johannes Tinctor wrote a lurid account of the Arras trials," said Dr. Sanderson. "His book, *Invectives contre la secte de vauderie*—or *Arguments Against the Sect of Waldensians*—was designed to convince his countrymen to find and stamp out witches. One of four existing copies sits at the University of Alberta. It predates the more famous *Malleus Maleficarum*, or *The Witches' Hammer*, by twenty-six years, and drew together the first descriptions of witches flying on brooms, having sex with Satan, and manipulating the weather to spoil crops. In essence, it became the template for identifying and persecuting witches."

According to Dr. Sanderson, the accused most often represented vulnerable members of society—prostitutes, paupers, and cooks—who were suspected of participating in unholy Sabbaths. Local clerics extracted confessions and additional accusations under torture, and before long people at all levels of society, including nobles and clerics, were being arrested. Although some residents of Arras protested the witch-hunt and questioned the methods and the confessions, the church leaders pressed ahead—a pattern that sadly repeated itself throughout the ages.

"The witch hysteria culminated most notoriously in Salem, Massachusetts. With unintentional irony, the Puritan settlers had named Salem after the Hebrew word *shalom*, meaning peace. They envisioned the settlement as God's shining city on the hill, a beacon of peace and light. In 1692, it became the antithesis."

The reasons for the hysteria were complex, but Dr. Sanderson identified several important factors. Fighting between the Puritan colonists and Native American groups, who were allies of the French Catholic settlers to the north—both of whom the Puritans considered to be in league with the devil—created a fearful mood in the colony. Tension between inhabitants of the more liberal, coastal Salem town, who favored a looser approach to religious attitudes, and the more conservative, stricter inhabitants of Salem village, who wanted more religious and economic autonomy from Salem town, created divisions. These divisions also fostered inter-family conflicts as individuals took sides to protect their economic interests. A sense of empowerment among the accusers, most of them women who were denied a voice in the society, likely fueled the hysteria as well. What started as just a very small number of tormented victims grew as young women found themselves suddenly at the center of attention, wielding important power that held the community in their thrall. But not only women brought forth accusations—it offered a way for anyone to settle a score, even against a spouse. "There were those who tried to resist the hysteria, who questioned the tactics and the use of shaky spectral evidence to prove guilt. But that was one of the fastest ways to be accused yourself of being in league with the Devil."

Dr. Sanderson clasped her hands and stood still. "Let's pause for a moment to consider some of the individuals who were accused of witchcraft." She took time between each name, letting the specifics of their circumstances sink in.

"Bridget Bishop, the first person to be convicted and hanged. She had been married to an abusive husband and was once punished in the public square—along with her husband—for having the audacity to complain to the authorities about his abuse."

Pause.

"John Proctor, who came under suspicion because he defended his wife against witchcraft accusations and—horror of horrors—allowed Native Americans to patronize his tavern."

Pause.

"Sarah Good, a homeless beggar who had been impoverished by debts from her first husband and had a troubled relationship with her second husband."

Pause.

"Sarah's four-year-old daughter Dorothy, whose timid responses to the interrogators were considered a confession of witchcraft."

A longer pause.

"Martha Corey, who, despite her piety and devotion to church, had an illegitimate mixed-race son and dared to denounce the witch trials."

Kendall felt a chill as Dr. Sanderson read each name, knowing they were only a fraction of those who had been persecuted. In all, more than two hundred individuals were accused of witchcraft. Nineteen of them were executed by hanging. Martha's husband Giles was crushed to death under stones for refusing to plead guilty; his last words were "More weight." At least five individuals died in jail. Confessions were extracted under torture. Neighbor turned against neighbor. Everyone became terrified because no telling who would next turn out to be a witch—ministers, devout churchgoers, even the governor's wife.

Dr. Sanderson resumed her pacing. "I know some of you—at least the older folks among you—are familiar with the satanic sex scandal in Martensville, Saskatchewan, in 1992. Exactly three centuries after Salem. You are probably aware that similar incidents occurred in the United States and in Europe during the nineteen-eighties and -nineties—the Satanic Panic. In the Saskatchewan incident, a mother alleged that a woman who ran a home day care center had sexually abused her child. The subsequent investigations, based on testimony from the children, uncovered a supposed satanic cult called The Brotherhood of the Ram that practiced ritual molestation and locked the children in cages to witness murders.

"More than a dozen persons in Martensville were charged with crimes. The only problem? None of it was real. The entire hysteria started with a book published in 1980 by Lawrence Pazder, the Canadian psychiatrist of a patient named Michelle Smith. The book, *Michelle Remembers*, purported to tell the true story of Ms. Smith's abuse in the nineteen-fifties when she was five and her mother forced her into a satanic cult. Soon, hundreds of Michelles were recalling similar buried memories of satanic cults. A common investigative pattern emerged. Investigators would interview children suspected of being satanic abuse victims and ask leading questions."

Dr. Sanderson went on to explain that, during this period, fear of these day care cults became so endemic that a talk show host could claim the U.S. was in the grip of a satanic underground with more than a million members. Even though there was never any evidence, medical professionals claimed that Satanists could be found in all ranks of society: politicians, lawyers, police, upstanding citizens. "It was the witch trials all over again. Although, at least this time, no one was executed. But many people served years in prison, their lives ruined. Even the accusation, despite being exonerated, hung around many individuals like the noose that hanged witches in Salem."

Dr. Sanderson gripped the edges of the lectern. "Fear is contagious, especially during unsettled times. The traditional concept of the witch brings together those things that unsettle us the most: wild beasts and unorthodox, outspoken women. The language used today in political campaigns and conspiracy theories like QAnon employs the same kind of language Tinctor used in his arguments

175

against witches. Using logic but starting from a flawed premise. Casting oneself in the role of Inquisitor and appropriating religious language to literally demonize one's opponents and create an atmosphere of paranoia, where imagination can run wild. The pace of technological change and economic disruption today are creating the same kind of unsettled conditions that we saw in the fourteen-hundreds and which we've seen throughout history. Modern-day witch hunts are a continuing danger as we project our fears onto those who unnerve or unsettle us, on those who are different or who are outsiders—whomever it is that we happen to distrust at a given cultural moment. Reading about Arras, or Salem, or the satanic sex scandals, you see time and time again how suggestible we are, how reluctantly we dissent for fear of being accused ourselves, and just how easily we may abandon our neighbors to the stake."

An enthusiastic applause met the conclusion of Dr. Sanderson's lecture. She responded to audience questions for the next twenty minutes. Kendall raised his hand, and when she called on him, he posed his question. "What can we do to keep from repeating these mistakes?"

Dr. Sanderson rested one elbow on the lectern. With her other hand she lifted the pendant that hung on the chain around her neck and held it out from her breast. "This is the Maori *pikorua*, a symbol representing the path of life, abiding loyalty, enduring love between two people or between cultures. The only way to fight fear of otherness is through love. It's not easy, and it takes constant vigilance, constant effort. Our natural fear as human beings is to fear what is different, what we do not understand. Love is the only bridge that can reach fear and neutralize it. And when that doesn't work"— she let the pendant drop back across her breast and looked Kendall directly in the eye, channeling the very words Lucy Lee had used— "keep your enemy confused and surprised."

Misery

Rooney

Rooney did not know what day it was, or how long she had been interred in the cell-like space with no windows. She had screamed herself hoarse when she first regained consciousness, but eventually tired when no one came to her rescue. She heard no sounds from the outside world—no birds singing, no jet planes, no water running—and deduced that she was in a soundproof room. Perhaps the room was out in the countryside, in the middle of nowhere. The only light came from a night light plugged into a solitary outlet.

The cold seeped into her bones. The shackles on her wrists and ankles chafed, but the chains had enough slack that she could stand, move around, and reach the toilet. Once a day, the creature came to visit, entering through the solitary door, bringing food and water, always wearing the great horned goat head concealing its face. Even though shadows draped its body in the room's weak light, she knew it was a man. But in all truth, had it been a mythological beast or some demon from hell, she would have believed it.

He never spoke. The first time she saw him after regaining consciousness, she asked him why he was keeping her imprisoned. But he did not answer. He just squatted on his haunches, watching her. Gloved hands hung limply over his knees, a claw protruding from the end of each finger. The concept of claws did not match the image of a goat, but it was effective—a touch of Freddie Krueger that frightened her even more than the mask.

The walls of her cell had been scribbled with fantastic drawings. Goat-headed men with massively muscular bodies mimicked the cover of a pulp novel or a comic book. Goat heads with fanciful horns traced a progression from realistic to stylized to abstract. Angular symbols that resembled runic letters, or what Rooney imagined such letters to look like, stretched like graffiti tags. The drawings were mediocre but ominous, something a mildly talented fourteen-year old boy might draw.

She felt grateful he had not harmed her physically, and wondered if his intent was only to terrorize her with uncertainty—the uncertainty of where she was, of who he was, of what he intended to do next. But what sprawled in the corner did not reassure her: a skull staring back, surrounded by scattered bones in disarray, evoking a scene ravaged by a wild animal. The presence of the skeleton suggested she would not get out of this room alive.

She dozed, dreamed of running through forests trying to evade some dark force, and awoke with a start. She imagined her friends trying to reach her on her phone, becoming distraught, and reporting her absence to the police. Although hunger pangs gnawed at her stomach, she had little appetite for the food that goat-man brought. She nibbled a little, then became nauseous. Soon her hip bones were pushing more sharply through her skin. She felt a hollowing out around her midsection. Her beautiful hands that danced through the air in her videos looked like the arthritic carpals of a crone. Perhaps she would just waste away, her unwashed body and clothes rotting in place.

She passed the time replaying her favorite songs in her mind. Sometimes she mumbled the tunes, unaware that the music had flowered out of the depth of her despair and released itself into actual sound. The music was the only thing that kept her from losing her mind. She remembered the first song to which she had slow-danced in eighth grade, the electronic dance tune that was everywhere two summers ago, all the songs on the first album her father bought for her when she was ten, the lullabies her mother used to sing to her, even the stupid song her college boyfriend used to play that drove her crazy.

Every so often she tested the shackles to see if she could squeeze her wrists through the clamps. She kept up the fantasy that sooner or later, as her weight dropped, she could slip out of the shackles. Not that it would make much difference, because she would never be able to release her feet. Still, the effort gave her something to do, especially when she felt a surge of panic at her inability to escape. Those moments were the worst. The walls and the darkness would close in, suffocating her. She could imagine with little difficulty sawing off her hands and feet, if a saw were available. Hadn't she read somewhere about animals chewing off a paw to get out of a trap? Anything to escape the claustrophobic panic.

She ran through a hundred scenarios where she turned the tables on goat-man, using the cup, the sandwich, the lid of the toilet tank, her shackled arm as a weapon. She fantasized being able to manage a spectacular trick like Hannibal Lecter. But when goat-man was actually there, each maneuver seemed futile, an ant trying to bite a giant. She lacked the inventiveness of Dr. Lecter. Such things only occurred in movies or books.

The sound of a key in the lock filled her with dread. The door swung open, and she struggled to see past it for some clue as to where she might be. All she could see was a dim antechamber. He carried a plastic bottle of water, which he poured into the plastic cup that had been left on top of the toilet tank, and handed the cup to her. Why he did not just give her the bottle she could not fathom. Probably part of his obsession with control. From the pocket of his jacket he extracted a sandwich wrapped in plastic. Store-bought white bread, some kind of cold cut, bright, tangy mustard. Always the same. He offered the sandwich, but she turned her head away, so he placed it on a decorative blue-and-white china plate sitting on top of the toilet tank. The plate reminded Rooney of something her grandmother might have displayed. It seemed so out of place in the dingy room, a creepy attempt at hominess that suggested he might not be completely ambivalent about what she thought. She wondered if the plate reminded him of his own grandmother. Perhaps later she would eat a bit, after he left.

He squatted and watched her drink from the cup.

"It's really cold in here," she said. "Do you think you could bring me a jacket or something?" She offered the question with as much humility as she could muster, hoping not to irritate him. "Please?"

He remained mute, just watching. She could not tell if the words even registered. She might as well have been talking to a real goat.

She held out the cup for more water, and he refilled it. She thought about kicking him in the groin, pummeling him with her fists, throwing the water at his face or tearing off the goat head. But he retreated six feet back from her. Besides, what would such a gesture accomplish other than to anger him? More than anything, she feared making him angry. She preferred this cold detente, as horrible as it was.

After a few minutes, he got up to leave.

Think, Rooney, she said to herself. *You're good at improvising.* She decided to try another tactic. "Wait."

He turned around.

"Is there something you want me to do? I'll do whatever you want." She inflected the suggestion with a touch of coyness. Maybe if she could get him up close, in a vulnerable position, she could make her Hannibal Lecter move.

But he just stood there. She could not tell if he was considering the offer or preferred to keep her terrified by the uncertainty of his purpose.

"Please, just say something. Anything."

He turned away and left the room. The lock clicked. Her sobs followed in convulsive waves.

7

Excerpt from Shockadelica Podcast
Episode 6: What Is Horror?
Guest: Author Elvira Woolsey

Kendall: There's a big online debate about whether your novel
           Unburied Ghosts is horror or not. How do you define
           horror?

Elvira: Well, I don't like to get caught up in labels. You'll never
           get everyone to agree on what horror is or isn't. At the
           edges it blends with other genres like fantasy, sci-fi,
           thrillers—even comedy. I know some people expect
           horror to have an element of dread, or fright. And it often
           does. At the very least, something in the story should
           make you feel uneasy. But there are plenty of stories that
           make you feel uneasy that *aren't* horror.

Kendall: So do you go along with Wikipedia's definition that
           horror is intended to or has the capacity to frighten, scare,
           startle, or disgust by inducing feelings of horror and
           terror?

Elvira: That's a pretty good definition for horror in its purest
           state, but as you get farther from the core, the definition
           falters. It's the problem with any categorization. Then
           what do you do with a story that has frightening scenes?
           Tommy Orange's *There There*, for example, describes
           spider legs burrowing inside human skin and a mass
           shooting at a powwow. That fits the Wikipedia definition
           of inducing feelings of terror, but most people would not
           call it a horror novel.

181

Jenna:	What do you think about Stephen King's three levels of horror?
Elvira:	You mean revulsion, horror, and terror?
Jenna:	Exactly. For the benefit of our listeners, King describes the first level as revulsion—something that makes us recoil in disgust, like spiders. The second level is horror, which is the graphic portrayal of the unbelievable—say, the appearance of a ghost. Then the third and highest level is terror, where the author induces fear through the suggestion of something unknown, and the reader's imagination fills in the details.
Elvira:	I think what King says—that it's not the physical or mental aberrations which horrify us, but the chaos, or lack of order, that these aberrations imply—has a lot of truth. It may be why horror so often reflects cultural anxieties—about otherness, about death, about the breakdown of order and logic. But that doesn't help us come up with a definition of horror that embraces every permutation.
Kendall:	You could always follow the example of the U.S. Supreme Court in the famous obscenity trial from the sixties: I can't define horror, but I know it when I see it.
Elvira:	Hah! Works for me.

The Oval Portrait

Kendall

In the spirit of Halloween, the Art Gallery of Ontario mounted a special exhibit of paintings by the artist Brian Bailey. Kendall and Jenna decided to spend one Saturday afternoon at the museum.

"Last weekend," said Jenna as they walked along Dundas Street, "when I visited LaoLao, she said she saw her mother, who warned me to beware of a goat."

"You're kidding."

"I wish. And I hope that's not a bad pun. I just wish I knew what all the strange occurrences mean. Everybody seeing goat-headed creatures. Voices in the walls. I just can't accept that it's actually a ghost."

"Then what is it?"

"Maybe Lilith has been conjuring something."

Kendall laughed. "You should hear yourself. Blaming witchcraft like you were in seventeenth-century Salem. Lilith took me to a lecture where I learned all about witchcraft paranoia." He watched Jenna frown and worried that he had struck a nerve. "What about the Bone Man, creeping around and breaking into locked rooms? It would be easier to believe that he was the goat-man."

"Okay, so maybe we're both letting our imaginations run away with us. Because neither explanation really makes any sense."

The informational brochure they picked up at the museum explained that Brian Bailey had been born in Ireland in 1847. His family had emigrated during the eighteen-fifties and settled in Cabbagetown with other Irish immigrants. His early works featured standard fare: scenes of farmland on the city's outskirts during different seasons; views from the bluffs overlooking the Don River; blacksmiths at work in their shops.

In his forties, however, he became obsessed with supernatural beings from Irish folklore. The banshee whose shrieks heralded someone's death. The selkie who possessed the ability to change from seal to human. Fairies, mermaids, and hybrid creatures that mixed animal and human form. The settings typically had no evidence of human habitation—just glades, riverbanks, rocky seashores, dark forests with mystical orbs of light. But sometimes the settings could be identified as actual locations in Canada, suggesting that the beings had been transplanted into North America almost as immigrants themselves. He died in 1914 at the age of sixty-seven.

Jenna and Kendall walked through the galleries, moving apart to look at different paintings, then regrouping to stare at a particular work and share comments. The paintings at the beginning of the century were bright and floral, imbued with an early Art Nouveau esthetic. Dappled sunlight filtered through the forest canopy and glittered on the iridescent wings of fairies. Mermaids lounged on rocky outcroppings against a wide expanse of turquoise sea and pastel sunsets.

"Reminds me of Maxfield Parrish," said Jenna.

Around 1910, the colors grew darker, the forests more claustrophobic, reflecting wider social anxieties as the world edged toward war and the collapse of order. The image that dominated those paintings was a goat-headed creature with long, curved horns.

Kendall stopped dead. "Oh my God. It's the image from the boiler room." He leaned close to read one of the labels.

> Brian Bailey (1847-1914)
> **Púca at Midnight, 1911**
> Oil on canvas
>
> The púca [alt. spelling puka, pooka, pookha, phuca] is a fearful, shapeshifting trickster in Irish folklore, most commonly assuming the form of a horse, rabbit, goat, dog, eagle, goblin, or human. Capable of being either malevolent or benevolent, the púca could be appeased by leaving a portion of the harvest on Samhain (Halloween) for "the púca's share."

He scrolled through his camera to find the photos he had taken. "Look, the technique looks similar. Do you think Bailey might have drawn the ones in our building?"

"Possibly. The building would have been, what, twenty or thirty years old when he did these paintings, so he could have lived there." Jenna folded back the brochure and read the description of Bailey's late period. "*Bailey began almost exclusively painting púcas in his last five years. While at first the settings were nonspecific rural locations, the púca increasingly appeared in urban settings that are often identifiably Toronto. The tension between folklore superstitions and modernity thus takes center stage in his mature work.*"

The púca's yellow eyes stared out with haunting focus, the only spot of vivid color in a canvas awash in inky blues, forest greens, charcoal grays, and black. Mimicking Rembrandt's use of lighting, a shaft from the upper left illuminated the goat-like face, bringing it out from the shadows as if the creature had stepped into moonlight. The black fur and tip of the nose glistened. The púca stood upright like a person, but fur covered its body. Whatever appendages it possessed, whether hands or hooves, faded into the undergrowth.

"Looks like that guy you dated last year," whispered Kendall.

They moved along to other paintings in the series. Some were populated symbolically with different animals associated with a púca. As in the boiler room, sometimes the goat head sat atop a male body. As they came to the end of the exhibit, Kendall grabbed Jenna's arm.

"Oh. My. God. That's him. That's Lucas, the guy I met in the laundry room."

Jenna looked back and forth between the painting and Kendall, as if uncertain whether he was joking again. But he put his hand on his forehead, said he was dizzy, and collapsed to his knees. She kneeled beside him as other patrons stared. "Breathe slowly, Kendall. You're hyperventilating."

"I'm having a panic attack. Oh my God." He put his hand to his chest. "I can't breathe."

A woman came up and asked if he needed medical attention.

"I think he'll be okay," said Jenna. She took Kendall's hand. "Focus on your breath. Inhale. Slowly. Exhale. That's it. You're going to be fine. Just take it slow."

Kendall's heartbeat settled down, but his hands still shook. "It's not possible. It can't be."

"And you're absolutely sure they're the same person?"

Kendall looked up at the painting. It was unmistakable. Same dark, wavy hair, and hazel eyes flecked with yellow. His lithe torso dissolved into the black backdrop, where dark, florid shapes swirled that barely stood out against the black paint. The label identified the painting's title as "Apotheosis (1913)."

A female security guard in a crisp uniform wandered over, drawn by the crowd that was forming. Kendall looked up and attempted a smile. "I bet you've never had anyone swoon over a painting before."

The guard snorted. "You'd be surprised."

Jenna helped Kendall to stand. "Maybe it's an ancestor. You said Lucas was Irish, right?"

Kendall nodded. "They both have that same mischievous grin." He shuddered. "I've got to get out of here. I feel like the walls are closing in."

"Where do you want to go?"

"I don't know. Just...outside."

A minute later they were on the sidewalk. Kendall paced back and forth with his head down, then stopped. "There's one person who might understand."

A half hour later they were sitting in Lilith's apartment. Kendall reviewed what they had seen at the museum, the drawings in the boiler room, and his encounters with Lucas, including the request for the dress.

"Well, if I didn't know better, I'd say you've been visited by a púca," said Lilith. "You can think of the púca as a variety of fairy with special characteristics. Fairies are essentially supernaturally gifted beings, and they come in all shapes and sizes. The púca is part of Irish folklore—ancient ideas passed down through the generations, perhaps from the Celts, perhaps even older."

"Do you believe in them?" asked Jenna.

"I've never seen actual evidence to prove that the legends are real. Nor has anyone I know. But I do believe there is an unseen world, filled with things beyond our comprehension. Sometimes the legends explain things for which we have no explanation."

"And what about the púca?" asked Kendall.

Lilith waved her hand. "Like so much folklore, the story is muddled with all manner of variation. These stories are not known for consistency. As with the púca's reputation, the details shape-shift depending on the region. But in general, the creature has a special association with autumn and with the turning of the year from summer to winter. It's a trickster, and some people believe it's associated with the origins of trick-or-treat. Leave it a treat, a share of the harvest, or it will play a wicked trick on you. One of its best-known incarnations is to appear as a horse and take some poor individual on a wild night ride."

"Like on a motorcycle, maybe?" Kendall offered with hesitation.

Lilith laughed. "I never heard of a púca that could ride a motorcycle, but why not? Even supernatural beings must keep up with the times, I suppose. There is a lovely Irish air, *The Púca's Lament*, that I learned from my mother. In Irish it's *Port na bPúcaí*. Sometimes the title is translated as *The Music of Ghosts*, or *The Fairy Lament*, or a number of other variations. Its provenance is perhaps as mysterious as the properties of the púca itself. Some people say the song originated in the Blasket Islands when islanders heard a mystical tune coming from the mists and believed it to be the music of restless spirits. Or maybe fishermen heard the singing of humpback whales reverberating in the hulls of their boats. Or maybe a fiddle player wrote the tune in the twentieth century and passed it off as traditional—although that's not likely, given the earliest recorded version. Whatever you want to believe, the lyrics tell about a woman who is taken at night by a fairy—taken away to the fairy mound—and her yearning to return to the mortal world." She fingered the amulet hanging around her neck. "You say he asked you to give him a dress you made?"

"Yes. I haven't finished it yet, but it's almost done. I was going to unveil it on Halloween."

"There's another variation of the púca legend: that the púca has high standards, and the gift of fine-quality clothing will make it go away. So everything you've told me fits with the legends. Or..."

"Or what?"

"Or it could be someone familiar with the legend who is playing with you."

Kendall shook his head. "But the sudden disappearances, the painting at the museum. It's..." He sunk back on the sofa, defeated. "I don't know what to believe."

187

That evening, Kendall put the final stitches on the silver dress. He kept mulling over all that had happened since the beginning of September, trying to make sense of the disparate threads. But of course it did not make sense. Was Lucas the goat creature that Jenna had been warned about, that had been stalking them? Or did he need to trust in the legend that Lilith had shared, and in what Lucas himself had said? It did not help that Lucas had such a mischievous streak. Perhaps that was part of the test. If the solution was obvious, the choice would be less an act of faith. He held out the dress, admiring his handiwork, and sighed. With Halloween just one week away, he still had a little time to come up with an alternative outfit. What the hell. Take the leap of faith.

Kendall heard the sound of dirt being thrown against his window. He looked out, and there stood Lucas, bedecked in leotards layered with tiny black feathers. A few white feathers were mixed in with the black, which complemented the tufts of white protruding from his behind. Over his eyes and nose he wore an eagle mask, its yellow beak turned sharply down at the end. Kendall opened the window.

Lucas raised his arms, and long, black wings unfolded. "What do you think?"

"Not bad. A touch of Las Vegas showgirl, but not bad."

"It's cold out here. Can I come in?"

Kendall let Lucas in through the building's back door. "Are you on the way to a costume party, or dressed like this just for the hell of it?"

"Costume party. The most fabulous one you can imagine." He removed the eagle mask and held it under one wing.

Kendall narrowed his eyes. "I'm still mad at you for disappearing on me the other night."

"Yes, well, I'm sorry about that."

"The ride home on the streetcar was much less nerve-wracking, though, so I shouldn't complain."

Lucas reached out to inspect the necklace Lilith had made for Kendall and held the pendant in his hand as feathers brushed against Kendall's arm. "The Irish triskelion. It pleases me to see you wearing this." He let the pendant fall back across Kendall's chest. "Unity. Integration with nature. Messages I too often see ignored, it pains me to say."

He wandered around the living room, inspecting Kendall's possessions, studying photos displayed on a bookshelf. He came upon the photo of Helen's wedding day. "Is this your mother?"

"Yes."

"I can see the likeness. Same bone structure. And the man next to her is your father?"

"Yes. I don't remember him at all. He's like a big zero to me."

"That's a shame. He's half of who you are, you know."

Kendall shrugged. "By blood, maybe. Not by soul."

"There's more to blood than you give credit, Kendall Akande."

Kendall approached Lucas and examined the feathered wings. "Nice work. Have you been out walking the streets dressed like this?"

"I've gotten some curious looks, but it's close to Halloween. No one thinks it odd. I just thought I'd drop by on the way to the party to see if you've given any more thought to my proposition."

"I have."

"And?"

"And I've decided to do it. I'll give you the dress."

Lucas gave a little bow. "Splendid. You will be grateful that you made such a wise choice."

"Foolish. Wise. I don't know the difference any longer. It seems completely crazy to be doing this."

Lucas made a gesture as if about to sit, but the tuft of obtrusive tail feathers must have convinced him to change his mind. Instead, he placed the mask back on his head and spread his arm wings. "What's crazy is putting yourself in a box. What do you think I am, Kendall? A man or an eagle?"

Kendall crossed his arms and eyed Lucas warily, looking for a trap. "An eagle-man?"

"Good answer. But I'm much more than that. I'm a hybrid, yes, but of many, many things. All of us are. Purity does not exist. It is a myth. My roots extend far back to ancient Norse traditions, before those ancestors mixed with others to become the Celts. And now here I am, a Canadian. And you know what else? I'm not Latino, but I celebrate *Día de los Muertos*, the Day of the Dead. Such a sensible holiday. Embrace your multiplicities. All of them. What was it Walt Whitman said? *Very well, then I contradict myself, I am large, I contain multitudes.* Don't ever let anyone tell you who you are, or put you into a neat little box. Boxes are coffins."

"Of course. I already know that."

"Do you?" He picked up a photo of Kendall posing in drag with several friends. "I think you probably realize it in occasional flashes, but you don't yet live it fully. Otherwise you would have recognized me earlier. And you would know more about your father."

Kendall snatched the photo out of Lucas' hand. "And who are you to lecture me? You're, what—twenty-one, twenty-two—and think you're such a fount of wisdom?"

Lucas laughed, the sound of a bow bouncing on the open A string of a fiddle. "No worries, my friend. Take whatever feels true for you yourself in what I've said and discard the rest. Unlike your fellow human beings, who are so good at telling others how to behave, I don't expect you to do everything I say."

"Except when it comes to the dress."

"But that's also your choice. I told you I would offer my protection in exchange for the outfit. There is someone who means you harm, who believes that he is purely one thing and one thing only, and his objective is to purify the world. If you really want to see crazy, then I can show you crazy."

"Do you want the dress now?"

Lucas held out his winged arms. "You will be glad you did it."

"I hope so. It doesn't feel that way at the moment." Kendall retrieved the dress and placed it in Lucas' arms. He caressed the fabric one last time.

Lucas cleared his throat. "The pumps, too."

"Not the pumps!"

"You would send me forth shoeless with an incomplete outfit?"

Kendall set the shoes atop the pile with an angry look and dismissively waved Lucas away. "Go. Quickly, before I change my mind." He accompanied Lucas to the back porch, and as the young man reached the bottom step, Kendall called out. "One last question. Who is this person? The one who means to do me harm?"

Lucas looked up at Kendall. "He'll be revealed to you very soon."

"So it's a man. Can I have another clue?"

"He is the one who foolishly believes he is me."

I Put a Spell on You

Jenna

As the streetcar accelerated, a woman lost her footing and slammed into Jenna, mumbling apologies. The sharp crack of electricity sounded above the roof where the connector attached to the overhead wires, and a blue flash illuminated the night. Jenna tensed, hunching her shoulders. As accustomed as she was to hearing that sound over the years, she still reacted the same way each time, as when hearing a car backfire. She glanced around the streetcar at Kendall and the other passengers. The sound seemed not to have bothered anyone else but her. She wondered if she was on her way to turning into a super-sensitive Morvena.

She and Kendall had exhausted their praise of the Todrick Hall concert they had just attended, and their conversation lagged. The audience had gone wild when he invited a young woman and her girlfriend onstage so the woman could propose marriage. The

girlfriend put her hands to her face and started crying as the woman
held out the ring box. *Not your average concert*, thought Jenna. But
then there was nothing average about Todrick Hall and his music,
which united straight, gay, trans, black, white, Asian, young, old.
Jenna still felt amped up by the exhilaration of the concert.

Kendall pressed the button to request the next stop.

"Why are we getting off here?" asked Jenna. "We should
transfer to the subway. It'll be faster."

"No, let's take the 506. We won't have to walk as far later."

"But the street's torn up with construction. We'll get delayed."

"It'll be fine."

Jenna looked out the window and saw a bus cross the street.
"No, it won't. We just missed our connection. And they're running
busses in place of the streetcar."

"Don't stress, diva. Another bus will come along in ten
minutes."

Jenna rolled her eyes. "If we're lucky."

"I saw that look, missy."

They stood on the corner waiting. Jenna kept looking
impatiently down the street, but she saw no headlights to suggest that
a bus was imminent. The night air was cold, and she shivered
beneath her light jacket. She could feel a wave of irritation building,
drowning the good vibes of the concert.

"I gave the dress to Lucas," said Kendall.

"Yes, you already told me, earlier this evening. You're getting
forgetful."

"No need to get huffy. Did I tell you that Lilith took me to her
favorite shop? She bought me a dark blue stone for protection. She's
teaching me about the different properties of crystals and herbs."

"Are you going to join her coven?" Jenna surprised herself
with the amount of sarcasm in her voice. If the statement had been a
tennis ball, it would have zinged with a mean curve.

"She's not part of any coven. And for your information, no,
I'm not planning on becoming a witch. I just think she's interesting."

"What is it with Lilith? You've been hanging out with her all
the time lately."

192

Kendall crossed his arms. "I think you're jealous."

"No, I'm not."

"Yes, you are."

"Let's change the subject. What time do you want to get together Friday after work to catch the ferry?"

Kendall gasped. "Oops, I forgot. I can't go Friday. I invited my mom over for dinner. What about Saturday?"

Jenna sighed heavily. "Saturday's no good for me. How could you forget? We agreed to go together to pick up Turnbull's permission letter so we can access any existing building plans from City Hall. I already called him and set it up."

"Sorry. It just slipped my mind."

"What about tomorrow night?"

"Can't. I was planning to ask Lilith to help me with my nightmares."

"See what I mean? You're infatuated with her. She's all you talk about. Lilith this, Lilith that. She must have cast a spell on you."

Kendall wagged his finger at her. "She would not do such a thing. You take that back."

"I will not."

"I can't believe you would say that. That is so insensitive, something I'd expect from a small mind."

Jenna spotted a streetcar heading toward the subway, the same line they had just gotten off ten minutes earlier. "You know what? You can wait here all night for the 506 for all I care. I'm going to the subway."

"Fine, if that's what you want."

"Fine. And I'll just get Elliott to go with me on Friday. Since you are clearly unreliable." She stuffed her hands in her jacket pockets. Kendall said nothing and turned away. She hesitated a moment, hoping for an apology, or even for the sight of a bus coming down the block. Nothing. She ran over to board the streetcar as it pulled up to the stop. She took her seat and looked out the window at Kendall standing alone on the street corner, his orange hair glowing like an angry flame. She already regretted her impetuous action and words, but his refusal to glance back her direction fueled a new wave of resentment. As the streetcar accelerated, he was still looking away.

Burnt Offerings
Kendall

Kendall stood in the alcove, looking through his mail. An offer for a credit card. The bill from his Internet provider, which still came like clockwork even though he had chosen paperless billing. Another credit card offer. Something more important was on his mind, but he was procrastinating, trying to summon the courage to ask Lilith for help with a spell. He had been visited by the recurring nightmare again the previous night, after his argument with Jenna, and had woken in a panic. At least the cleansing ceremony seemed to have prevented a repetition of the sleep paralysis.

Maybe Lilith had something to help him with the nightmares. He wasn't quite sure why he hesitated, though. It wasn't that he felt ambivalent about the existence of magic. It wasn't that he was nervous about whatever he imagined the procedure of a spell to entail. It wasn't even that he had seen too many horror movies about witches. Sure, each of these factors were a little bit true. And he could even acknowledge that they contradicted each other. Perhaps it was the dichotomy between two extremes that tugged him in two directions, each as implausible as the other. On one side there was *Harry Potter* and *The Worst Witch*: quaint, fantastical worlds peopled with plenty of good-natured folk where magic could make astonishing things happen. On the other side was *Suspiria* and *The Craft*, where dabbling in witchcraft would bring dangerous, awful repercussions.

He saw Lilith coming up the stairs and stepped out of the way so she could open her mailbox. "I was just thinking about you."

"You must have sent out vibrations to summon me."

He held up his envelopes. "Does anything interesting ever come by mail anymore?"

Lilith laughed and retrieved a single envelope from her mailbox. She looked at the address with surprise, then presented it like a trophy. "You were saying?"

Although addressed to her neighbor in apartment ten, the letter had been mistakenly delivered to her box. Kendall read the name aloud: "*Marvin Gumbal.*" It took a moment for the name to register, then he repeated it as if calling out the name of a naughty child. "Marvin Gumbal! Oh my God, do you know who that is?"

"My mystery neighbor."

"No—I mean, yes—but he's also the infamous author of *I Dined with Satan.*" Lilith must have assumed he was joking, because she laughed. "It's no joke, I swear."

"It sounds like the title of a comedy sketch."

"He passed the novel off as a real-life story about a cult of witches who practiced human sacrifice. It was supposedly a first-person account of a woman who was seduced into joining the cult. But it didn't exist. He made the whole thing up—although you can still find people who believe it really happened and there was a cover-up. The cult practiced increasingly horrific acts that started out small-scale—for example, killing a cat—then slowly escalated to abduction, torture, child abuse, and ultimately murder."

Lilith lost her smile. "That's precisely the thing that inflames the public against us. Those aren't witches—they're sociopaths."

Kendall took the envelope from her hand. "It's from his publishing company. I think we should pay Mr. Gumbal a little visit."

They went down to the basement, Kendall leading the way with a triumphant air. At Marvin's door, Kendall called out, "Mail delivery for Mr. Marvin Gumbal."

A moment later, a sheepish Marvin opened the door. Kendall held out the envelope, but when Marvin reached for it, Kendall snatched his hand back. "Uh-uh. First you're going to invite us in to talk."

"You can't withhold my mail. That's illegal."

"So what are you going to do—call the police?"

Lilith took the envelope from Kendall and handed it to Marvin. "Please, Marvin. Now that we know who you are, you don't need to be so secretive."

Marvin seemed to weigh the offer, then grudgingly opened the door wider so they could enter. The apartment's clutter felt claustrophobic, a Jackson Pollock splatter of color that assaulted Kendall's senses. Ornate Belle Époque furniture squatted on bowed legs, with curving, delicate filigree and gilded scrollwork. Ceramic harlequin figurines and fairies in coy poses populated every inch of the half-dozen display cases and tabletops, along with translucent Depression-era glassware in shades of rose, amber, canary, ruby, and emerald. Elaborate lace doilies lolled across the backs of chairs and the arms of the sofa. It was an overcrowded antiques shop.

"All right, you're in," said Marvin. "Now what do you want to talk about? My book, I suppose. That's all anyone ever wants to talk about, so they can shove their opinions down my throat. Have you followed what people have written online, seen the vulgar comments, the death threats?"

Kendall sat on the couch with his legs primly pressed together and hands folded in his lap. "Actually, that wasn't my objective. But now that you've brought it up, why did you pretend as if it really happened? It was a pretty good story, without all the pretense."

Marvin sat down in an armchair with flowery stitching in the fabric. "That's what sells. Few people paid attention to any of my previous books. You can't imagine the frustration I felt, all through my life, sending out the result of my blood, sweat, and tears into the world where it was ignored."

"And I imagine it wasn't any more satisfying when people began to ridicule *I Dined with Satan*."

Marvin picked at a piece of lint on his pants. "Ultimately, no. But it was amusing while it lasted, to have my little revenge."

"I'm sure it wasn't amusing to the people who the police investigated based on the details in your plot."

"That was unintentional. I didn't think people would take it so seriously that they would track down the actual location and make complaints to the police. That just shows you how stupid people are.

I only used the location to provide a veneer of realism. For a little *frisson*."

"Yes, and it created a mess," said Kendall. "So now you hide here from the world."

On the table beside him, Marvin dragged a figurine back two inches from the edge. It seemed to Kendall to be such a transparently symbolic gesture that he wanted to laugh.

"I've always been something of a hermit," said Marvin. "This is really nothing new."

Kendall sensed a familiar refrain in Marvin's voice, the sound of someone who had been hurt too many times. Probably doomed to chase the wrong kind of men who stole his figurines for drug money. A wave of sympathy began to form in Kendall's heart. A moment later, however, it was flattened when Marvin announced, "I find humanity rather despicable."

Marvin's negativity punched Kendall in the gut. He looked at Lilith, who seemed to be trying to deflect the negativity by directing her attention elsewhere. She was absorbed in one of the display cases, whose mirrored shelves gave the impression that the figurines packed the case as tightly as Times Square partiers on New Year's Eve.

"I'm certain you think I grew rich off all the attention the book received," Marvin continued. "My publisher agreed to give refunds to anyone who purchased the novel and felt deceived." He emitted a single, bitter guffaw, nasal like the honk of a Canada goose. "So I ended up with a bestseller that made little money."

"Well, you certainly can't blame others for that."

"No. But what I didn't expect was all the vulgarity, the death threats, people saying I should die a painful death like the victims in my story. Someone made a video of me as a voodoo doll being dismembered."

"People can be unbelievably cruel, I know. I'm really sorry to hear that."

Lilith bent closer to examine a fairy with delicately veined transparent wings.

Marvin's mood softened. "I see you like my fairies."

197

"Yes. The *aos sí*. That's what my mother called them. The fair folk. They come in many forms, not just these diminutive, winged fairies that most people equate with the term."

Kendall spread out his arms. "And you have one variety sitting right here." Lilith ignored his attempt at humor. Marvin coughed and shifted in his chair. Probably closeted and uncomfortable with Kendall's brash gayness. Kendall folded his hands back on his lap. "Normally that joke would get a better reaction from the audience."

"Sorry, Kendall," said Lilith. "It's just that fairies are not something to laugh at."

"Don't tell me you believe in them," scoffed Marvin.

"I believe there is a world of unseen things. Ghosts, banshees, fairy folk—call them what you will. I'm not saying the images in this case necessarily reflect that world with absolute accuracy, or that little fairy creatures go zipping around like dragonflies. These are just one of the ways in which we imperfectly try to represent that hidden world."

"What about you, Marvin?" Kendall asked. "Do you believe in ghosts?"

Marvin gripped the end of the armrests, looking very much the monarch ruling his little kingdom and doling out judgments. "I believe they are a projection of the evil within men's hearts. Personifications of our guilt and cruelty, if you will."

"So you've never seen anything unusual or experienced something unexplainable in this building?"

Marvin eyed him suspiciously. "What are you getting at?"

"Have you heard the rumors—that Covington Terrace is haunted?"

"Haunted by what, exactly?"

"I don't know. The ghost of the man with a goat head, or those who were murdered by him."

Marvin slapped his hands against the armrests and pushed himself to his feet. His hands balled into fists. "I resent what you're implying. I only used the disappearances and the boiler room drawings as inspiration for my novel. I had nothing to do with any of it."

198

"I'm not implying anything. So you've seen the drawings?"

"Yes. Several years ago, when the boiler was being fixed. I happened to look in the open door, and what I saw gave me the idea for a satanic cult that practiced human sacrifice. And since there had been two disappearances in the building—"

"Wait. What do you mean, *two* disappearances? Your book was published before Rooney disappeared."

He cleared his throat. "There were two others before her. One not quite two years ago, the first one five years ago. I assumed you knew about them both."

"Turnbull only mentioned one disappearance, and that was because Jenna and I asked him specifically about it."

"Maybe he didn't acknowledge the other one because he was worried it would scare you off," Lilith offered. "Then he might lose you both as tenants."

Marvin started toward the door. "Anyway, I'll have to ask you both to leave now."

"Why? What's wrong?" asked Kendall.

"I know what you're up to with your implications. Trying to criticize and blame me, just like everyone else."

Kendall stood. "You're wrong. I think you've become so accustomed to assuming the worst that you see bad intent in every little gesture. Like that's all you can see anymore. But we'll go."

Marvin slammed the door shut behind them, followed by the exclamation point of the dead bolt clicking shut.

"He's a tad sensitive," said Lilith.

"You think?" Kendall remembered his nightmares and his interest in obtaining Lilith's help. "Listen, I wanted to ask you something. Do you—do you have a way to cure my panic attacks and nightmares?"

Lilith rubbed her chin, thinking, then held up a finger. "I know something that can help. But first of all, you need to reorient your attitude about what spells are. They aren't a magick wand you wave and the world suddenly changes. Spells help you focus the energy of the universe to guide you to a desired outcome. And the universe gives you what you need, not what you want or think you need. For example, if you desire transportation in your life, you don't cast a spell asking for a Ferrari. You ask the universe to help you find transportation. Maybe a new bus line will be routed past your door. Maybe you'll find a good deal on a used car. You have to remain open to whatever the universe presents to you. We can certainly cast a spell to help you understand your nightmares. Just don't be surprised if the answer arrives in an unexpected way."

Lilith dispatched Kendall to his apartment to retrieve his aventurine stone. By the time he came back, she had gathered everything for the spell. Widely placed colored candles representing each of the cardinal directions created a circle with the altar in the center. "This is our circle," she explained. "You must not break the circle once the candles are lit. Now write down on a slip of paper what you would like the spell to accomplish."

Kendall took a moment, then wrote out a sentence and handed the paper to Lilith. He sat on the floor facing the altar.

"The first thing we need to do is cleanse ourselves and purify the circle with some sage." She lit an incense cone, and lifted the holder to waft the smoke toward her. Then she instructed Kendall to do the same. The sage smelled sweet and earthy. "Now we're ready to open the circle."

Lilith lit the green candle. "Welcome, Elementals of the North, of earth. I ask that you bring your gifts of patience, endurance, stability, and prosperity to this circle." She moved to the yellow candle. "Welcome, Elementals of the East, of air. I ask that you bring your gifts of wisdom, intellect, perception, and inspiration to this circle." Next, the red candle. "Welcome, Elementals of the South, of fire. I ask that you bring your gifts of passion, strength, energy, and willpower to this circle." Finally, she lit the blue candle. "Welcome, Elementals of the West, of water. I ask that you bring your gifts of emotion, pleasure, abundance, and receptivity to this circle."

She returned to the center of the circle and dripped some essential oil on a purple tea candle in the middle of the altar. "Welcome, Elementals of the Center, of the universe. I ask that you bring guidance and protection to this circle." She lit the candle. "This circle is now protected, and protected it shall stay." She sat on the floor beside Kendall. "The candle in the center serves as the focus for our spell. Purple is good for banishing negative energy and bad influences. It's also used for wisdom and to treat sleep disorders. There are other colors we could have chosen, but I think purple will be the most effective."

Kendall stared at the flame as it hovered almost motionless. Lilith made him state the purpose of the ritual. Then she asked him to pick up his aventurine stone. She told him to thank the universe for its guidance and concentrate for several minutes on feeling a connection to the stone. She did the same with her own amulet. When she gave the word, they placed both items back on the altar.

The sage released its last wisp of smoke. Lilith selected a different incense cone and placed it beside the ash pyramid of the sage. The new scent was more potent. "Dragon's blood," she explained. "It augments the power of the spell." Kendall made a face, and Lilith chuckled. "Not real dragon's blood, obviously. It's just the name of a red resin obtained from various plants."

She picked up a piece of paper and read the words of protection she had written down. Kendall helped as she folded the paper into a tiny square. She held the square over the flame of the purple candle until it caught fire, then dropped it into the small cast-iron cauldron. A serpent's tongue of flame grew higher, licking the air.

Once the paper had blackened and the flames subsided, Kendall read from his paper. "I ask the universe to help me understand my nightmares and panic attacks, and release me from their power." Together they folded the paper and repeated the steps to burn it. Again forked flames lapped at the sides of the cauldron, growing higher as the fire consumed the paper and released its energy into the air. This time the twin flames reminded Kendall of the horns of the goat-man. He imagined the goat-man being consumed and vanquished by the fire. Lilith picked up a dried bay leaf on which she had written the word *nightmare* and crumbled it, sprinkling the pieces over the flame.

201

Kendall expected a wind to blow suddenly through the room, like in the movies. But nothing out of the ordinary happened. The process of casting the spell seemed much more natural than he had anticipated. Probably he'd seen too many horror films with strange incantations and the arrival of occult spirits. This seemed little different than a Buddhist monk lighting a joss stick and meditating, or a Catholic priest reciting Latin while swinging a censor. Just different rituals to create mindfulness and connect to something deeply spiritual.

The scent of the bay leaf and the incense relaxed Kendall. Lilith told him to meditate on the spell—on what he had requested from the universe. He concentrated on the words: *help me understand my nightmares and panic attacks and release me from their power*. He thought about the night when he had awakened in a panic and seen the goat-man in the Jungle, and of his phone call to his mother, her reassuring words. Tomorrow she was coming over for dinner. He started thinking about his grocery list, the items he needed to pick up for the dishes he planned to make. He realized he had wandered far from thoughts of the spell and forced his mind to concentrate once again. *Help release me from their power.*

If only he could figure out the cause. Not the triggers—that was obvious, with all the talk of ghosts and goat-men. What was it that caused the nightmare in the first place? The spell felt a bit like praying. Actually, he could not identify any difference. They were both simply ways to ask for help and guidance. What was it Lilith had said? *The magick lies not in bending the universe to one's will, but in focusing one's energy to enable a solution to be found.* The nightmare and panic attacks emerged from feelings of vulnerability—that much seemed clear. He thought about Robbie, and about having allowed Robbie to make him feel vulnerable. He kept replaying the scene in his mind when Robbie told him he was not masculine enough.

Lilith must have sensed his waning concentration, because she said, "Refocus your mind on the meditation. It's normal for random thoughts to intrude. The mind is like a hyperactive child, jumping from thought to thought, telling itself ridiculous things like *I'll never be any good* or *Why doesn't he love me?*" She picked up a small mallet and rubbed it along the rim of her Tibetan singing bowl. "This will help. Concentrate on the motion of my hand and the sound of the bowl."

The steady rotation did indeed quiet his mind. A soothing alto hum filled the room and banished Robbie and the grocery list.

When the wax of the candle had burned away, Lilith rose to close the circle, extinguishing each candle in the reverse order from west to north and thanking the Elementals for their presence. The candles left wispy trails of smoke and a slight burnt smell that cut through the lingering scent of the incense but was not unpleasant. Then she stood in the center to thank the universe, and blew out the purple candle. "The final step is to ground ourselves. Place your palms against the floor, close your eyes, and let the energy drain back into the earth."

They remained like that for about fifteen minutes. All Kendall could think was, *I hope this works.*

Bone White

Rooney

Rooney's body ached from sleeping on the concrete floor. Her skin was dirty, her hair matted. She had named the skeleton in the corner Phyllis, and found it no longer frightened her. She had long conversations with Phyllis. She told her about her life growing up, the men she had dated, how she could not stand her sister, only now she'd give anything to hear her sister's voice.

Phyllis was a good listener. Rooney decided there was no point in lying to Phyllis. At first, she started to spin her usual tales. She said her mother was related to England's royal family. That's what she had told other kids in elementary school. Nathaniel Brownstone had been the only one to challenge her. *Then why are you living in Barrie, Ontario, instead of a castle?* She had gotten so angry, and cooked up revenge, putting water on his chair so it looked like he wet himself when he sat down.

Then she realized Phyllis didn't care if she had royal blood, if she had completed college, if she'd been voted the prettiest girl in high school. She didn't care if Rooney made a living lying about products and businesses. So Rooney apologized, and started saying what she really felt. Phyllis grinned in the weak light, indifferent either way.

The cell smelled like death. Rooney expected it would be where she lived out her final days, whether that came tomorrow or a year from now. Initially, she managed to keep a small flame of hope burning, but now she resigned herself to her fate. She used to think she would be one of those people who never give up hope no matter how dire the circumstances. She would tell herself, *As long as you're still alive, there will always be hope.* But she found it harder to sustain that belief now. Surely Phyllis once thought there was a reason to be hopeful, too. And now there she lay. If something happened to the goat-man, Rooney was certain this would become her grave, too.

Goat-man continued to bring her food and water, and to squat and watch. She tried on different attitudes, much like the way she selected clothes from her wardrobe, to see if anything broke through his mysterious silence. She threw out a look of disgust one day. Another day she tried to grovel. Once she acted like she didn't care. She tried smiling. She tried acting ill. He remained as indifferent as Phyllis. He never touched her, but his penetrating gaze made her feel as if she had been violated. Surely he would eventually tire of this game, but she tried not to dwell on the thought, because what would happen to her then?

Her only sense of time came through the rhythms of her body. Her menstrual cycle. The urge to urinate. Her hunger and thirst. She integrated goat-man into these rhythms, a certain predictability in his visits. Each visit tormented her. The watching, watching, watching. She counted the seconds until she could be alone again with Phyllis. She never thought of herself as a murderer before, but she knew if she ever had the opportunity she would kill him as calmly as flipping off a light switch.

She accidentally knocked the plate with the blue-and-white designs off the toilet tank. It shattered on the floor. At first, she feared that the broken plate would anger goat-man and prompt some terrible reaction. Then she noticed the shards with their sharp points. She grabbed one particularly vicious looking shard and hid the other pieces behind her. Although she had not formulated a plan for how she might use it, the object in her hand bolstered her confidence, and she waited.

She heard the key being inserted in the lock, and her muscles tensed. A moment later he stepped into the gloom, his monstrous form all shadow. But today was different. He was in a state of agitation. He did not hand her the food like usual on the blue-and-white plate but tossed the tightly wrapped sandwich at her feet, not even noticing the absent plate. Instead of squatting to watch her, he paced the cell. She could not tell what this change in his demeanor signified, but it was an ominous sign. He stomped on Phyllis' ribs with his heavy boots, shattering them. Rooney gasped, as if he had stomped on a friend. She tried not to look at him, afraid that would anger him more. He approached her and squatted, the goat head only inches from her face. She leaned away, trembling. The goat head moved in response, pushing itself in her face, demanding she look. She did not want to look. She smelled his stale, unwashed breath. He placed his palms against the wall on either side of her head. He had not put on his claw gloves yet, perhaps distracted from his routine by whatever was troubling him.

The reflex happened so fast, almost before she was aware of what she was doing. She did not think of the consequences. She only knew she hated him and wanted this ordeal to end, one way or another. She jabbed the shard into the base of his neck, but the mask head prevented it from puncturing too deeply. With one hand he grabbed the wound, while the other hand grabbed her wrist to try to shake loose the weapon. She thought about using her free hand to strangle him with the shackle's chain, but the goat horns protruded too high. Instead, she grabbed one of the horns and yanked off the mask. His hand moved from the neck wound and tried to grab for the mask as it dropped to the floor. That was her chance. Her hand looped the chain around his neck. He tried to slip one hand beneath the chain while his other hand slammed her wrist on the floor until she let go of the shard. She pulled more tightly—pulled him forward onto his knees. Then she recognized who he was and gasped.

He flicked the shard across the floor, away from her, and grabbed her throat. His other hand pulled against the chain, resisting its pressure. The strength in his hands surprised her. She wondered who would succumb first, but already she could not breathe. He shook her back and forth, pushed one knee into her stomach, then rammed the knee hard. Her leverage loosened, and he wrenched free.

He stood, breathing heavily, and pressed the spot where she had stabbed him. "You're like all the rest."

She clutched her throat, coughing. "What do you want from me?" she sobbed, fearing the worst from her failed attempt to overpower him. Despite the dark line of blood soaking into his collar, she could tell the mask had saved him from a more debilitating wound.

Still holding his throat, he retrieved the mask with his other hand and placed it back over his head, but said nothing else. Instead, he picked up Phyllis' skull and turned it slowly in his hand, as if admiring a rare object. He tossed it once in the air and caught it. Then his rage exploded and he threw the skull with brutal force at Rooney's feet. She winced as it shattered, small pieces of bone striking her cheek.

He snatched the uneaten sandwich off the floor and left her with hunger and fear devouring her insides.

8

Excerpt from Shockadelica Podcast
Episode 51: Horror Music
Guest: The Bone Man

Jenna: Hello, ghoulies and goblins. I'm here today minus Kendall, but with a special guest, a musician who writes music on dark themes and goes by the name the Bone Man. Welcome.

Vince: Thanks. It's great to be on your podcast after listening for the past two years.

Jenna: You've released your first album, titled *Box of Bones*, a collection of horror-themed songs. What inspired you?

Vince: All the myths and stories about the dark side of the world.

Jenna: Each song represents a classic horror creature. Frankenstein's monster, werewolf, vampire, witch...

Vince: Ghost, devil, zombie. They're all there.

Jenna: The scariest song for me is the one about the boogeyman. The song titled "Box of Bones."

Vince: Yeah. The killer lurking in the shadows, waiting to steal you away.

Jenna: What are your musical influences? I hear rap, rock, and electronica in your sound. But, interestingly, no black metal or death metal, which usually goes hand in hand with horror themes. I'm thinking of Cannibal Corpse, Pantera, Wan...

Vince: Yeah, that music is great, but I'm more eclectic in my tastes. And I didn't want to do the obvious, the kind of thing you'd expect.

Jenna: I like how your lyrics aren't obvious, either. Take
            "Frankenstein Monster," which could be a song about the
            mad scientist building the Creature, or it could be a
            metaphor for social dysfunction and the rise of
            conspiracy theories.
Vince: The current state of the world.
Jenna: Exactly.

Psycho

Jenna

Jenna had not spoken to Kendall since their argument a few
nights earlier. She was grateful that Elliott Bernbaum agreed to
accompany her to Ward's Island. She did not want to confront the
house of curiosities alone. That was what she called it when telling
Elliott about Turnbull's residence. She warned Elliott to expect a
parlor filled with the oddest collection imaginable. Then she
remembered his teasing comment about the boiler room, and added,
"I won't tell you exactly what. That would spoil the surprise."

Elliott laughed and said, "*Touché.*"

Twilight was settling in as they boarded the ferry, creating a
Halloween sky with bony fingers of cloud pointing toward the
unknown. They took the ferry directly to Ward's Island. The few
other passengers all appeared to be residents who had come into the
city for shopping or work, and were returning home with nightfall.
They clustered in small groups, talking and sharing news, with their
grocery bags, briefcases, and roller carts at their sides. Jenna thought
how nice it would be to live in a close-knit community like Ward's
Island. She was glad she was getting to know her neighbors better,
even if something unpleasant like ghost sightings provided the
impetus that brought them together.

The streetlights were on, lending a cozy feeling to the narrow
lanes of Ward's Island. Within a few minutes of stepping off the
ferry, they were standing at Turnbull's door. He invited them in and

excused himself to retrieve the letter of permission so they could access whatever building records existed at City Hall.

"See what I mean?" said Jenna, nodding toward the room's contents. In the day's waning light, the collection looked even more sinister than the day she had visited with Kendall. So many items crowded the room that they swallowed the light from the lone Tiffany lamp, leaving secluded spaces in shadow. Jenna noticed objects she had overlooked before: skeletons of birds arrayed on a shelf, a hand in a glass jar. "What must it have been like for Wade to grow up in a house like this?"

She had not heard Turnbull step back into the room and reddened as she realized he had heard her.

"Wade has not returned home for several days," he said. "I don't know where he is and I'm worried."

Jenna took the letter from Turnbull's outstretched hand. "Okay, now things are getting scary. That's two disappearances."

"Three," Elliott reminder her, "counting the tenant two years ago."

"Actually, that would make four," admitted Turnbull. "I didn't want to mention the first disappearance when you were here last time. That happened five years ago. Maybe the property is haunted after all. Or at least cursed." Turnbull went to one of the cabinets and retrieved a goat skull decorated with black swirls and veined with branching black lines. Black dots outlined the eye sockets and nose holes, which were painted a rust-colored red. Black horns curved up out of the skull. "Do you know the history, the legend of the goat-man murders?" Jenna and Elliott nodded. "We never gave it much credence, my wife and me. I even amused myself with a special interest in collecting objects like this, because of the legend. There are more objects I could show you. Playing cards. Illustrations. A statue of Baphomet. I treated it as a joke."

"And you actually think the goat-man's ghost is responsible for what's been happening?" asked Jenna.

"I don't know what to believe."

Jenna was about to ask him who painted the drawings in the boiler room, but a knock on the door interrupted their conversation.

Two detectives identified themselves, and Turnbull invited them inside. He introduced Jenna and Elliott as two of his tenants. Jenna remembered seeing the men on the ferry, but had assumed they were residents.

"We just want to ask a few questions about your son Wade," said one of the men.

"Has something happened to him?" Turnbull asked with alarm.

"Not that we know of. We were also hoping to question him as well."

Turnbull explained that he had not seen his son in several days. The detectives revealed that Wade was a person of interest in a murder investigation involving a family in Cabbagetown. The Syrian family, Jenna realized. It had been all over the news a month ago, but still no suspect had been identified.

The detectives asked a few questions of Elliott and Jenna, but neither she nor Elliott had any useful information, other than pointing out Rooney's disappearance three weeks earlier.

"Yes, we're aware of that," said one of the men.

Jenna thought of the other strange occurrences and sightings. She considered saying something but stopped herself, unsure how it all would sound. Would they think she was crazy? Her head was filled with too much conflicting information, a mess of jigsaw pieces. Then all at once it fit together—or at least enough of it that she suspected the solution. She might not be able to explain everything, but she knew the broad outline. The recurring images. The noises and voices. The disappearances. The access to tenant's apartments. Turnbull's collection and the boiler room.

One of the detectives had his hand on the doorknob as the two men prepared to leave.

"Wait," Jenna called out. Everyone turned to look at her. "This is going to sound bizarre, but strange things have been happening at Covington Terrace. Sightings of a man wearing a goat mask. Threatening voices coming from the walls. Disappearances. Strange visitations and things happening inside our units. I think they're all connected. Connected to someone who has keys to our apartments."

She glanced at Turnbull, who already looked stricken by what she was about to say. "Wade Turnbull."

Turnbull sagged against the wall. The two detectives looked at each other, assessing Jenna's claim. She could sense something unspoken in their look that suggested they were not surprised. One said, "I don't mean to alarm you, but if what you say is accurate, it may not be safe for you or the other tenants to remain in the building at the moment."

She took out her phone. "We've got to warn Kendall. And the others."

Get Out

Kendall

The cell phone on the table rang. Kendall leaned away from the stove and saw Jenna's face on the screen. "Not now," he said aloud to himself, brandishing a wooden spoon. He let the call go to voicemail and returned to his stir fry. But a minute later, the phone rang again. He could sense the urgency in the ring and imagined Jenna's voice saying *pick up pick up pick up*. He pressed the answer button and put the phone on speaker, careful to temper any warmth in his voice so she knew he was still angry at her. "I'm in the middle of cooking. What do you want?"

Jenna's disembodied voice floated up from the speaker. "Kendall, we're at Turnbull's house. The police came to question him about Wade. You've got to get out of there."

The vegetables sizzled and popped in the frying pan, as agitated as Jenna sounded. "What's the matter?"

"Wade is a suspect in the killing of that immigrant family in Cabbagetown. And he probably killed Vince's girlfriend, and Rooney, too."

The spoon froze in Kendall's hand. "Okay. So why do I have to leave right now?"

"He's got keys to all of the apartments. It's not safe to stay there until the locks are changed."

Kendall moved the pan away from the burner and turned off the heat. He looked over at the door, and a chill went down his spine.

"Kendall. Are you still there?"

"Yes. I just..."

Elliott's voice came over the speaker, loud and insistent. "You've got to get out of there, man. It's not safe at the moment."

Kendall grabbed the phone and pressed off the speaker button, his voice dropping to a murmur, although he wasn't sure why he felt compelled to whisper. "Okay, I'll leave shortly. Are you guys coming back?"

Jenna's voice again: "Yeah, we'll catch the seven o'clock ferry and just stop by to gather some things. Do you have somewhere to spend the night?"

"My mother's on her way over for dinner. I can stay at her place." The apartment plunged into darkness. "Oh, God, the lights just went off." Kendall scurried to the kitchen window. "I see lights on next door, though, and in other houses."

He heard Elliott's voice in the background asking Jenna what was happening, followed by Jenna's explanation. Then he heard jostling sounds as Jenna passed the phone to Elliott. "Kendall, I don't think it's an accident that the lights have gone off. Get out of there now, man!"

Kendall heard a key being inserted into his apartment door. The deadbolt slipped open and a hand wiggled the knob from the other side. The handle was locked, but he knew it provided only a momentary reprieve. "I think it's him, coming into my apartment."

He heard Jenna's voice in the background shouting at someone to call the police. Elliott said, "Try to get out the window, or find somewhere to hide."

Think fast, he thought to himself. *The bathroom door locks. No, not the bathroom. There's no other way out. The closet. No, he could find me if I hide there.* The front door was already opening. Kendall needed something to incapacitate Wade, give him just enough time to open a window before he was trapped. The kitchen, with its two entry points from the living room and hall, was the best place to stay for the moment. The one place he could not be cornered. He looked down at the frying pan filled with hot oil and vegetables. That might give him just the edge he needed. He grabbed the handle and backed up against the refrigerator, just out of sight.

The footsteps on the hardwood floor approached, slow and deliberate, a predator moving with caution, sniffing out its prey. Kendall knew the smell of the stir fry would draw the intruder to the kitchen. A floorboard squeaked. A moment later, Kendall saw the shape of a man in the doorway, but where he expected to see Wade's face, instead there was the head of a goat with curving horns. One hand gripped a hunting knife. Kendall tossed the contents of the frying pan at the goat face. Some of the contents must have managed to enter the eye holes, because the intruder held his palms up to the eye sockets and cried out. Kendall whacked the mask's forehead with the frying pan, then kicked the goat-man in the groin. The intruder bent over with pain, swiping the blade through the air, which grazed Kendall's leg. The sharp pain momentarily stunned Kendall. He felt a warmth seeping through his pants. He raised the frying pan high and brought it down on the back of the goat-man's head, hoping it would momentarily stun him at least long enough to escape.

Kendall dropped the pan and tried to run out through the hall toward the front door, but Wade was already staggering into the hall from the other direction, anticipating Kendall's move. Instead, Kendall fled to the bedroom, the pain where he had been sliced shooting through his leg. He struggled to unlock the window tabs, his hands shaking. He could hear Wade stumbling in the hall, pursuing him. All he could think was to get through that window as quickly as possible. The sash grated as he raised it. Then it got stuck half-way up in its old wooden grooves. He cursed at the window and the rundown property. He was doing it too fast. It always got stuck if he did not raise it slowly. Damn! Too late now. Wade entered the bedroom, exuding anger, the knife in his hand.

Kendall picked up any item he could find and threw it at Wade. The dressmaker's dummy. A chair. The lamp. The nightstand. Wade deflected each missile and kept advancing. Kendall was

213

running out of options. He picked up his vintage sewing machine, struggling with its heft. They didn't make sewing machines like that anymore. He launched it at Wade and it landed squarely in Wade's chest, sending him reeling backwards onto the floor. It had knocked the wind out of him. Temporarily. Kendall forced the sash a few inches higher—not all the way open, but it would have to do. He crawled through the window, legs first, face down. His elbows scraped against the ledge and his head banged the window frame, but that pain was eclipsed by the pain in his leg when he dropped several feet and his heels hit the pavement of his garden court. He lost his balance and toppled onto his behind.

He knew what would happen next. Any moment, Wade would likely charge through the building's back door. Kendall limped to his feet and looked around the yard. He doubted his condition would enable him to scale the seven-foot-high fence or outrun Wade through the gate that led into the alley. He grabbed one of the patio folding chairs and yelled for help. A window opened on the second story, and the Bone Man peered out. "It's Wade Turnbull," Kendall shouted. "He's trying to kill me."

The back door flew open and Wade came down the steps with his knife. The two circled one another around the patio table. Each time Wade lunged one direction, Kendall moved the other way. Wade gripped the table, and with a bestial yell yanked the table aside, sending it clattering into the Jungle. Just as he lunged forward, a microwave oven hurtled from above, grazing his shoulder, and knocked him to his knees. Kendall raised the chair and brought it down on Wade's head, but it only knocked him on all fours, its flimsy wire frame insufficient to knock him out.

Wade crouched at Kendall's feet, the blade still gripped in one hand that was pressed against the ground. The blade glistened in the moonlight. And suddenly Kendall remembered. He looked down at this man who wanted to kill him and it all came back, a tsunami that had been gathering strength for twenty-three years. He saw the masked figures, the firelight, the angry faces, the flash of the blade, and the eyes of another man who wanted to kill him. Because he was different.

A siren grew closer. Kendall tossed aside the chair and picked up the battered microwave oven. He raised it over his head. Wade staggered to his feet and jumped back. Kendall threw the microwave at him, but Wade was already running back into the building.

The Bone Man scurried down the fire escape. "Are you all right?"

Kendall looked down at his leg. The blood had seeped through the tear where the knife had sliced open his pants. "Just one cut, but hurts like hell."

A police officer appeared at the bedroom window with her gun drawn. She shouted for Kendall and Vince to put up their hands. Only after they had been cuffed did the police sort out the story of what had happened, and released them. Helen arrived for dinner in the midst of the hubbub, finding police swarming the building in search of Wade. An ambulance was summoned to transport Kendall to the hospital. His mother climbed in the ambulance with him. He had not known how banged up he was until the other points of pain began to throb. An attendant cut open his pant leg and wrapped the wound with gauze.

Just before the doors of the ambulance closed, Kendall looked at the Bone Man and said, "Thanks for helping me out there."

The Bone Man shrugged nonchalantly. "Any time, my friend."

Witchfinder General

Kendall

Helen Akande sat next to her son's hospital bed, waiting for him to be discharged after the wound had been stitched up.

"I had a vision while Wade was trying to kill me," Kendall said. "It's happened before, hasn't it?" He saw the distress in his mother's eyes. "Tell me. I need to know what happened back in Nigeria."

She looked out the window and took a deep breath. "The people in our town always resented me. I was too modern, too

215

independent. College educated. Married a white man, broke too many taboos. Then you came along. Even as a small child, I could tell you were different from the other boys." She smiled at the memory. "You liked playing with dolls. Our differences—yours and mine—did not sit well with some of those small-minded people. The rumors started after your father died and I had to return to live with your aunt and uncle. Some people said we were witches."

"So why didn't you just leave?"

"That's what I did. Eventually. But not before some of the villagers tried to kill us. I'll tell you what happened."

The witchfinder, prophet Moses Okon, slipped the three boys some money and told them to run to suspicious houses looking for witch medicine. "You know who is hiding it," he said. "Bring it all back to me."

Everyone had heard about Okon's arrival. His periodic visits were eagerly anticipated as he made the circuit through different towns. A crowd gathered in the plaza, waiting to hear his revelations. He paced back and forth, his chest puffed out like a strutting quail. A short time later the boys returned with several gourds and placed them on the ground at Okon's feet. He picked up the first gourd and held it to his nose. "Who is the owner of this gourd?"

One of the boys pointed to Abeni Bankole. Okon sniffed the gourd and declared it to be good. He repeated the process with the second gourd. The owner, Mary Oluranti, fell to her knees pleading and sobbing. Okon sniffed the gourd and waited dramatically before declaring it to be bad. Mary confessed to being a witch. Okon asked her what objects she had used to practice witchcraft. *An old lantern to light the way, a wooden staff, a piece of stone.* He made her promise before God to stop practicing, and told her she must surrender two chickens, a goat, and a liter of palm wine, as well as pay a small fine. He held his hand over her head and pronounced her cured.

"Is there anyone else who joined you as a witch?" he asked.

Mary remained silent, staring at the ground.

"You know there is someone else." Okon's voice was confident and insistent. "Don't hide the truth, woman. The evil must be rooted out. If you want God's forgiveness."

She named Helen Akande.

Okon picked up the third gourd and tossed it casually in his hand like a ball. He asked the boys to identify the owner, and one pointed to Helen. She had one arm draped over Kendall's shoulder as he clutched her leg.

"That belonged to my husband," said Helen. "He liked to collect cultural objects."

A woman in the crowd called out, "She killed him with her medicine," and the villagers shifted uncomfortably on their feet.

Pastor Azebry stood in the back of the crowd, a tall, thin man who towered over the others. He wore a shimmering blue jacket edged in gold that would not have been out of place on an eighties rock star. A large gold cross with a diamond on each point hung from a heavy chain around his neck. One hand grasped the iron Opa Osooro, the Yoruban salvation staff. He nodded silently to Okon.

Okon sniffed the gourd and drew back as if bitten. "This gourd... This gourd is very bad. It has bad medicine."

"There's nothing in it. It's empty," protested Helen.

Okon let the gourd fall back to the earth. "It's empty now. But not before, when it contained your witch medicine. Helen Akande, confess your sin before God, that you and your son are witches. If you confess, I will cleanse you and return you to good standing, just like Mary Oluranti."

Kendall hid his face in Helen's pant leg.

"I will do no such thing. I'm not a witch, and neither is my son. I've done nothing wrong."

"Oye Taiwo saw you sitting in a tree eating the flesh of her dying uncle. Others say that you turn into an owl at night and fly over the houses spreading evil, and that your son caused Abeni Bankole's daughter to die by looking at her with an evil eye."

A male voice called out from the crowd. "I had a dream where she summoned me to play my drum at an assembly of witches."

A gruff, male voice spoke up, and Helen's brother Gideon stepped forward. "Neighbors, this is nonsense. Helen goes to church, like most of us."

"But not Pastor Azebry's church," someone called out.

"Are you saying that as a Christian there is only one church a godly person can attend?"

Okon was not dissuaded. "How else do we know that she goes to church, then? Or that she does not secretly worship Satan in her heart?"

Helen raised her head defiantly. "Going to one particular church doesn't make you a devout person any more than going to a certain garage makes you a mechanic."

217

Gideon addressed Okon. "Look at you. More interested in the money and gifts you can earn through your cleansing ritual than in saving souls. Pretending you can smell a witch's medicine in an old gourd." He spat on the ground.

Murmurs and gasps rippled through the crowd at Gideon's affront to Okon's honor.

Pastor Azebry stamped the Opa Osooro three times on the ground. The agogo at the end of the staff tinkled with each thump. "Brother Okon has spoken truthfully. Bad things have been happening, and someone is to blame. If Helen Akande will not confess to her sin, then I cannot protect her. God cannot protect her." He turned away.

Okon glared at Helen. "We are not finished with you, woman."

Helen returned with Gideon to his house, expressing regret that she had come back to the town to stay with him and his wife. She announced that she would leave in the morning and return to Lagos to find work. It would be difficult, a young widow with a four-year-old son, but what alternative did she have? She had heard the stories about what happened to others who had been accused of witchcraft, despite the official laws on the books that prohibited such accusations. Beatings. Ostracism. Banishment. Occasionally murder. Children abandoned and left to die in the bush.

But late that night, five men entered their house and kidnapped Helen and Kendall. One of the men kept Gideon and his wife at bay with a machete.

The men took Helen and Kendall to a clearing just outside town where Okon waited before a fire with two men wearing Gelede masks atop their heads. A white cloth hung from the masks, covering their faces like a shroud. The abductors bound the hands and feet of both Helen and Kendall with twine while the Gelede dancers stamped and twirled their protection ritual against witches. One man ripped open the back of Helen's blouse while another held a knife to Kendall's throat and told him not to move or cry out.

Prophet Okon squatted by the fire, heating a machete in its flames. "Now you have another chance to confess, Helen Akande." He lifted the blade of the machete, glowing a bright red, and held it over her back. "Confess. Confess that you are a witch."

"How can I lie before God and say I am something that I am not?"

Okon pressed the blade against her skin, releasing the smell of burning flesh. Helen screamed. "In the name of God, have mercy! I swear I am innocent!"

The blade left its imprint across her back. "Confess, Helen Akande, and God will forgive you."

A group of men emerged into the clearing, led by Gideon. His voice boomed out. "You are outnumbered, Brother Okon. Put down the machete and release them. I promise they will leave tomorrow and not return."

Okon rose to his feet, the machete glowing like Satan's branding iron. He surveyed the other band of men, saw their stern and unforgiving faces in the firelight. Okon instructed his men to untie Helen and Kendall. She clutched the back of her blouse to keep it from slipping off, and with the other hand led Kendall to her protectors.

"There are no witches here," continued Gideon. "But I do see devils."

"We are only bringing back purity to a corrupt world," said Okon.

Helen spun around, her eyes flashing with anger. "You are the corruption that the world laments. May God have mercy on you for what you have done in his name."

Helen finished the story. "And so we left. We went back to Lagos for a short time. Then your Aunt Abbie urged us to join her in Canada, and that's how we ended up here."

"Why didn't you tell me all of this before?"

"I wanted to protect you from the memory. You were so young, I thought perhaps you would forget about it eventually. I didn't want it to hang over you like a machete, the way it has with me." She reached around to touch her back. "I still have the scar. Your scar is different, but you have one all the same."

Kendall took his mother's hand. "Now it all makes sense. It's like completing a huge puzzle. The panic, the nightmares." He thought of the photo of his mother and father taken in Nigeria on their wedding day. His mother in white, with lace-embroidered sleeves that came down just below the elbows. His father broadly smiling, dark wavy hair down to his collar, sensuous lips. "Tell me about my father. What was he like?"

Helen looked at him with surprise. She thought a moment, then shook her head and smiled. "Funny. Always making me laugh.

He had a wonderful sense of humor. I brought him to our town a few times. He did a hilarious imitation of Brother Okon for me and Uncle Gideon. He knew every tic, strutting back and forth with his chin sticking out and making us laugh until my stomach hurt. A kind man. So gentle. He loved to quote Chinua Achebe. Let me see if I can remember it. Mmm." She closed her eyes. "Yes. *The world is like a Mask dancing. If you want to see it well, you do not stand in one place.*"

"I wish I'd known him."

"He loved you very much. He called you his little turnip."

Jenna appeared in the doorway. "Thank God you're all right. The police told us you'd been taken to St. Michael's."

Kendall modeled the gauze patch over his wound. "Stitched up like Frankenstein, but almost as good as new. It was just a light slash. But so much blood, diva. My pants are ruined."

Jenna greeted Helen and came over to stand beside the bed. "The police are still there. They poured over the building but can't find any trace of Wade. Turnbull is coming in the morning to change all the locks."

"He must be devastated. I can't imagine the humiliation." He looked at his mother, who patted his good leg.

Jenna fingered a fold in the bed sheet, then smoothed it out. "I owe you an apology. I'm sorry for the things I said the other night. The truth is, I *am* a little jealous of your relationship with Lilith."

Kendall took her hand. "Diva, no one is going to replace you in my life. Not even a boyfriend. We are like this." With his other hand, he crossed two fingers. "And anyway, you're not the only one who exercised poor judgment. I owe you an apology. You were right about the Bone Man. I was wrong. He helped me fight Wade."

"Well, then, I feel at least partly vindicated."

Helen looked from Kendall to Jenna. "Who on earth is the Bone Man?"

Kendall and Jenna laughed, then provided a rundown on Vince's background and the incidents that had made Kendall so suspicious.

The nurse came in and said the hospital was ready to release Kendall. She held out a clipboard with some papers to sign. "You got off easy with that knife wound. It could have been much worse. You're a very lucky man, Mr. Akande."

Kendall reached his hands out to touch Helen and Jenna. "Yes, I certainly am."

9

Excerpt from Shockadelica Podcast
Episode 53: The Púca in Film and Literature

Jenna: The most famous example of a púca in film is the 1950 comedy-drama *Harvey* starring James Stewart, who starts having visions of a giant rabbit named Harvey. In the film, the púca is a benign presence who is fond of social outcasts.

Kendall: The 2001 film *Donnie Darko*, directed by Richard Kelly, offers a very different take. Jake Gyllenhaal plays a troubled teen who is plagued by visions of a man in a frightening rabbit suit—it's hard to imagine what could be frightening about a rabbit costume unless you've seen the movie—who manipulates him to commit a series of crimes.

Jenna: It's not the cuddly rabbit from *Harvey*.

Kendall: No! Not at all.

Jenna: When I saw the movie I had no idea that was a púca.

Kendall: I don't think most people did. It's not explicit. How many people even know what a púca is? I certainly didn't until recently.

Jenna: In 2018, the series *Into the Dark* featured an episode titled *Pooka!*, in which an unemployed actor accepts a job portraying a stuffed toy, but the pooka costume starts taking over his life with terrifying results.

Kendall: So popular culture equates púcas with giant rabbits, whether they're cuddly or scary.

Jenna: But that's only one of the púca's manifestations.

Kendall: From what I've learned, it's better known as a supernatural horse that gives wild night rides.

Jenna: There's a fifteen-minute German short titled *Puca* from 2004, directed by Tanja Böning. Have you seen it?

Kendall: No.

Jenna: A fourteen-year-old girl follows an enticing, androgynous character into a fantasy realm to escape from her constricted life. It has echoes of a macabre *Alice in Wonderland*. The androgynous character is kind of like the white rabbit that beckons Alice. And like in *Donnie Darko*, once inside the strange world of the púca, she is inspired to commit a violent act.

Kendall: Sounds interesting. I've got to check that out.

Jenna: Apart from children's books and folk tale collections, it's hard to find examples of púcas in literature. Certainly nothing that has the visibility of the films we mentioned. But Flann O'Brien, who is a major figure in twentieth-century Irish literature, wrote a modernist, satirical novel, *At Swim-Two-Birds*, that has a character named The Pooka MacPhellimey, who is a sort of devilish human. Not a púca in the traditional sense, but drawing on certain associations. Then some people consider Puck in *A Midsummer Night's Dream* to be related to a púca. He's a clever, mischievous fairy.

Kendall: And there's the similarity between the names Puck and púca.

Jenna: Exactly.

Kendall: So is a púca frightening or comedic? I see both threads in film and literature.

Jenna: That's the interesting thing. Like many trickster characters, the púca has one foot in both the comic and the horrific.

Kendall: And if you happen to run into a púca, treat it with a lot of respect. Believe me, you'll be glad you did.

Wrong Bitch

Kendall

After being released from the hospital, Kendall spent Friday night at his mother's house. Jenna did likewise with her family. He texted Lilith, concerned about her welfare, and she replied that she was staying with a friend. Where the other tenants spent the night, he had no idea.

Turnbull had promised everyone that the locks would be changed first thing Saturday morning. Kendall met up with Jenna at noon at Covington Terrace. Turnbull sat at Rooney's kitchen table with the door open, dispensing keys. His shock of white hair looked disheveled, as if he had not slept well.

"It's such a nuisance to have to do this to every single lock throughout the building," said Turnbull, handing each of them their new keys. "Not to mention the expense."

Kendall though it odd that the man would express his regret about changing the locks but not a word about his son the wanted killer. Then again, what could he say—*Sorry that my son tried to kill you yesterday*? If Turnbull knew that Wade had attacked Kendall, he did not mention it. Perhaps he wanted to believe that someone else might have been under the goat mask. After all, when the police had questioned Kendall, he had mentioned Wade's name and said his attacker wore a goat mask. Had he seen the face of the person beneath the goat mask? Well, no... But who else could it have been?

"Do you have any idea where your son might have gone?" asked Jenna.

"The police asked me the same thing. I have no idea. He still hasn't been home."

Jenna shifted her duffel bag to her other hand. "Do they think he might have—you know—killed Rooney?"

Turnbull sighed wearily. "They didn't say. But clearly it's a possibility." He looked down at the floor and muttered something inaudible. Then he lifted his head. "Do you have time to come see me on the island later after I'm finished here? I have something I would like to show you."

Kendall shrugged. "Sure, I guess so."

"Good. I discovered it last night in Wade's room, after the detectives left. I haven't shown it to anyone." He excused himself to answer a knock on the building's front door.

Kendall looked out the window and saw Mrs. Gupta's daughter carrying two suitcases. He limped into the hall, and as soon as the door opened he shouted Mrs. Gupta's name. They hugged.

"Ah, Kenny, it's good to be back. I came as soon as Mr. Turnbull contacted me this morning."

"And we're so happy you've returned," said Kendall.

"I knew I wasn't imagining things," said Mrs. Gupta as she followed Turnbull into Rooney's apartment for her new keys. "You believe me now?"

"We always believed you," said Jenna. "We were just trying to figure out what the logical explanation was."

Mrs. Gupta looked around the apartment. "Where's Rooney?"

"She disappeared several weeks ago," Kendall said. He lowered his voice to a whisper, even though Turnbull could likely hear. "We think Wade killed her."

Mrs. Gupta drew a sharp breath. "Oh, how awful."

Kendall rolled up his pant leg to reveal his bandage. "He attacked me, too." Kendall looked back at Turnbull, feeling sheepish for talking so openly about the misdeeds of his son.

Mrs. Gupta expressed her shock, saying she had not known any of the details of the incident, only that Wade had attacked a tenant and fled. Kendall reassured her that they would be secure with the new locks.

Mrs. Gupta's daughter picked up the suitcases that had been resting at her feet. "Okay, mother, let's get you settled back in. I still have to go in to the office to catch up on some work this afternoon."

Kendall followed Jenna upstairs. He wanted to see if the Bone Man had returned home yet. Kendall found it hard to suppress a smile when Vince opened the door. "That was quite an adventure yesterday."

"Did everything check out at the hospital?"

"Oh, yeah. It was not a deep cut, fortunately."

The Bone Man invited them in. Kendall had not been back to the apartment since the day when boxes lay scattered about. The home recording studio stood in a corner of the living room, black monitor speakers perched above the desk like huge crows on either side of a computer screen. Cables snaked from the desk to a fortress of electronic keyboards. A Fender electric guitar rested in a stand against the wall.

"So this is where the musical mayhem happens."

"Yep. It's my own little musical Frankenstein lab."

"I have to confess something, Kendall," said Jenna. "I recorded an interview with Vince for the podcast. Without you."

Kendall bent over one of the keyboards, studying the array of knobs. "Fair enough. I deserved that after..." He looked at the Bone Man and swallowed hard. It was not easy to admit to prejudice. "That brings me to what I came up here to say. First off, I want to thank you again."

"Yeah, no worries, dude."

"And then I owe you an apology."

"For what?"

"I misjudged you. I thought you were the person I needed to fear instead of the real culprit. But I still don't understand, why did you want to move in here?"

"I thought I could figure out what happened to Alyssa. I had my suspicions that something happened to her here. She vanished during the night, while she was at home, and I believed this place held the key. It was my way to try to achieve closure. Now I have a pretty good idea what happened to her, even if I don't have the complete picture."

"You think she still might be alive?"

The Bone Man played a melancholy musical riff on the keyboard. He said nothing, but just shook his head.

"I saw you sneaking around the basement one night. You didn't see me, but I watched you break into the storage room."

"Ah, so you were spying on me."

227

Kendall smiled guiltily. "Yes. I admit it. Feel free to put me in the stocks so people can laugh and throw tomatoes at me."

"No, man, it's okay. I'm just teasing. I understand why you would be suspicious. I was trying to figure out the layout of this place. Something still doesn't add up, but whatever. I'll keep trying to poke around down there."

Kendall leaned back and looked into the kitchen. "I suppose I owe you a new microwave."

The Bone Man let out a raucous laugh. "We'll make Turnbull pay for it. After all, his son is to blame." The smile vanished in a flash, leaving behind the Bone Man's normally gruff look. "Are you worried that Wade will show up again?"

"A little. I always try to look at all the possibilities. I don't think it's likely, but he could steal the new master keys from his dad."

"Tell you what. I'm going to install a security chain on my door. I'll help you both put one in, too, if you want."

"That would be fantastic. Maybe we should recommend it for everybody in the building."

His House

Jenna

The brisk, cold wind kept them on the protected lower level of the ferry. Only a handful of other passengers occupied the wooden benches, huddled in their dark coats and knitted tuques, silent like statues. *Almost like mourners on their way to a funeral*, thought Jenna. One teenage girl apparently had not expected the temperature to plunge so much, and shivered in a charcoal pullover. Snow flurries danced in the air on their way tumbling down from the low, grey clouds.

"I can't believe winter is coming so early this year," said Jenna.

228

Kendall mumbled his assent and stuffed his hands deeper in his pockets. "In all the hubbub, I forgot to tell you, I found out who the mystery tenant is."

"Who?"

"Marvin Gumbal."

"Not *the* Marvin Gumbal?"

"One and the same. Lilith and I got to talk to him a couple of days ago when she accidentally received some of his mail." Kendall shared what little he had learned before Marvin kicked them out. "The images in the boiler room and the disappearances inspired him to write the novel and gave him the idea for a satanic cult that abducted people."

"To think that the author was in our very own backyard."

"Little did he know his fictional creation has a real-life counterpart. Not a satanic cult, but something demonic all the same."

As they walked to Turnbull's house, Jenna pulled her tuque down more tightly over her ears. Snowflakes tickled her nose. Those that reached the ground immediately melted, vanishing into the asphalt. Neither of them spoke, the mood as leaden as the sky.

The inside of the house felt only marginally warmer than outside. Kendall and Jenna kept on their coats. Turnbull motioned for them to sit and disappeared into the back.

Jenna pointed to a painting sitting on the floor that had not been there during previous visits. "Kendall, look! It's a púca painting by Brian Bailey."

The painting of a man with the head of a goat looked much like those in the museum, but with two sets of arms and legs outstretched like Da Vinci's *Vitruvian Man*. In similar fashion, the body was naked and covered everywhere except the genitals in fine black hair.

Turnbull returned to the room carrying a book. "Oh, I see you've noticed the painting. I don't keep it out because of, obviously, the—well, the sensitive depiction of the..." He trailed off and gestured toward the goat-man's groin.

"How did you get a hold of this?" asked Jenna.

"Brian Bailey was Emma's—my wife's—great-grandfather. He used to live at Covington Terrace when he was a poor, starving artist. Never made much money from his art. But late in his life he met a patron, a woman from a prominent Irish family. They married, and bought the property to preserve the drawings he had made on the walls in the boiler room." He held out the book to Jenna. "I brought the painting out because of what I saw in this journal."

Jenna opened the journal, which was filled with scribblings and crude drawings of goat-men. She thumbed through the pages, reading some of the entries.

> *Goat = Vitality Virility Visibility Vindication.*

> *Goat = Horn. The horn that brought down the walls of Jericho.*

> *The horned beasts. Goat. Gazelle. Marchor. Oryx. Ibex. Saiga. Bharal. Blackbuck. Addax. Antelope. Mouflon. Roan. Reedbuck. Eland. Springbok. Gemsbok. Impala. Nyala. Takin. Wildebeest. Chamois. Duiker. Tur. Kudu. Kob. Oribi.*

> *He is the beginning and the end. The ancient one. Coming to purify the world. He will restore balance, and separate the pure from the corrupt.*

> *I am destined to carry out his wishes. I have been chosen. He reached out to me through the drawings, telling me this will be my purpose.*

> *I've been going to Monmouth's grave at the Necropolis, waiting for the goat-man to enter me. I felt the spirit rise up out of the earth, freed from its chains, and enter my body.*

List of Undesirables

Marvin Gumbal
Elliott Bernbaum
Lucy Lee
V. Gupta
Lilith Adebayo
Jenna Chen
Kendall Akande
Vince Fournier

"I take it Wade knew about the building's history, and Monmouth's journal?" asked Jenna.

Turnbull nodded. "The stories were passed down through the family." He retrieved the goat skull that Jenna had seen during her last visit with Elliott. "Wade loved all of the goat images in my collection. When he was older, and I trusted him to come into the parlor alone, sometimes I would find him just sitting in here, staring at this skull."

"Do you know what happened to Monmouth?" asked Kendall. "What made him become obsessed?"

"He found the drawings in the boiler room. It must have sparked something in his mind. He began to think he was the incarnation of the goat-man. But the real question—why those drawings spoke to him in that way—no one can ever know."

"And the same thing happened to Wade," said Jenna, closing the journal.

Turnbull stood before them, looking broken and pitiful. "I've gone over things a thousand times. I can't figure out where Emma and I went wrong. I didn't want to say this before, and it's even hard to say it now, but she killed herself. Maybe it was the shock of her suicide that did something to his young psyche."

"Sometimes there aren't easy answers," said Kendall. "It might not have been anything you and your wife did or didn't do. Maybe people sometimes just catch bad ideas like viruses that are always around us, floating in the air."

231

"History repeats itself," Turnbull muttered.

Jenna reached out and touched his arm as the old man wept.

A Head Full of Ghosts
Wade

I remember the first time I saw the goat-man drawings. I was thirteen. My father had started teaching me to help him with simple repairs. He showed me how to hold two-by-fours while he measured and sawed. How to turn off the water. How to unscrew the light fixture. "Someday this will all be your responsibility," he said. He took me into the boiler room to show me the heating system. With its gauges and pipes, it excited me like nothing I had ever seen. And there, scribbled on the wall, were the images. Just black lines against the white wall, but coursing with energy. Like the heat surging through the boiler pipes. They filled me with an electric rush. The sinewy muscles. The long, erect horns. I placed my finger on one of the drawings, tracing its outline.

"Don't do that," my father said. "Those are family artifacts." I looked at the tip of my finger where the graphite had rubbed onto me. "When we get home, I'll show you a painting I have in storage," he said. "You'll see the same type of image, painted by your great-great-grandfather."

As I grew older, I would borrow my father's keys and go into the boiler room, just to sit and stare at the drawings. I tried sketching them in a notebook. They lacked the refinement of the wall drawings. But they still had power.

I remember once, when I was a child, I overheard the adults talk about William Monmouth and what happened in apartment six. "Do you think he should be hearing this?" someone asked my mother, nodding toward me. She took me out of the room. That just made me burn with curiosity. Later I learned the details. How he lured victims to his apartment and murdered them. He never wore a goat mask, as far as I know, but he wrote that the drawings had inspired him.

My mother died a year after I first saw the drawings. Killed herself. I knew I was supposed to feel sad, but I felt nothing. I sat in my bedroom, trying to force myself to cry. The adults seemed to be able to cry so easily. Even my father was able to turn on the waterworks. Me? Nothing. I kept expecting something to happen. After enough time passed, I just accepted that nothing would come and moved on. My father would tell people that I was taking it especially hard. Told them I was in denial. I think he made that up because he was embarrassed by my apathy.

After her death, my father started to withdraw from Covington Terrace, little by little. He spent more and more time focusing on his collection. Every week some new item would appear. He spent days scouting for antiques all over the Greater Toronto Area, or ordering things on the Internet. As a kid, I had wanted to play with the animated execution scene and other objects, but he always warned me not to touch anything and stay out of the room. He would sometimes give me permission to drop a coin into the mechanism in his presence. Together we would watch the trap door open up and the miniature body drop, swinging from the noose. Not until after my mother died did he let me go into that room on my own. I remember the day he brought home the goat skull. I was sixteen. Now, looking back, I know it was a sign, showing me my future.

In those years right after my mother's death, my father still visited Covington Terrace whenever a repair was needed, with me in tow. If we were in the common areas, Marvin Gumbal would creep out of his apartment to watch us. He reminded me of a hairy trapdoor spider. He'd bring me sodas and try to talk, all friendly like. I've never been much for talk, so I'd basically just listen. I knew what he wanted, but I wasn't about to go for that crap. One day he was so upset. Something had set him off, I could tell. He didn't reveal the details, but he felt compelled to share his bitterness about whatever had happened to him.

"People disappoint you," he said. "They're vile and cruel, and they want nothing better than to hurt you. The sooner you learn that, the better off you'll be. I'd just as soon see them all wiped off the face of the earth."

What he said reminded me of Monmouth. I didn't yet know what I was destined for. But another seed had been planted.

My father asked me what I wanted to be after high school. I shrugged my shoulders. I fell into construction work without intending to. It just happened, the way water follows a path downhill. That's the way everything happened to me. It was that way with the girls I dated. It was that way with becoming the maintenance man for Covington Terrace. With becoming the goat-man. All I had to do was open myself like a receptacle and let whatever waited out there fill me up.

You can spend hours on the Internet. One thing leads to another. Click, click, click. That's how I came across the forum where people complained how certain groups were taking over the world. Minorities. Gays. Jews. Foreigners. I thought about the kinds of people we were renting to at Covington Terrace. It was true. I'd never given it much thought before. But they were right. *Undesirables*. Just like Monmouth had written.

I found the goat head mask on one of the curio sites my father frequented. It was constructed out of wire mesh and papier-mâché, covered with real fur and sprouting two authentic horns. When I put it on, it made me feel powerful. Transformed. Like I was somebody else. A superhero putting on his costume. It made me feel destined for something special. I still did not know what shape that would take, but it was another seed planted inside me. The drawings. The gritty goat images my father collected. My great-great-grandfather's paintings. They were all messages, just for me, pointing the way.

I did not intend to kill the woman who lived in apartment six. I'm not talking about the one with the musician boyfriend—I'll get to her in a minute. I'm talking about the first one. We dated for a few months. Then one day I drugged her and took her to my secret space. Why did I do it? She didn't discover my network of passageways like Rooney did, which forced me to lock Rooney up (and which I regretted having to do). But she was going to dump me. I heard her say that to a friend on the phone when I was hiding in the wall, listening. She was getting ready to leave me, just like my mother had.

I can hear you thinking right now, *Oh, so that explains it, he has abandonment issues.* But that explains nothing. I felt nothing when my mother died. I already told you that. Anyway, it's too simplistic a reason. What I believe is that Monmouth's ghost was speaking to me, because he had lived in that apartment. He gave me the idea. Not that I mean his ghost was actually stalking the apartment. I don't believe in ghosts. I'm just speaking symbolically.

I laid the body out in my lab. I wanted to see what made her tick. I wanted to find some explanation for why she wanted to leave me. My father was so stupid. He never figured out what I had built when I did the renovation. Too obsessed with his collection by that time to notice. I opened up the torso using a circular saw, and examined all of the organs. The stomach. The sausage-like intestines. The slimy brown bulge of the liver. I held the heart in my hand, turning it around and around. It didn't look like the drawing a kid makes on Valentine's Day. It looked like a dark red blob. A small nothing. I put it in a glass jar with preservative. Then I cut up the body. I put the head in a container of acid and watched the tissue melt away, turning to skull.

I know you must think that I had planned this all along. Why else would I have built the lab? It's true, I was curious to know what made people act the way they did. I wanted to cut them up and see what was on the inside. But I never intended that she would be the one I would end up studying. I always thought it would be some stranger.

When the musician's girlfriend moved into that apartment— Alyssa, that was her name—I started spying on her. I would watch her through a tiny hole in the bedroom wall. I took Alyssa away from the musician because she reminded me of the girl who had preceded her. I didn't think ahead to how things would end. Once I had her chained up in the cell, letting her go was out of the question. I stupidly thought if she saw me dressed as the goat-man she would recognize my power. She would be overcome with desire, and let me have her. I never touched her, though, I swear. But when she refused my advances, I stopped feeding her. Each day, with her life draining away, I felt less and less emotion. My desire for her withered with her body. By the time she died, I no longer felt anything at all.

I'm not much of a reader, so I never read that book, *I Dined with Satan*, that everybody was talking about. For a while it was all over the news. But I'd heard the controversy and knew what it was about from what people posted online. People said it was part of a big conspiracy, part of QAnon. Abductions, child sacrifice, mind control. Stuff like that. The evil reached into the highest levels of the government, they said. *A cult of liberal elites hell-bent on converting the world to their twisted lifestyle.* That's what some people had written. It reminded me again of Monmouth and undesirables. When news broke claiming that the book was a made-up story, people started saying that the cult was trying to cover its tracks. They said the cult got scared because the truth had been exposed. Another seed. Soon these seeds would burst forth and my purpose would come to fruition.

I had been going to Monmouth's grave in the Necropolis ever since I found out about him. I would sit on the grass beside the tombstone, in a kind of meditation, waiting for his spirit to speak to me. My finger traced the carved letters of his name, just as my finger had traced the goat-man drawings. *What is my purpose?* I began bringing the goat mask with me, hoping it would help channel his spirit. Nothing. I grew frustrated with the silence, and one day defaced the tombstone with a crowbar. Then I knocked it off its foundation. I know you'll think it was planned because I had brought a crowbar with me, but I swear to you it wasn't planned. All at once, I felt something enter my body, filling my empty receptacle. I finally understood my purpose. I realized that, by breaking open the grave marker, I had broken the seal to allow his spirit to pass into me. It took an act of violence to bring him alive.

A great joy filled me. I understood my mission was to continue what he had started over eight decades earlier. To rid the world of its impurity. That was it. So straightforward. I was amazed I hadn't realized it sooner. The easiest place to start was Covington Terrace, infested with impurity. I figured out I had the perfect opportunity to fulfill my destiny. Plus I could get a rush frightening the undesirables in the process. It was all part of the grand design.

Killing the Syrian family that hired me to fix up their property turned out to be an unexpected bonus. But I never should have rented to the musician. That was my mistake. I should have torn up his application. Then the musician wouldn't have been there to interfere with my plan. Well, it was only a temporary setback. They would all soon find out.

10

Excerpt from Shockadelica Podcast
Episode 19: Diversity and Horror Fiction
Guest: Author Tenisha Wilson

Jenna: One of the things you hear from people who object to
            efforts to encourage all forms of diversity is, "I don't care
            about the sexuality, gender, color, et cetera, of the
            writer—I just care about good stories."

Tenisha: As long as the writing is attentive to diversity in a
            thoughtful way, sure, you don't have to know anything
            about the author. But it matters to me because it's
            important to fight the tendency to ignore voices from
            backgrounds different from your own. We all have that
            tendency—which cultural institutions often magnify—so
            explicit encouragement is a helpful antidote.

Kendall: You're a gay, black, female author. What's the biggest
            misconception about your writing, or about the writing by
            your colleagues from diverse backgrounds?

Tenisha: That you have to be gay, or black, or a woman, or
            whatever to appreciate it.

Kendall: Here, here. I know when I read horror novels, I like to see
            characters from diverse backgrounds, not just my own or
            that of the author. In your opinion, what mistake do
            authors make when portraying characters who are from
            backgrounds different from their own?

Tenisha: The trap for any author is falling back on tropes rather
            than imaging how a character would behave as an actual
            human being. You know, the screaming woman who

always trips as she flees the killer. The black or Asian sidekick whose main purpose is to say to the white protagonist, "Are you okay?"

Jenna: Why do you write horror?

Tenisha: Fear is one of our most primitive, powerful emotions. It can motivate us to make positive change or it can spook us to cause harm. Horror speaks directly to these deep impulses. But horror resonates with me in another way as well. Because it often deals with the supernatural—with aspects of reality hidden behind a veil, or with things that may not be what they appear—it addresses our uncertainty about the world. It explores that fluid boundary between what is "real" and what is imagined. When you hear that knocking on the wall, is it really just old pipes, or something else?

Halloween

Kendall

Kendall sat at the vanity desk in his bedroom, his version of a star's dressing room with large round bulbs framing the mirror, and examined his face. The makeup had turned out quite well, and he felt pride at having pulled off this alternate look after having surrendered his original idea when he gave the dress to Lucas a week earlier. He also credited Lucas, or at least certain things Lucas had said, with prompting this burst of creativity that stared back at him. Inspired by Nina Bo'nina Brown's skull-face look—which he had first seen on the ninth season of RuPaul's *Drag Race*—and by the horror looks of local drag artist Yovska, Kendall had developed his own variation: dark kohl encircling the eyes against a turquoise base; skeletal teeth painted over the lips; and rhinestones, dots, and flourishes outlining cheekbones, eye sockets, and eyebrows like a *Día de Los Muertos* sugar skull. He rose from the vanity to don the rest of his outfit. Framing the skull face would be an elaborate gold headpiece with two twisting goat horns modeled after those of the púca. Beneath a black and purple Maleficent cloak he would wear a black body suit painted with bones in psychedelic colors. Wide turquoise soutache bracelets would adorn his wrists.

In the other room, he heard Jenna welcoming the neighbors as they arrived. She had dressed as a black cat: a furry head piece with cat ears, a long-sleeved black dress cinched at the waist, black leggings, and paw-like gloves with her fingertips poking through the finger holes. A limp tail protruded from the rear of the dress. Black makeup smudged the tip of her nose, and she had drawn black whisker-like lines across her cheeks. Lilith was the first to arrive. Kendall knew she was planning to dress as a witch, albeit a colorful, festive one. Elliott arrived next, and Kendall heard him say to Jenna, "Oh, I get it. You're supposed to be Lilith's black cat."

"No, I'm just a cat," explained Jenna. "We didn't coordinate our costumes."

As a finishing touch, Kendall strapped on his heels. Inspired by the Manolo Blahnick design he had seen at the Bata Shoe Museum, he had tied small bones to the strip of shoe that climbed up his ankle. It was a subtle touch, because most people would only see his upper body as he paraded through the crowds on Church Street. But he knew the shoes were there.

Morvena arrived and said to Jenna, "And you must be Lilith's familiar."

Jenna, with a touch of annoyance: "No, I'm just a cat. A plain old black cat, not anyone's familiar."

Kendall waited for the others to assemble so he could make his grand entrance. He had tacked up a bedsheet as a makeshift curtain where the hall connected to the living room, and stood behind it, trying to control his breathing.

Once the last neighbor arrived, Jenna made the announcement. "And now, ladies and gentlemen, the unveiling. Tonight marks the demise of La Chandelle. I present to you, instead, the fabulous—ta dah!"—Kendall swept aside the curtain and stepped through— "Shockadelica!"

Kendall struck his best pose, body twisted slightly to the side, chin held high, one arm stretched up toward the ceiling. Everyone applauded, with oohs and ahs. He had to admit, the outfit was even more striking than what he had originally planned with the silver dress. Surrendering those plans had been a blessing in disguise. He still did not know what to make of his encounters with Lucas. It had all been so uncanny, the kind of thing that happened only in old tales from another time and place. Yet it had happened to him. He would never reveal the details to anyone but Jenna and Lilith. Who would believe it?

Morvena, reprising her bell-bottom look from the photo on her wall, held an unlit cigarette in her hand, eager for one last smoke before they succumbed to the rigors of a smoke-free bar. "What happened to the silver dress? Not that you don't still look fabulous, darling, but I was all ready for a vision in silver."

Kendall read the look of amusement in Jenna's face—the look that said, *Try to explain that one.* "It's a long story. Let's just say I had to improvise a different solution late in the game."

Vince had put on his full Bone Man drag: a top hat ringed with small skulls; a long, black cloak; and the skull face makeup. His black-and-white look complemented Kendall's fiesta skeleton.

Lilith showed off her costume. "As an act of power, I'm reclaiming the image of the witch from its appropriation by society-at-large." A cross between what a witch and a princess might wear, the dress and pointed hat were a blend of green, turquoise, and purple material, the dress covered by a transparent overlay sporting a black spiral motif. Puffy short sleeves and black boots completed the look.

Lucy had dressed as an eggplant, covering her torso and upper legs with an assembly of dark purple garbage bags that Jenna had helped her make. Wires inside the costume supported the eggplant shape. She had painted her face purple and wore a green beret with a stem poking out of the top. Instead of a costume, Mrs. Gupta displayed intricate henna designs on her face and hands. She looked like a piece of art. Elliott had placed on his head a band with two red devil horns and called it a day.

Naturally, Marvin had chosen not to come.

Walking over to Church Street, Kendall's gaily painted skull face turned heads and generated smiles. Arriving at Dante's, they ran into Tipsy Hedrin, who did a doubletake when she saw Kendall.

"Tonight, I am reborn as Shockadelica," Kendall explained.

Tipsy delicately applauded her gloved hands. "What happened to La Chandelle?"

"Oh, she's dead, child. She was cut up in a fight."

"I heard about that. You were apparently quite fierce."

"Word travels fast."

"Almost as fast as V.D. through your string of boyfriends." Tipsy flashed a big smile and primped the back of her wig.

"Ooh, that was shady. I'm gonna get you for that, girl."

Tipsy surveyed the rest of Kendall's group. "I see a devil, a skeleton man, a Bollywood actress, a vegetable, a sixties fashion model, a witch..." She stopped at Jenna. "And you must be the witch's black cat."

Jenna sighed. "I give up. Yeah, you guessed it."

Church Street was packed with Halloween revelers. There were skeletons, superheroes, unicorns, fairies, witches, a guy wearing a hat from which dangled planets of the solar system, a girl dressed as an Easter Island monolith, another as a giant smartphone. One group supported a fifteen-foot tall giant puppet, the figure of an old crone carrying a lantern. Seeing the crowd's diversity, Kendall swelled with pride for his city and his community, individuals from all manner of backgrounds coming together to celebrate creativity and difference.

They stayed out a couple of hours, until the crowd grew uncomfortably dense, and headed home, laughing and talking about the wild visions they had seen.

Elliott pulled Kendall aside as they reached the quieter streets of Cabbagetown. "I picked up the building plans for Covington Terrace—the plans from ten years ago when the basement was renovated. Have you ever noticed that there are eleven mailboxes but only ten apartments?"

"No. Why?"

"There used to be a third apartment in the basement. The same floor plan as the other floors, with the fourth quadrant comprising the laundry, storage lockers, and boiler room. But that apartment's not there anymore."

Kendall halted and faced Elliott. "It couldn't have disappeared. What happened to it?"

"I don't know. It's like it was just sealed off. We ought to check out the basement tomorrow, see what we can find."

After Kendall removed his makeup, he collapsed into bed. It was almost one in the morning, November first. It had been a successful debut for his new persona. But thoughts of the missing apartment nagged at him. He drifted into sleep, pleased with how the evening had turned out, and secure with the extra precaution of a new chain on the apartment door, which the Bone Man had helped install.

The nightmare came quickly. It began as usual, with masked figures and the firelight ritual. This time, however, an enormous black goat appeared. The goat lowered its head, aimed its huge horns, and charged the masked men, knocking some to the ground just as Kendall had once witnessed at Riverdale Farm, and scattering the others into the night. The goat spoke to Kendall, and it was the voice of Lucas. "I want to show you something." A moment later, Lucas appeared in place of the goat, wearing the silver dress that Kendall had sewn. The firelight played off his face like the light in the painting in the museum and made the silver sparkle like diamonds.

"Looks good on me, doesn't it?" Lucas asked.

Kendall's hands had been bound at the beginning of the dream. Now they were free, and he smoothed out and readjusted the fit of the dress on Lucas. "Fits you like a glove."

And suddenly they were in Kendall's bedroom.

"He's coming," said Lucas.

"Who?"

"The one who imagines he is me but is not. The one who wants to harm you."

"You mean Wade? But we changed the locks. He can't get in."

"He is about to enter your bedroom through a small door cut into the back of the closet. That is where he has been hiding, creeping around inside the walls."

"What do you mean, inside the walls?"

"He intends to slaughter you and others in the building, starting now."

"I don't understand how that's possible."

Lucas placed his finger against Kendall's lips. "Shhhhh. It's time to wake up."

Kendall removed his sleep mask and opened his eyes. The radiator was emitting a soft whistling noise. He got out of bed, Lucas' words still on his mind. He flicked the light switch several times, but the room remained dark. The same tactic Wade used last time. That convinced him the warning in his dream had been real. He used his cell phone's flashlight to illuminate the closet and saw the small door. He had never paid much attention to it before now. It had a pull tab like one would find on a utility cabinet. Then Kendall heard a sound from behind the door, the sound of something rustling.

He slipped on his robe and ran across the hall to Elliott's door. The lights were out in the hall as well. After the third knock and two buzzes, a groggy Elliott opened the door.

Kendall's words flew out in a breathless rush. "I know where Wade is. He didn't run away. He's been hiding here in the building this whole time. And he can get into all our apartments through a small door in the back of the closet. He intends to kill us. I heard him just now."

It took Elliott a moment to digest the information. "You sure it's not the ghost?"

"He *is* the ghost. It has been him all along, trying to terrorize us."

"Okay. Pull the fire alarm to rouse everybody. It's on a separate circuit from the building's power, but since it's not hooked up to the fire department, I'll have to call the police."

The alarm's loud, old-fashioned clang rang through the hall. Kendall ran up the stairs, pounding on doors to underscore the emergency. He led everyone down to Elliott's apartment, trying to give a quick summary of the danger above the sound of the alarm. Bergie struggled in Lucy's arms, her eyes wild. Morvena pressed her hands over her ears, grimacing. Mrs. Gupta joined them as they reached the bottom of the stairs.

Elliott grabbed a flashlight and a baseball bat and gave a quick rundown of what he had discovered about the renovation plans. "There used to be a third apartment down there. It was reconfigured, apparently by Wade. It must be his hideaway." The alarm stopped. "That was probably him, down in the basement."

"Where's Lilith?" asked Jenna. "And Marvin?"

Kendall followed Elliott and the Bone Man downstairs to the basement. They found both apartment doors open. Marvin lay sprawled at his entry, his throat slit, a lake of blood pooling on the floor. There was no sign of Lilith, and when they called her name they heard no response. The fire alarm panel flashed a yellow caution light, its glass door ajar. The circuit breaker box nearby, however, had apparently been re-locked after Wade turned off the power, rendering it inaccessible. Elliott gestured with his flashlight beam toward the supply closet. "The entrance to the hideaway could be through there."

"No, I've looked in there, dude," said the Bone Man. "It's just garden tools. There's no other door."

"There's probably a concealed entrance somewhere," said Elliott. "Something he wanted to keep hidden."

"We could try the entrance through Lilith's closet," suggested Kendall.

Jenna and Lucy stood at the top of the stairs, listening to the conversation. "Shouldn't we wait for the police?" Jenna shouted down to them.

"It may be too late when they arrive," said Elliott.

"I'll go," volunteered the Bone Man. "I'm sure the fucker killed my girlfriend."

"I'll go with you," said Kendall.

"We'll all go together," said Elliott.

Jenna scampered down the stairs. "Then I'm going, too."

Lucy called down after her. "Kendall, Jenna, remember—keep your enemy confused and surprised."

They found their way to the door in the back of Lilith's closet. Elliott handed the bat to the Bone Man and crawled through first with the flashlight. He stood and motioned with his hand for the others to follow.

Elliott's girth made it difficult for him to squeeze through the passageway, so he gave the flashlight to Kendall and sent his skinnier neighbors ahead. "I'll go back out and bring the police down here when they arrive."

The Bone Man led the way, followed by Jenna and Kendall. Within a short distance they located an opening in the wall and stepped through it into a narrow, windowless chamber with a door to the left and right. The Bone Man tried to open the door on the left, but it was locked. The door on the right, however, opened into a darkened room. Kendall's heart raced, dreading what they would find inside.

The beam from the flashlight illuminated a primitive lab that occupied another windowless space, evidently soundproofed. Animal skulls, beakers, and jars of brownish liquid lined the shelves. Filling each jar were various items: hand, jawbone, heart, eyeballs, other body parts that Kendall could not identify. Tools lay scattered on a work table. A power drill. A circular saw. An eighteenth-century trepan, which Kendall recognized from a horror movie, for opening a hole in the skull. A grimy white smock hung from a hook on the wall. Dark blood stained a slab in the middle of the room. The smell of death and human remains hung in the air. It all reminded him of a gruesome version of Arthur Turnbull's house of curiosities. Jenna pulled on Kendall's elbow and pointed to drawings on the walls. The goat-man. The realization that this horrific place existed beneath the floor on which he lived sickened him. What horrors had gone on here while he slept above, oblivious?

Another door led out of the room. It was not locked. But with every new door, Kendall felt they were drawing closer to the source of some profound evil. Kendall turned the knob and threw open the door. This room, too, was dark, but the flashlight beam swept over a soiled mattress, crumpled bags of chips, bottles of soda, and crumbs scattered on the floor. The beam settled on Lilith, standing on the far side of the room, her hands tied. Behind her loomed Wade with the goat head mask. He held a hunting knife to Lilith's throat. Kendall recognized the scene. He had been in her position once.

Wade's voice emerged through the mask, muted. "If you come closer I will kill her."

Kendall thought of that other confrontation over two decades earlier, which he remembered only vaguely but which his mother had described to him. "You are outnumbered, Wade. Put down the knife and release her."

Wade pulled back Lilith's head and with his other hand pressed the blade more firmly against her throat.

Kendall handed the flashlight to Jenna and got down on his hands and knees. "I know what you are. You're the púca. Ancient and eternal. But I am also the púca. Unlike you, I can become an eagle, or a rabbit, or a horse, or a dog. I can become a man, or a woman, or a skeleton, or a witch. My powers are greater than yours. You can only become a goat." He started to crawl toward Wade.

"Stay back."

Jenna swung the flashlight in a slow spiral, its beam circling the goat mask. "Let her go, púca. We will let you gallop away, but only if you release her unharmed."

The beam circled in smaller and smaller spirals until Jenna was aiming the light directly into Wade's eyes. He let go of Lilith's head and held his hand up to block the light.

Lilith began singing a mournful Irish air. Her voice sounded like the ring of the Tibetan singing bowl on her altar.

> *Is bean ón slua sí mé*
> *Do tháinig thar toinn*
> *Is do goideadh san oíche mé*
> *Tamall thar lear*
> *Is go bhfuilim as riocht so*
> *Fé gheasa mná sí*

Is ní bheidh ar an saol so
Go nglaofaidh an coileach

Wade slowly lowered the arm holding the knife, as if mesmerized. On the last note, Lilith sprang away before he could react. The Bone Man rushed forward with the bat, but Wade raised the knife and drew it across his own throat. The blood spurted out as he sagged to his knees, then he collapsed sideways, the goat head still concealing his face.

The Bone Man used the bat to fish the knife out of Wade's hand. When it was safely out of reach, he retrieved a set of keys from Wade's pocket. "I want to see what's in that first locked room."

"Are you sure you're ready for what you might find?" asked Jenna.

The Bone Man shrugged. "I think I already know." He headed back into the maze of rooms.

Kendall untied Lilith's hands and hugged her. "I'm so glad you're all right. What song was that?"

"The Irish tune I told you about. *The Púca's Lament.*"

Jenna located an exit. When she opened the door, Kendall recognized the supply room with the gardening tools. The other side of the door had been disguised to look just like part of the wall with shelving. A secret passage right out of an old horror movie. They heard voices and scuffling in the hallway beyond the supply room, then the door was kicked open and someone shouted "Police!"

With their hands in the air, Kendall, Jenna, and Lilith explained that Wade had slit his own throat. They left out the detail about the song and crawling on the floor. Who would have believed that part? No one asked how they had managed to overpower Wade. Kendall mentioned that one of their companions had gone further back into the secret space to explore a locked room. "Don't shoot him," he cautioned.

One of the officers must have broken into the circuit breaker box, because the lights came back on. As Kendall walked through the supply room into the hallway, he felt a wave of relief for the first time. The ordeal was over. But his entire body still trembled.

249

Elliott stood in the hallway, and relaxed once he saw that his neighbors were okay. A moment later, the Bone Man emerged from the chamber of horrors with an officer. "Rooney's in the other room," he said, "but she's too weak to stand. They're calling an ambulance."

"And your girlfriend?" asked Kendall.

His face looked somber and drained of color. "I think she's in there, too. At least, what's left of her."

Kendall looked one last time at Marvin's body before they went upstairs. He felt guilty that he had been able to prevent the deaths of all of his neighbors except one. Perhaps if Marvin had survived, Kendall would eventually have been able to wear down Marvin's defenses and let him know that someone appreciated his talent as a writer, the deceptions notwithstanding. Perhaps they might even have become friends. Kendall said a silent blessing for his spirit. He wasn't sure if he believed in God, or Brigid, or Oshun, or some enigmatic force that animated the universe. He didn't know if people had souls, or what happened after death, or whether spirits lingered in the land of the living. But he knew that he and his neighbors were stronger together than they were apart.

The police took statements from each of the tenants—except for Rooney, who was whisked away after being hooked up to an I.V. drip. They could not remain in the building, of course. It was an active crime scene. The police offered to make arrangements with the Red Cross for those who had nowhere else to go.

"We're a family now," said Kendall. "We'll make sure everyone has lodging. Right, Jenna?"

"Right, Kendall. Or, rather, Shockadelica."

They looked at each other and in unison said, "This will make an awesome podcast."

Epilogue: The Evil Dead

Excerpt from Shockadelica Podcast
Episode 52: The Haunting of Covington Terrace
Guests: Lilith Adebayo and Vince Fournier (aka the Bone Man)

Jenna: So, ghoulies and goblins, you might be wondering: was the building really haunted after all, or not?

Kendall: Well, here's the kicker. That night—or really, it was, like, three in the morning at that point—we gathered in the Bone Man's apartment to, you know, get ready to leave with some of our belongings.

Jenna: Some of us were going to stay at my parent's house, and some of us were going to Kendall's mother's house.

Vince: I was throwing some clothes into a sports bag, when all of a sudden I heard a noise behind me. I turned around, and swear to God, I almost jumped out of my fucking skin. Oh, sorry—can I say "fucking" on a podcast?

Lilith: We heard Vince shout and ran into his bedroom.

Jenna: And standing in the corner we saw Wade. I mean, just picture that for a minute if you can.

Kendall: We had just watched him kill himself down in the basement, so you can imagine the shock.

Jenna: It was the most freaky-deaky thing I've ever experienced. I would not have believed it if I had not seen it with my own eyes.

Lilith: The weird thing was, the color had been drained out of his body, like in those sun-faded photos you see in the window of a beauty parlor.

Vince: You could see the gash in his neck, and where the blood had stained his shirt in dark patches.

Jenna: He just stood there a moment, turned, and walked into the open closet.

Lilith: We immediately ran after him to see where he went, but he had already vanished. I knew at that moment what it meant—that his spirit would remain with this world a long time. Dead, but not quite dead. He would linger to haunt the living, which means we will always need to stay vigilant.

Kendall: And honey, you can bet that the next day I was out looking for a new apartment. Ooh, diva, if there's one thing I fear more than a bigoted killer, it's a bigoted killer's ghost.